THE REMEDY

ASHER ELLIS

DEADITE PRESS
PORTLAND, OREGON

deadite press

DEADITE PRESS
833 SE Main Street #342
Portland, OR 97214
www.DEADITEPRESS.com

AN ERASERHEAD PRESS COMPANY
www.ERASERHEADPRESS.com

ISBN: 978-1-62105-322-4

Printed in the USA.

THE REMEDY

"Look deep into nature, and then you will understand everything better."
—*Albert Einstein*

PROLOGUE

Dale Preston had always loved fire. But one couldn't justly label his fascination as pyromania, since he'd never found any perverse pleasure in burning down what others had built. Dale simply enjoyed being near the sight and smell of blazing wood, losing himself as he stared into the hypnotic dance of the tangled flames. He did this now, guzzling his third beer while sitting at a campsite nestled in the woods of Vermont's Northeast Kingdom. Red Hogan, his hunting companion, and brother-in-law had yet to return. The guy was taking the longest piss in recorded history.

The combination of cheap beer and the campfire's earthy smoke urged Dale's mind to drift. As he stared unblinking into the yellowish-orange center of the cinders, he reminisced about his senior year of high school, and the night he got to second base with Cindy Burnett, the hottest piece of ass at Embry High. Dale made his move the night of the big bonfire, Halloween weekend. He squeezed the beer can in his hand, remembering how Cindy had gone braless that night, her nipples visible through her white blouse as she perspired from the heat of the fire. When he followed her away from the bonfire into the surrounding woods and ripped away the buttons of her blouse with one aggressive pull, she'd immediately grabbed the back of his head and shoved his mouth to her breasts. His lips attached themselves to those silver dollar nipples and began furiously sucking.

She moaned…

CRACK!

Dale's lust-filled memory vaporized as a log on the campfire let loose a deafening pop. The sudden noise so badly startled the distracted hunter that he spilled half his can of beer.

"Ah, shit," Dale muttered, brushing the liquid off his bright orange hunting vest. "What a waste," referring both to his spilled beer and the memory-induced hard-on that he could do nothing about.

Dale could feel the beer soaking through to his camouflaged sweatshirt underneath, so he removed the orange vest and turned to grab a nearby rag to sop up the fluid.

And saw the black eyes of a white-tailed deer staring into his own a mere inch from his face.

"Gah!" Dale's heart nearly beat itself to exhaustion from the stress of two scares back-to-back. But the fright instantly vanished when he noticed the limp tongue hanging from the deer's open mouth, and realized that it was Red Hogan who held up the animal's dead body.

"C'mon, Dale! Give us a kiss!" Red's raspy laugh, the result of years and years of endless Marlboros, echoed through the tall spruce trees surrounding their campsite. The older man lifted the deer's hoof next to his scruffy, graying beard and made it wave to Dale.

"Fuck you, Red." Dale picked himself off the ground, fully aware of how close his right hand had just come to landing in the fire's hot coals.

"Fuck me?" Red chuckled. "Wouldn't you rather fuck this little beauty right here?"

Dale brushed the deer away. "Would you quit it with that shit? Bestiality may run in your family, but not mine."

"Ah, what's the matter?" Red taunted. "Is the cry-baby jealous of my kill?"

"Yeah, right." Dale poked at the fire, embarrassed that he'd been spooked and unable to meet Red's eyes. "I bet that'll be the only one you get all weekend. I'm surprised a fat ass like you even managed to sneak up on this one here!"

Red tied a rope around the buck's rear feet. "You mean the same fat ass that just scared the panties off of you? Hell, I didn't need to do any sneakin' anyhow. There I was, drainin' the lizard, when this sucker just came moseying along. All I had to do was unsling my rifle and *bam*! Didn't even put my dick away."

While Red guffawed again at his own remark and then loudly belched, Dale rolled his eyes and reached for another piece of firewood. "Well, good for you, Red. But we'll see who's laughing when we compare bucks tomorr—AAH!" Dale yelped yet again when a large bowie knife suddenly planted itself in the firewood he gripped, landing a mere centimeter from his thumb.

Dale turned to see Red aiming his hand like a pistol directly at the wood. "Bullseye!" he shouted. But before Dale could react to this most recent display of crass carelessness, Red spoke again. "I suppose if you somehow happen to kill *anything* tomorrow, we'll see how it stacks up to this ten-point puppy."

Red threw the rope over a nearby tree branch and hoisted the deer's carcass into the air. After positioning a large metal bucket under the dangling corpse, he pointed to the knife.

"In the meantime, why don't you make yourself useful and go clean that blade in the lake. You didn't get to see me take down this buck, but I can at least show you how a real hunter guts one."

Smirking, Dale yanked the blade from the wood. "Didn't realize I was in the presence of a *real* hunter."

Red's condescending grin finally dropped for the first time since returning to the campsite. He paused, struggling with the right words to retort, but after a moment of face twitching, he simply blurted out, "Get moving!"

Dale resented the idea of taking orders from Red, a man he had never cared for, even though he had been married to his sister for many years now. It wasn't easy walking away from the incessantly annoying redneck while conveniently gripping the handle of a large knife, but Dale knew he'd never actually let himself get to such a point. He would continue to put up with Red's bullshit for as long as it made his sister, Cathy, happy. That was the only reason he always agreed to go on these trips in the first place: Cathy was the only family he had left, and he felt he owed it to her. He had no idea what she saw in the over-the-hill asshole, but as far as Dale could tell, Red treated her well enough.

But if Dale ever found Cathy with a shiner...

He strengthened his grip on the knife. *Well,* he thought, *let's just hope it never comes to that.*

The heavy brush soon gave way, and the lake came into view. Neither Dale nor Red knew the name of this particular lagoon, but it seemed like the perfect place to pitch a tent. A quick dip and a pot full of crystal-clear cooking water were just a short walk away, with enough available space to get away from highly irritating company.

Dale squatted at the water's edge and dunked the blade under the surface. He retrieved a bandana from his back pocket and wiped the dirt and grime away, whistling an improvised tune. Red had managed to get under his skin back there, but in the face of the total serenity offered by this new lakeside view, Dale felt his mood improving. The perfectly still, glasslike surface of the lake reflected the surrounding mountains just like the photography of Ansel Adams, but in color.

Chuckling, Dale stared out onto the lake and the reflected greenery. *And here we're going to make a happy little tree...*

SPLASH!

To Dale's left, the surface rippled with the flash of a fish's tail. Dale twitched in surprise, the spasm jerking the knife's point into his hand that held the bandana.

"Ow!" Dale yanked his hand up and saw he'd cut a tiny, triangle-shaped wound on the tip of his thumb. "God damnit," he whispered, shaking his hand and sucking the cut. He put aside the knife to clean his wound and dunked his entire hand into the cold lake.

Tiny ribbons of blood expanded and trailed off in the clear water. Dale hoped the bleeding would stop before he returned to the campsite—the last thing he wanted was to give Red another reason to give him shit. He looked down and sighed with relief when he saw the flow slowing.

But he stopped mid-sigh when he realized that despite the ice-cold temperature of the lake, his thumb burned as if on fire.

Dale jerked his thumb from the water. At first glance, it appeared that a scab had somehow *already* formed over the incision. But upon further inspection, Dale could see that it was something else. The triangle-shaped cut was covered with a thick, green coat of fuzz that prevented any further blood from leaking out. The skin bordering the wound had also taken on a green tint, a strange discoloration that didn't at all resemble the usual pinkish hue of a skin infection.

"What the fuck?" Dale mumbled, staring in total disbelief as before his eyes the fuzz continued to spread down to his knuckle. His thumb simultaneously itched and burned, reminding him of the few times in his life he had contracted poison ivy. This had to be something similar—some allergenic plant-life in the water, or perhaps a weed growing on the bottom of the lake.

Dale desperately wanted to scratch at the fuzzy green inflammation that was now engulfing his thumb, but he knew that scratching only spread infection. Not like this stuff needed any help with that. It was like watching shag carpeting knit itself—thick green fibrous strands that no one would want in their living room, let alone the back of their hand. But that's exactly where this fungus was heading as it continued to feast on his flesh.

Dale grabbed the knife and hurriedly made his way back through the trees. He'd have to call off the trip if this rash from hell didn't immediately stop spreading. Red would be pissed for sure, but he'd get over it. Besides, he had already nabbed that trophy buck. Dale would be the one going home empty-handed, but at this point, he really didn't care—he was more concerned with having hands at all. He could already picture the doctor's blank expression as he delivered the news with professional apathy.

I'm sorry, Mr. Preston. Our only option is amputation.

Dale stumbled into camp, stopping in his tracks when he saw Red standing a few paces from the campsite's perimeter, his rifle aimed at an unknown target.

"Must be my lucky day," Red whispered. "Dale is gonna shit himself when he sees you."

God, don't tell me he's spotted another one.

Dale took a soft step forward and pulled apart the branches impeding his vision. He gasped.

The head of a black bear stuck up from behind some thick blackberry bushes. It stared at Red, but didn't move.

Red breathed deeply, steadying his aim as he stared down the rifle's scope. *He must be shitting bricks,* Dale thought as his eyes darted back and forth between the bear and Red. *Well, if he pulls this one off, it should help when he hears the bad news that we have to go home.* Remembering his thumb again, Dale looked back down to discover that the fungus had yet to cease its crusade across his flesh. It might've been his imagination, but Dale swore he could even feel the fungus growing *underneath* his skin now.

He glanced up again at the sound of Red's voice saying "Goodbye, Smokey," to see him grinning like an idiot as he prepared to take the shot. Dale silently urged him to just hurry up and do it already; his legs were beginning to cramp from crouching behind this bush. And that was the least of his body's problems.

He looked at the bear's head, bracing himself for the rifle's booming report, when Red screamed. Dale tore his gaze away from the bear over to Red, clutching at his leg, blood spurting between his fingers like oil from a freshly drilled well.

A serrated metallic disc protruded from the hemorrhaging wound, embedded in Red's leg like the knife he'd chucked at Dale's firewood.

Someone had thrown the circular saw blade and hit Red square in the thigh.

"Red!" Dale swiped at the bushes, desperately trying to find the quickest route to his brother-in-law. But just as he shouted, Red fired blindly into the woods, the gun blast completely drowning out Dale's voice.

Dale was almost free of the dense undergrowth when he happened to glance over in the direction of the black bear… and almost choked from lack of breath.

The "bear" was getting to its feet—its two *human* feet, that is. Human feet attached to a gigantic human body. Now towering above the blackberry bushes that had previously concealed him, it was clear that the gargantuan man was wearing a bear head as a mask. He lifted something long and black and pointed it towards Red. Distracted with pain and panic, Red did not see the double-barreled shotgun aimed at his chest.

"NO!" Dale screamed as the bear-masked man fired, knocking Red to the ground with one powerful shot. The bear man turned toward Dale, who darted back into the bushes, praying that the huge stranger hadn't heard his shout over the gun's explosion. Through the leafy and thorny undergrowth, Dale held his breath as he watched the "bear" take a step towards his hiding place, scan the area, and then take another. Dale trembled, squeezing the hilt of the knife, his only weapon. But what good would it do against a seven-foot, shotgun-wielding giant?

Just as the colossal brute was a mere step away, a bullet whizzed overhead, burying itself into the side of a nearby birch tree. The masked monster turned to find Red aiming his rifle with one shaky arm.

"Fuck you," Red yelled, a wet gurgle making his voice even raspier than usual. "I'm gonna fuck you up!"

Before Red could get off another shot, a flash of sparks bloomed halfway down the rifle's barrel. As half of the severed weapon fell to the ground, Red spun his head around to a nearby tree stump. Embedded in its rotted wood was another circular saw blade, and the man throwing them finally emerged.

"Grizzly, you dumb sack of shit!"

The second man was shorter and much thinner than his massive companion, his skin clinging tightly to his slender form like stretched rawhide. He was clad in dirty mechanic's overalls with the sleeves tied around his waist. A faded, brown baseball cap sat cockeyed on his head, concealing all but a few tuffs of scraggly black hair.

The vice grip squeezing Dale's heart loosened slightly as Grizzly backed away from Dale's hiding place and joined his partner, who towered above Red.

"This codger almost got the jump on you!" The shorter man shouted and punched Grizzly's arm. "You're mighty lucky Bugger was watching your back! What the fuck would you do without your big brother?" Grizzly only shrugged.

"Well, fuck it, just tie him up," Bugger ordered his brother and walked over to where the campfire still smoldered. With buckshot embedded in his side and his weapon now useless, Red could offer little resistance against the giant that hefted him from the ground. His punches to Grizzly's face and chest might as well have been mosquito bites as Grizzly tied up his legs and swung the remaining rope over one of the higher branches of a maple tree. Meanwhile, Bugger retrieved the metal bucket from underneath the hanging deer.

Dale looked on in horror, afraid to move or even breathe. He desperately wanted to help Red, but knew he didn't stand a chance against two armed thugs. He cursed himself for not bringing along his rifle when he went to the lake. Red had brought his gun with him just to take a piss and ended up with a prize buck. If only Dale had been so smart.

But thank god I spilled beer on my vest. His total camouflage garb was the only thing keeping him alive. Dale felt a mosquito land on his left eyebrow but made no move to brush it away. Maybe if he could just keep quiet and out of sight for a little longer, these two assholes would just take their stuff—weapons, beer, whatever—and be on their way.

From his hiding place, Dale watched the one called Bugger place the bucket underneath Red, who now dangled upside down.

"Now, Grizzly," Bugger said as he removed a knife even larger than the one Dale held from his belt. "Pay attention and watch how a real hunter guts his kill." Bugger plunged the blade into Red's stomach, all the way to the hilt. Red couldn't even scream at the brutal attack, only gargle wordlessly as blood clogged his airway. Dale pressed a hand over his mouth as Bugger tore the blade down the entire length of Red's gut, leaving a long, gaping hole from which a torrent of blood gushed down Red's body into the bucket below. Red twitched for about ten seconds, shaking like a fish on a line before going completely limp. The gurgling noises ceased as well, leaving the splash of Red's blood dripping into the metal tub as the only sound in the quiet forest.

The two brothers just stared at the bloody waterfall, mesmerized by the crimson torrent. Bugger's trance was finally broken when Grizzly grunted and pointed to his brother's forearm.

Dale saw that the same green fungus still eating away at his own thumb had reached slightly above Bugger's wrist.

"Well, look at that." Bugger shrugged, as if the ailment was nothing more than a horsefly bite. "Guess I better have a piece of this one here before it spreads."

Dale instinctually took a deep breath through his nose, a trick he'd once learned at the dentist's office as a way to control his gag reflex. The exercise barely worked now as he watched Bugger reach into the wound in Red's stomach, pull out a rope of intestine, and take an enthusiastic bite. Blood smeared Bugger's mouth as he smiled and chewed, offering a piece of the intestinal coil to his partner. Grizzly accepted the organ and carefully inserted it into the mouth of his bear mask, sucking it into his own concealed mouth like it was a string of spaghetti.

As soon as the slippery sound of Red's intestine snaking its way into Grizzly's hungry maw reached Dale's ears, he simply could not take it anymore. He gagged, releasing the slightest airy cough into the serene stillness.

Bugger slapped Grizzly in the chest.

"Did you hear something?"

Dale jumped out the backside of the brambles and began to sprint. He was sure the two attackers could see the bush shake with his exit, but perhaps they would not actually see him leave the shrubs. Either way, he ran harder than he ever had in his entire life. Tree limbs smacked his face, thorn bushes scratched his skin, but none of it slowed him in the least.

The lake, however, brought him to a dead stop.

He could hear his pursuers getting closer and panic squeezed his chest like a socket wrench. A patch of cattails stuck out of the water's surface to his right. It was his only chance.

Dale plunged into the cold water and reached the cover of the tall green stems just as Bugger emerged on the shore. From the way his eyes scanned the lake, Dale could tell Bugger hadn't failed to notice the ripples from Dale's frantic movements. A moment later, Grizzly joined him by his side.

"Look at the water," Bugger said, pointing to the ripples. "Something's out there."

Suddenly, a fish broke the surface with a strident splash. Grizzly pointed his finger at the source of movement.

"Yeah, it could've been a fish," Bugger said quietly. "But just in case there's something out there that isn't a critter," he paused and then drastically raised his voice, as if speaking directly to Dale, "I wouldn't be taking a dip if I were you!"

Dale clenched his jaw to silent the sound of his chattering teeth. A gentle wind came and blew at his weak cover, making the brown cattail cones sway side to side.

"You're not gonna like how you look when you come out!" Bugger continued. "I can promise you that. But if you show yourself now, Grizzly and I can fix you up! We have the cure to what ails you!"

With that, Bugger raised his arm to reveal that his skin no longer showed any sign of the green fungus. There wasn't the slightest hint of fuzz anywhere on his limb.

He popped the remaining chunk of Red's organ into his mouth and licked a bloody finger. "Mmm! Just what the doctor ordered!"

Dale squeezed his eyes shut.

"Hell," Bugger shouted with a laugh. "Even if we do kill ya, I can downright guarantee it'll be far less painful than what you've got ahead of you!" Bugger waited for three beats of silence and then elbowed his larger companion. "Fuck it, Grizzly. Man or marmot, it's not worth our time. Let's get that meat back to the house."

Without another word, both of the men disappeared from sight.

Dale waited another thirty minutes before emerging from the cattail patch. There was no way of knowing if the killers were still at the campsite, but he didn't dare find out. The other side of the lake wasn't too far away, and he'd always been a decent swimmer. Without a second thought, he began an overarm stroke towards the far shore.

It did not take long for feeling to return to Dale's numbed body as blood pumped back into his muscles. And as his nerves began to reawaken to the sole sensation of burning flesh, Dale realized what a grave mistake he'd made. He should have taken Red's murderers up on their offer.

His arms, legs, neck, and face were now covered in the insatiable fungus. When his vision blurred and his eyes began to burn, he knew it had found its way behind his eyelids. He could feel it reaching back toward his retinas, searching for his brain.

CHAPTER ONE

Leigh Swanson looked up from her Dean Koontz novel just in time to see the disgusting leftovers of a squished raccoon flash past the car window. She'd been ignoring her present company for almost the entire ride back from Montreal, and instantly regretted coming up for air now. While it was indeed engrossing, her attachment to the book was spurred mostly by the one glaringly obvious fact that Leigh had been trying to overlook the entire weekend:

There were worse things than being a third wheel. Sometimes third wheels served an important purpose, like on a tricycle or wheelbarrow. But this was not the case for Leigh.

She was a fifth wheel, a metaphor so absurd it had no literal counterpart.

"Oh, shit!" Rob clutched the steering wheel and momentarily whipped his head around to follow the mangled corpse of the dead animal disappearing behind them "Did you guys see that?"

His girlfriend, Eliza, laughed from the passenger seat. "Well, I, for one, don't mind if you want to go back and get it."

Rob turned to the girl sitting directly behind Eliza—her sister, Alexandra. "Didn't you say were hungry, Alex?"

"Ugh, it looked like it got hit by a steamroller," Alex said to the couple in the front seat. "You guys are sick."

Bemused, Leigh shook her head and pretended to return to her book. She'd been quietly tolerating Rob's childish antics since she'd first boarded his van back at the University of Vermont's campus. She hadn't known much about him except that he was a recent transfer student from somewhere out of state, who had started dating her best friend's twin sister almost immediately after stepping foot into their first shared class. This didn't surprise Leigh in the slightest, since Rob was exactly the type Eliza always fell for: the wanna-be rocker, consistently clad in a trucker's cap and denim vest covered in Black Flag and Misfits patches. And while it didn't seem to bother Eliza, Leigh never failed to notice how suspiciously well-groomed he kept his perfectly "scruffy" five o'clock shadow.

Lastly, and most importantly, Rob was eternally obnoxious, especially after he'd had a few drinks. If it weren't for Alex's incessant pleading, there was no way Leigh would've agreed to be in the same vehicle with this loudmouth poser for two-plus hours.

"Come with us!" Alex had said in her usual, bubbly tone. "I know you don't like Rob very much, but Marshall and Eliza will be there too. You'll have fun!" Even though she and Leigh had been roommates since sophomore year, they were an unlikely pair: polar opposites in appearance and social habits. While Leigh preferred to keep to herself and concentrate on maintaining her *magna cum laude* status, Alex was the epitome of a social butterfly. Blonde, busty, and perpetually twirling her hair in that flirtatious fashion that guys somehow still fell for, Alex was a fantasy co-ed come to life. If it weren't for the fact that Leigh had been blessed with attractive features as well—namely her slender body and striking eyes—Alex probably wouldn't have given her the time of day.

Fortunately, the utter superficiality of Leigh's roommate never bothered her enough to affect their friendship. Minor character flaws aside, Alex was fun, even if Leigh had to hold her hair back after a night of excessive drinking a few too many times. She was Leigh's link to the outside world; a valuable resource that kept her in touch with people her age. Not to mention that it was nice having someone call you the "sexiest librarian she'd ever seen," due to the tortoise shell glasses Leigh always wore.

This time, Leigh had let Alex's charisma and forceful personality get the best of her, too easily giving in to her pleading and whining to spend Labor Day weekend with her and the rest of the gang up in Montreal. While she didn't care for Alex's suggestion to have a fling with a "cute, French-Canadian boy," the trip seemed like a better way to spend her break than doing chores at her parents' house. She knew her therapist would've been proud of her, having many times suggested that Leigh try to cut down on her chronic pessimism. Naturally, Dr. Blaine was right, as Leigh's increasingly cynical attitude since graduating high school had spurred her to seek treatment in the first place.

"Do you know what fear stands for?" Dr. Blaine had once asked. "False events appearing real. We can't always trust our inner voices because they have a tendency to lie to us. You have to learn to trust *people* once in a while, too."

So Leigh heeded her doctor's advice, reminded herself that fun only happens when you let it, and hopped aboard the Montreal express.

And now here she was, wishing Rob would just shut up and press the gas pedal to the floor so this trip could be over already. Well, at least she had tried.

"Hey, Marshall." Rob glanced in the rearview mirror. "I'm sick of driving. You about ready to switch?"

Marshall sat next to Alex, behind Rob. Tanned with shaggy, dusty blond hair, Marshall was yet another piece of evidence that proved Alex was all about appearances. They'd been dating since junior year, and it hadn't taken long for Alex to fall for his surfer physique and "chill" attitude. Marshall was from San Diego. A shark's tooth necklace always hung around his neck. Simply put, Marshall was the spitting image of Chris Hemsworth on a surfboard. But to his credit, he wasn't at all unpleasant to be around, and he was certainly better than many of Alex's past boyfriends.

"Dude, I thought we agreed that I'd take over after we cross the border." Marshall leaned between the two front seats.

Eliza turned from the window. "He's right, Rob. That is what you said."

Leigh had secretly resented Eliza since the beginning of the school year for introducing Rob into their circle of friends. For the most part, she enjoyed being around Alex's twin sister and the accompanying sibling banter and bickering. Eliza and Alex were the yin to each other's yang. While Eliza dyed her light hair jet-black and wore leather outfits and black eye shadow, the blonde Alex maintained the plaid-skirted, solidly preppy look. And as far as Leigh could tell, Eliza liked having her around since she commonly sided with Eliza during the frequent arguments that arose between the twins.

"What can I say?" Leigh always explained to Alex. "You're my best friend, but your sister and I are just more like-minded. That's all."

Then why had Eliza been so foolish to shack up with the king of all posers? Still, there were times that Eliza stuck to her honest nature, as was the case now, and Leigh was always grateful not to miss these moments.

Rob sighed. "Yeah, I know that's what I said. It just feels like we've been on this road forever."

"Well, whose bright idea was it not to take the highway?."

Leigh regretted saying the words even as they were leaving her mouth.

Everyone except Rob, who eyed her in the rearview mirror, turned to face Leigh in the van's rear seat which she shared with no one.

"What was that?" Rob asked, turning down the volume of the van's stereo.

Leigh darted her eyes out the window. "Nothing."

"She said you didn't want to take the interstate," Marshall said. A mischievous grin spread across his face. Both he and Alex loved to be entertained by the drama of others.

Alex slapped Marshall's shoulder and gave him a harsh "Sshh!" getting an "Ow! What did I do?" in response.

"Yes, Leigh," Rob shouted over the squabbling couple. "You're correct. I didn't want to take the interstate. Do you know why?"

He didn't wait for Leigh to reply.

"Because taking the highway would've been a stupid fucking idea."

Marshall grabbed Alex's wrists. She playfully struggled against him. "And why would that be a stupid fucking idea?" she asked with a giggle.

Rob's annoyed expression transformed into a genuine smile. He turned to Eliza and said, "Why don't you tell them again."

Eliza's lips parted to expose her bright, white teeth in a large grin. She punched the button on the glove compartment in front of her and reached all the way to the back. Like a magician pulling a rabbit from a hat, she retrieved a very large plastic baggie, filled to the brim with marijuana.

"Because how the hell would we get this past the border patrol?" She threw the bag over her shoulder to her sister, who caught it eagerly. "Yeah, baby!" she yelled.

Marshall leaned forward, practically suffocating himself with the bag's clear shell, and inhaled deeply. "Shit, dude." He nudged Rob. "I still can't believe you were able to score this much!"

Shrugging, Rob rolled down his window and rested his arm in the cool wind battering the van as they whipped along the backwoods dirt road. "Man, what did I tell you about Canada? Do you know how much that amount of weed would've cost me in the States?"

Marshall shook his head. "I don't even want to think about it."

Leigh placed her bookmark in the novel. She felt a headache coming on and desperately rubbed her eyes, trying to suppress it. On their last night in Montreal, Rob and Marshall had told the girls to wait in the room while they went and ran what they referred to as an "errand." Eliza seemed to know what the boys were up to, but whenever Alex or Leigh asked what was going on, she would only wink and say, "It's a surprise." An hour later, the guys returned with the largest quantity of pot Leigh had ever seen in her life. Although she'd bitten her tongue, Leigh found herself with yet another reason to regret joining this escapade: possible imprisonment.

And now, as she eyed the copious amount of marijuana, she couldn't keep silent any longer. She had to voice her concerns or she'd have only herself to blame later if they faced the consequences of their foolish actions.

Leigh decided to try a coy approach to voicing her concerns. "Well maybe," she said, leaning forward, closer to Marshall's ear, "what you should be thinking about is what you're going to do with that big bag of illegal drugs if we discover this road does indeed have a border patrol."

Eliza responded before anyone else could. "Oh, give us a break, Leigh! Like they'd really bother with a road in the middle of nowhere that gets hardly any traffic."

Alex spun her head and met Leigh's eyes with a nervous expression. It seemed that she, at least, was finally starting to come to her senses.

"But what if she's right?" Alex looked from one passenger to another, searching their faces for signs of agreement. "I can't get busted, you guys. My parents would fucking kill me!"

"Would you guys quit it with this shit?" Rob said, a slight hint of doubt in his voice. "Look, I've been on this road before. My family used to take it on every vacation to Quebec."

Leigh scoffed. "Yeah, when you were a kid."

"Yeah. So what?"

Marshall impressed Leigh by immediately realizing her point. He answered Rob's question without hesitation. "Dude, that was back in the days before 9/11."

Even over the whistling wind and the radio, Leigh heard Rob mutter, "Shit," and saw his hands grip the wheel a little tighter. Despite her awareness that their shared problem was no laughing matter, she could do nothing to stop the smirk that automatically shaped her mouth when she noticed his frustration.

Rob had now completely taken all of his attention off the road as he stared at her through the rearview mirror. Although she'd tried her best to hide her look of satisfaction behind the cover of her novel, Rob hadn't been fooled.

"Oh, what?" He said as the van began to drift. "I suppose you have a better idea. Let's hear it!"

Eliza's hand suddenly gripped her boyfriend's arm. "Rob…"

"C'mon! She thinks she's so fucking smart all the time."

"No, ROB! Look out!"

"FUCK!"

Rob slammed on the breaks. Everyone lurched forward as the van violently rocked, throwing its passengers into the seats in front of them. The van fishtailed, turning a complete one hundred and eighty degrees before screeching to a stop.

Though everyone else moaned as if stepping off a faulty carnival ride, Leigh could only hear her internal alarm system screaming in red alert. Her vision had gone blurry, a common result of severe head trauma. Had she hit her head and was in too much shock to feel it? Was she bleeding? She brought her fingers to her skull, praying they wouldn't come back red.

Relief replaced panic in an instant. This wasn't a concussion or something even worse. Her glasses had simply fallen off.

As she found her eyewear resting on the seat beside her, Leigh thanked herself for not voicing her initial concern out loud She was also grateful for the seatbelth that had kept her securely in place. Her friends hadn't been so lucky.

Marshall ran his fingers through his mop of hair, gently massaging his scalp. "Damn," he grumbled. "That sucked. You okay, babe?"

Groaning, Alex gingerly rotated her neck. "Yeah, I'm all right." Marshall brushed the tangled locks of blond hair from her eyes, but she pushed past him and punched Rob's right bicep, hard.

"What the FUCK was that all about?!" she screamed.

Rob ignored the blow and looked straight ahead. With his index finger pointing past the windshield, he said, "Why don't you ask him?"

Leigh's eyes followed the direction of Rob's finger.

Fifteen feet ahead in the middle of the road, a stranger was walking slowly towards them.

CHAPTER
TWO

Alex's dainty hand reached for the handle of the van's sliding door and pulled hard. The door slid open loudly, letting in a cloud of unsettled dirt still hanging in the air after the van's screeching stop.

The stranger appeared to be their age—his youth evident in his energetic eyes and attractive smile. He sauntered in a relaxed manner, hands resting on the beltloops of his worn-out jeans. An old army jacket covered his upper torso, the solid olive green kind one would expect to find in any vintage clothing store. It was complete with a sewn-in nametag above the right breast that read "TUCKER." A battered backpack hung from one shoulder and dangled by his waist. Its color matched the old, faded blue Montreal Expos hat that concealed his brown hair, except for a few tufts that peeked out near his ears.

"Hey," the boy said casually.

No one in the van seemed to know how to reply to his nonchalant greeting. Just moments before, he'd come perilously close to the same fate as the smashed raccoon they'd passed.

After a rather long, awkward moment of silence, it was Alex who finally asked, "Hey, man. Are you all right?"

The boy just shrugged. "No harm done."

Marshall leaned over and stuck his head over Alex's shoulder. "Sorry, dude. We totally didn't see you."

The stranger's eyes scanned the surrounding wilderness. "I do suppose I kind of blend in around here, don't I?"

"Or maybe you shouldn't have been standing so close to the road," Rob grumbled just quietly enough that only those in the van could hear his complaint.

"You hitchin'?" Marshall yelled over to the young man.

"I guess you could call it that," he answered. "Though you're the only car I've seen all day."

Eliza rolled down her window. "Where you headed?"

"Burlington, or thereabouts anyway. Back to school."

"No shit," Alex spoke up. "What school?"

"JCV."

Even in the back of the van, Leigh could hear Rob mumble, "What a surprise." JCV stood for the Junior College of Vermont. Rob, in typical fashion, must have taken one look at their new friend and assumed he wasn't university material. Leigh wanted to berate Rob for his condescending remark, but Marshall beat her to it.

"Hey, watch your mouth!" Marshall shot Rob a dirty look but it soon changed to his trademark mischievous smile when he added, "I may have an idea." He turned back to the kid standing outside. "So, are you from this neck of the woods?"

He nodded. "Yeah…more or less."

"But you know this area, right?"

"I suppose I do." The boy looked around as if he could confirm that statement by checking the familiarity of the surrounding wilderness.

"Well then," Marshall said as he extended his hand outward and waved the stranger forward. "Maybe we can help each other."

"Whoa!" Rob spun in his seat and grabbed Marshall's arm. "Hold on. What the hell are you talking about?"

Leigh watched as Marshall discretely lifted up the bag of marijuana and gave Rob a wink. "I think we found the answer to our little import problem."

Rob's furrowed brow and dramatic frown immediately flipped into a foolish grin.

Alex, too, seemed to have caught on right away. She whispered, "Ooh, nice thinking, baby."

Leigh wasn't exactly certain what her cohorts were plotting, but it was obvious it involved this unknown man approaching their vehicle. While Leigh wouldn't have called herself a distrusting person, putting her future in the hands of someone they knew absolutely nothing about seemed to fall short of intelligent.

"Hey, wait!" Leigh tried to quietly yell from the backseat, unsure as to what exactly she was objecting to. "We should… think about this."

But as the words were leaving her mouth, the stranger reached the van and leaned on the sliding door frame. Viewing him from this close up, Leigh had to second guess herself. Perhaps she had read one too many thriller novels in her life, heard one too many urban legends at the sleepovers of her adolescence. This clearly wasn't the hitchhiker of campfire tales, dressed in all black and brandishing a hook for a hand. On the contrary, Leigh only thinks of one way to describe the college kid who stood against their van:

He seems nice enough.

As if to further suggest this point, the boy raised the brim of his cap, lifting the heavy shadow from his eyes. "What'd you folks have in mind?"

Alex flashed her perfectly white teeth. "Why don't you get in and we'll tell you *allll* about it."

"Whoa!" Rob raised a hand towards the boy like a Force-wielding Jedi, apparently less trusting than Alex, to Leigh's relief. "Now just hold up there, pal. We haven't exactly voted on anything yet."

Leigh found herself surprised to be siding with Rob for the first time since meeting him. While he and Marshall seemed to have been on the same page before, Rob hadn't considered that the plan would involve giving something to this outsider in return, even something as mundane as a ride. That, of course, was in direct violation of the "asshole code," which clearly stated one should never fall victim to the follies of generosity.

"Who says we have to vote on anything?" Alex snarled back. "Is this your van? I didn't think so."

Eliza gently placed a hand on Rob's bicep in a coaxing manner. "Oh c'mon, Rob. It's no big deal; we can trust him. There's plenty of room next to *Leigh*."

Leigh's head darted to the girl in the front seat. Her eyes widened as she stared daggers at Eliza, her heart rate increasing to a steady, hammering thump. Was her friend innocently trying to play matchmaker...or might there be an ulterior motive behind Eliza's eyes?

Two nights ago, the group had snuck into their hotel's pool after hours with a bottle of whiskey. By chance, Marshall discovered the staff had failed to lock the door of the spa, allowing them access to both the heated pool and spacious hot tub. Bloodstreams coursing with alcohol, the college students practiced their cannonballs and splashed chlorinated water at each other, all the while expecting to be kicked out at any moment. And even though Leigh was not as drunk as any of her friends, she was actually enjoying herself for the first time since arriving in the Canadian city.

But eventually and inevitably, the last auburn drop of Jack Daniels had fallen from the bottle, leaving Leigh's companions wanting more. Unfortunately, Montreal liquor stores and gas stations wouldn't sell alcohol after 11 PM—a fact that deeply upset everyone except Leigh, prompting Marshall to repeat "fuckin' Canadians" several times throughout their trip. After visiting their fifth sports bar to find only more hockey on the TV and more gravy on their French fries instead of ketchup, Marshall had turned the expression into something of a catch phrase. If anyone wanted anything further alcoholic to drink, someone was going to have to hustle back to the hotel suite.

"I'll go," Marshall offered, and was immediately echoed by Alex's announcement that she'd be going with him. As the two grabbed towels and threw t-shirts over their semi-damp bodies, Eliza pulled herself out of the hot tub as well.

"I'm gonna have a quick smoke," she said, pushing her feet though a pair of lime green flip-flops. Perhaps it was due to the alcoholic fog slowing her thought processes, but Leigh didn't even realize that she'd be alone with Rob until after everyone else had already left. Perhaps it was for this same reason that she didn't realize he had wrapped his arm around her shoulder the moment Eliza walked out the door, and his face was suddenly a mere inch from hers.

"What are you doing?" Leigh asked, trying to hide the concern in her voice with a forced chuckle.

"You're lookin' good t'night, Leigh." Rob's voice came out a sloppy slur. He'd had far more to drink than anyone else.

"Uh, thanks Rob." Leigh was growing more uncomfortable with each passing second. What did this guy think he was doing?

"It must suck bein' all 'lone on dis trip wit' two couples."

"It's okay. I'm having a good time."

"Bullshit!" Rob laughed and raised a hand out of the water to poke her shoulder, splashing her face. A drop landed on her bottom eyelid, the chlorine stinging. "But hey, we gotta moment here, don't we? If you want to use it, I'd be down."

"Rob…" Leigh tried to inch her way out of the cradle of his heavy arm. "You're drunk. You know Eliza wouldn't like this very much."

"Well, hey!" The stench of booze radiating from his mouth was nauseating. "Friends share, don't they?"

Before Leigh could answer that ridiculous question, the sound of the pool area's glass door swinging open echoed off the room's high ceiling. Leigh turned, expecting to finally see a hotel staff member wagging his finger at the two trespassers. But it wasn't a maid or a bellboy that stood staring incredulously at the cozy couple.

It was Eliza.

"I forgot my lighter," she said, not taking her eyes off Leigh as she slowly reached into her sweatshirt pocket.

Leigh jumped out from under Rob's arm and kicked herself to the other side of the hot tub. She was unaware she had even begun speaking when the first lie that came into her head was coming out her mouth.

"Rob was telling me a secret," she said, forcing herself to smile. She then made a drinking motion with her hand that she was certain Rob couldn't see with her back to him.

Eliza slowly nodded. "Oh," she said. It was clear she'd identified Leigh's gesture. Whether or not she believed it was up for debate. She turned to Rob.

"Was it about me?"

Rob winked. "*Maaaaybe*," he replied, stretching the word out like a parent teasing their child about what their Christmas present might be. "What will you give me if I tell ya?"

Eliza smirked and lifted up her pack of Camel Lights. "How about a cigarette."

Rob's response was to jump out of the hot tub and land a deep kiss on his girlfriend's lips in a one deft movement. It was actually quite impressive considering his drunken state. Rob didn't even bother drying himself off before escorting Eliza out the door, his hand around her waist.

Leigh remained in the hot tub, wondering if Eliza suspected anything. Wondering what Rob would tell her if she questioned him. Not that he would be a reliable source at all in his current state, but she knew never to understatement a jealous girlfriend.

Not that there was anything to deny! Christ, how do I get myself into these things?

Fortunately, when the couple returned, their behavior was as normal as ever, and nothing further was mentioned about the subject for the remainder of the trip. When the group discussed their fun night over breakfast the next morning, a very hung-over Rob rubbed his aching temples and confessed, "I totally blacked out. I don't remember anything." The statement was awarded a high five from Marshall and secret relief from Leigh, who felt she'd put the awkward situation behind her.

Until now.

It seemed likely that Eliza had suspected her the entire time, and saw this as her opportunity to exact revenge. She was undoubtedly fully aware of Leigh's discomfort, something Leigh had never been able to hide when placed in situations she couldn't control. What better way to exploit her neurosis than to place her in extremely close quarters with someone who was most probably going to turn out to be a gigantic creep?

Leigh stared into Alex's beaming blue eyes as she too twirled around in her seat. "Looks like we found you a date after all!" she said, giggling.

All Leigh could do was turn her face towards the window in embarrassment. She didn't need to see the satisfied expression on Rob's face to know what he was about to say to the stranger.

"On second thought, why don't you *squeeze* in next to Leigh? I think she's getting lonely back there."

His intonation of the word "squeeze" sent a shiver down Leigh's spine. She was starting to doubt Rob's claim that he had no recollection of the night in the hot tub. It was beginning to seem more plausible that he too was using this stranger as a form of payback, a way to retaliate for her rejection of his advances.

"Only if you don't mind."

Leigh spotted the brim of the boy's faded cap in her peripheral vision and realized he was speaking to her. She looked up, immediately startled by the indisputable warmth in his eyes. She still didn't feel one hundred percent comfortable inviting a stranger onto the seat next to her, but she also couldn't deny the strange yet pleasurable warmth that resonated throughout her entire body just from catching his gaze.

They all think this is hilarious, don't they? "We're really putting her on the spot here, aren't we?" Well, fuck them.

Straightening her shoulders and ignoring the sneering Rob in the rearview mirror, Leigh took a deep breath and answered as confidently as she could.

"Go ahead."

Rob clapped his hands. "Well all right! What's your name, man?"

"Samuel Tucker." The boy pinched the brim of his cap and tugged it down. "But everyone calls me Sam. Nice to meet all of you."

Leigh moved over to make room for Sam, who took his place next to her with a welcoming smile. Rob waited for Alex to slide the door shut behind him before turning to face their new companion.

"Well, Sammy-boy, that's Marshall sitting in front of you and he's gonna fill you in on what we need from you in exchange for this ride."

Sam nodded. "All ears."

Rob yanked the gearshift into drive and stomped the accelerator. The back tires spun up a cloud of dirt and stones that clinked loudly against the undercarriage of the van as it jerked forward.

Leigh stared at Sam's inquisitive face as he listened to Marshall's proposal and felt something drop at the pit of her stomach.

She had been hesitant to invite the nice looking stranger into their car, worrying he might bring more trouble than he was worth. But now, as their van sped along under trees so tall they blocked out the sun, she found herself thinking it was Sam who was getting himself in trouble. Wasn't he the one taking the greater risk, entrusting his fate to a group of strangers who outnumbered him five to one? The possible repercussions for his involvement in their illegal scheme were far, far worse than the risk they were taking.

Her stomach rolled again

CHAPTER THREE

Despite having been a devoted Chevy man his entire life, Jake Spire had to admit that Ford was capable of making a decent truck. Perhaps it wasn't "Like a Rock," but his shiny, new, dark green F-150 was meeting his expectations in every other regard. When he had given up his company allegiance only to take advantage of the dealership's Ford sale, he expected to be yet another victim of that old axiom, "you get what you pay for." But here it was two weeks later and the truck had given him a single reason to regret. It even had a kick-ass stereo system, which was currently blasting CCR's "Green River" as he ripped along Route 6 to the ranger headquarters.

"I can hear the bullfrog callin' me!" Jake sang, pounding his fist to the beat on the steering wheel. With a hearty breakfast sitting in his belly and his favorite band playing on his way to work, Jake's mood was exceptionally high for a Monday morning. It also wasn't every weekend he got to get away from his responsibilities as a Vermont State forest ranger, and the previous one he had spent visiting his twin brother Jack for a couple days in Portland, Maine. After a fun few days of lobster and microbrews, it was time to get back to the "office." But the unmistakable fragrance of pine and the welcoming songs of birds and insects made it far from the worst office in the world.

Jake gently applied pressure to the brake as he turned the last corner in the road before the Vermont State Forest HQ came into view. Phil Carson's truck was already parked in his usual space, but that, of course, came as no surprise. Phil hadn't been able to take on any field work since he'd stumbled into that bear trap a month and three days ago. There was an aftertaste of guilt every time Jake recollected the day Phil suffered his horrible accident. Although he felt immensely sorry for his old coworker, Jake couldn't deny how eternally grateful he was that it had been Phil's foot snapping between the trap's rusted teeth, and not his own. Sure, broken bones healed, but to be restricted to the indoors for more than a month's time was hell on Earth for rangers like Jake and Phil. They had all signed up for this job for one reason and one reason only: an unconditional love for primeval wilderness, despite the endless risks that come into play when one exposes oneself to the elements.

Jake could only imagine how thankful Phil must be that his cast was scheduled to come off next week after being sidelined for so long. On the day of the accident, the two had been checking out yet another abandoned campsite, an unfortunate trend that had become a plague on their neck of the woods. Tourists these days just didn't have any respect for the maintenance of wild country, constantly leaving their campsites littered with beer cans, discarded clothing, and even smoldering campfires. Those cases were the worst of all, of course. It was far too easy for a renegade spark to escape the stone circle and ignite a single dry leaf or pine needle. Next thing you know, the entire forest is on fire.

Fucking flatlanders, Jake thought for the millionth time in his career, a phrase usually inspired by catching someone fishing without a license or attempting to feed the wildlife. But after discovering a copy of *Field and Stream* and a bottle of deer musk near the stone circle of the campsite's fire pit, Jake wasn't so sure he was looking at the leftovers of out-of-staters. Nine times out of ten, poaching was done by locals who knew the best areas to get away with their illegal hunting practices. But even poaching rednecks were usually smart enough not to leave behind a stockpile of incriminating evidence. Maybe it had been the mistake of a drunken stupor.

Jake had heard the metallic snap of the cast iron jaws and knew the scream was coming even before Phil began to holler a second later. He'd heard that horrific sound before and it had never left the audio archives of his mind. Hunting was one thing, especially when a rifle was in the hands of a seasoned marksman. Sometimes the animal would drop to the ground and find itself in critter heaven before it even knew it had been hit.

But traps?

Traps were cruel. Hell, they were straight out sadistic as far as Jake was concerned. But even more so, traps were dangerous—deadly, gnashing mouths hidden in the underbrush like landmines. A forgotten bear trap or snare could spell serious trouble for a strolling hiker or a hunting sportsman—or an unfortunate forest ranger patrolling the parameter.

Thank God the two men had been patrolling together. Phil would've been in an even worse spot if Jake hadn't been there to help him pry the trap apart and assist him to his four-wheeler. Even through the blinding pain of severed flesh and shattered bones, Phil could acknowledge how lucky he was that by chance on that day Jake had decided to tag along instead of staying behind during his lunch break.

"Who the *fuck* still uses old-school bear traps?" Phil bellowed as Jake sped him to the emergency room. Had it been Jake with the crushed foot, the intense pain would've surely stopped him from forming coherent words. But apparently it took far more to stop this tough old man from slinging obscenities. "I'm gonna catch the motherfucker who set that thing. I'll kill him!"

Jake ignored his partner's outburst while he radioed for the rookie, Doug, to go retrieve the other four-wheeler they'd been forced to leave behind at the campsite.

Doug hadn't found any further traps, but Phil's question still burned in his mind.

Who set that trap?

But nothing short of fancy police equipment and computer databases could solve the case, and their department didn't have the time or money to devote to such a detailed investigation. With miles and miles of rugged, wooded landscape, there was a whole world in which the perpetrator could hide. The rangers had no choice but to let the case go and just pray it would remain an isolated incident. Besides, the most important thing at the moment was that Phil was okay and that his injuries were not permanent.

The screen door of the headquarters swung open as Jake entered, its springs squealing a pathetic plea for some WD-40. The fact the screen was still attached to the door frame at all proved just how high the temperature had remained, even in the first week of September. In past years, Jake would've put the extra-ventilated door back into storage, along with the AC unit that still presently hummed in one of building's rear windows. He didn't even need to wear his windbreaker, and hung it on the coat hooks near the entrance as Phil registered a pair of day hikers. They were an attractive couple, probably in their late twenties, clad in color-coordinated L.L. Bean outfits.

Phil addressed the man and pointed at a form attached to a clipboard. "Just sign here and you'll be all set."

"Super," the man said, scribbling a line on the bottom of the paper before handing it back to Phil. Phil accepted the clipboard, gave it one final check, and added, "Before you go, may I interest you in any complimentary provisions?"

He gestured to a small display rack of dried meats and trail mix.

"Why thank you," the man said, grabbing a package of dried beef nuggets.

"I'll to have to pass," the woman said. "That's very generous, but I brought my own."

Phil winked at her like a mall Santa Clause trying to coerce a Christmas wish out of a shy child. "Well, how about a cup of coffee to start your day? I promise you won't find a cup this good at Starbucks."

The young woman smiled coyly. "Well, okay. I am still a bit groggy thanks to this one." She playfully elbowed her companion.

"Hey!" the man said. "You'll thank me later when we have the whole trail to ourselves this morning."

Phil handed her the cup of coffee. "Have fun, you two. And remember, even though it still feels like summer, the sun is setting earlier as the days get shorter. So give yourselves plenty of time to get out of the woods before dark."

"Of course, sir. Thanks again."

Jake gave the couple a friendly nod as they passed by and turned to the other ranger.

"How we doin' this morning, Phil?"

Without asking, Phil handed Jake a fresh cup of coffee. Jake accepted it like he did at the start of every workday, inhaling its aroma with an euphoric "*Mmm.*" Phil leaned back, placing his hands behind his balding head in a relaxed pose. With an ear-to-ear grin stretching across the forty-five year old's face, he exclaimed, "Cast comes off tomorrow!"

"Really? I thought you still had another week. That's great."

"You're telling me!" Phil hit a few keys on the computer then stood up, pulling his shoulders back and pushing his overweight belly forward, audibly popping several of his vertebrae in the process. "If I was stuck behind this desk another day, I'd go off the deep end. I belong out there."

"Well, maybe you'll watch your step from now on," Jake said, teasing his coworker.

But Phil didn't take the bait, directing his anger at the ones responsible for his condition. "Goddamned poachers! I would just love to catch the fucking bastard who set that trap!"

"You and me both, Phil. But like I've been telling you,

you're only going to riase your blood pressure if you don't let it go. Just consider yourself lucky that the teeth on that trap were as dull as they were or you might've lost a foot."

Phil retook his seat behind the computer, grumbling, "Tell me something I *don't* know."

The Ham radio to his left suddenly erupted with the fuzzy transmission of a ranger at another outpost.

"*HQ, this is Maple Ridge station requesting confirmation of radio test. Come back. Over.*"

Phil leaned his head towards the radio's microphone and pressed the appropriate button. "This is HQ. Radio communications are open. You may conclude testing. Over."

"*Test complete, HQ. Over and out.*"

Motioning with the steaming cup of coffee in his hand, Jake pointed at the radio. "Was that Doug?"

"Yeah," Phil answered. "I sent him up to Maple Ridge to have a quick look at the generator. Thing's been on the fritz lately. I asked him to do a radio test on his way out so he should be on his way back now."

Jake nodded. "Good. I'm sure Doug will figure out what's wrong. The kid's a whiz with small engines." Jake realized the heat emanating through the thin cup was starting to burn his hand. "Well, I guess I'll take this time to do some paper work while I wait for him."

Jake walked around a partitioned wall that separated his and Phil's work stations. He sat down at his desk, placing the cup of coffee on top of a yellow pad of sticky notes. As he waited for his computer to boot up, Jake sipped the dark, delicious brew. He'd already had a cup with his breakfast that morning at the Spruce Moose Diner, but Jake could never resist Phil's special blend. It was the only cup that Jake never bothered adding cream or sugar to, preferring to savor the drink's distinct flavor.

The computer's home screen sparked to life, a breathtaking Vermont mountaintop landscape offsetting the usual icons and toolbar. Before Jake placed the cup back down on the desk, he took one more generous gulp. He could already feel the caffeine taking effect, and felt truly awake for the first time that morning. Jake suspected that Phil added a secret shot of espresso to the concoction, but Phil always insisted that it was "for him to know and Jake to wonder." Still, there was no denying that the instant revitalization was something you'd never find in a cup of Folger's Crystals.

It wasn't long before Jake had reached the bottom of his mug. Though he could smell the steaming pot around the corner beckoning to him to take another, Jake purposely distracted himself with an email from the regional headquarters. For the thousandth time in his life, he'd made a promise to himself to cut back on the caffeine.

You beat nicotine addiction over a year ago, so cutting back on coffee should be a walk in the park, right?

Then again, Phil didn't greet Jake with a lit cigarette every morning.

The screen door sang its screeching song once more and then slammed shut as the youngest and newest ranger, Douglas Graham, made his usual noisy entrance. The twenty-something removed his hat to reveal a mop of bushy black hair that hung in front of his eyes. Doug's laid-back, bed-head style completely contradicted his straight-laced official uniform. Jake had known right away that the recent college graduate would be an ideal addition to their team after one look at his impressive résumé. Multiple internships, and high marks in every environmental science course offered at his school, paired well with his easy-going personality.

"Hey there Doug," Jake greeted the rookie. "Were you able to fix the generator at Maple Ridge?"

Doug finished his Vitamin Water bottle and nodded. "Yeah, it should be good to go. I gave it a good cleaning and it seems to be working." He shot his empty bottle at the trash bin. It bounced off the back rim and fell in.

Jake raised his eyebrows. "Nice one. You ready to go?"

"Just let me grab a cup of coffee and I'll be all set." Doug then turned to Phil. "So do you think you'll be able to hold down the fort while we're gone?"

Phil shook his head, keeping his eyes trained on the computer screen. "Har har. Enjoy it while you can, newbie. After tomorrow, it'll be your ass stuck behind this desk."

Doug filled his coffee thermos and smiled. Phil had him there. If not for the veteran's foot injury, Doug would've started out in the office doing all the grunt work. As it was, Doug received a month's worth of fieldwork and enjoyed every second of it, temporary as it may be.

Doug took a challenging step towards Phil's desk. "But you know it won't last for long, old man. I bet you'll step into another trap the first day you forget your glasses." He grinned, raising up three fingers. "How many, Phil?"

Phil raised his middle finger in return. "You tell me."

Jake's hand wasn't quick enough to stifle a laugh at the childish behavior.

"And you can kiss my ass too." Phil said, turning the hand gesture in Jake's direction.

"I'm sorry, Phil, but he's got your number."

Phil narrowed his eyes at his associates and muttered, "Yeah, whatever. We'll see who gets the last laugh when *you're* the one twiddling your thumbs between radio tests.

Doug scoffed and tapped the side of the metal box. "Why do we even still use this ancient technology? Would it kill us to get with the times?"

Phil finished the coffee in his paper cup, crumpling it into a tight ball and throwing it at the cocky newbie. "Well, Douglas, why don't you write the State and request an increase in our funding so we might be able to afford such an improvement. I mean, they haven't bothered to throw a cent our way in the last five years, but maybe your irresistible charm is just what we need."

Before Doug could offer up a clever comeback, Jake interfered to put the bickering to an end. "In all seriousness, the Ham radio is reliable. It works when our walkie talkies and phones fail." He unlocked the wooden door of the station's gun cabinet and handed a rifle to Doug before taking one for himself. "All right, all right. What do you say we get out of here already? We've got work to do."

Doug rolled his eyes and accepted the firearm "Ah yes, our trusty rifles. The most unnecessary equipment we could possible carry. I bet I could work here for thirty years without ever having to take a single shot."

"You should be so lucky," Phil mumbled, not bothering to look away from the papers on his desk. "I'd step in a bear trap everyday if it guaranteed we'd never have to use those things."

"Yeah, well, I think I'd rather shoot a bear everyday than step in its trap, but that's just me," said Doug.

"I'm not talking about shooting bears, kid. We carry pepper spray on our belts for a reason." Phil's eyes rose to meet Doug's.

"What, you shoot *people*? I guess didn't realize I was working alongside Judge Dredd."

Phil reverted his gaze to his computer. With a volume just over a whisper he replied, "Not me."

Phil's last comment hung in the air like a paper bag floating in the breeze. When Doug finally realized what the older man was saying, his head jerked to where Jake stood waiting at the door. Instead of offering an explanation, Jake only said, "Come on. Let's go."

Although it was obvious judging by the probing look in Doug's eyes that he wanted to know the story between Jake Spire and the weapon resting on his shoulder, the rookie bit his tongue and followed his superior's order. As he took his first step towards the building's exit, Phil waved goodbye, saying, "Enjoy yourselves out there, boys! I'll be here...having a blast."

Doug looked back over his shoulder. "Don't sweat it, Phil. Without you around to entertain us, I'm sure nothing interesting is going to happen today. Right, Jake?"

Jake caressed the smooth, freshly oiled wood of the rifle's stock resting on his shoulder. Years ago, as a rookie, he'd been tasked with oiling the rifles the same day Phil asked if he wanted to accompany him on his route for the first time. He remembered inhaling the heavy aroma of the varnish only an hour later as he took aim at another human being. He'd never enjoy the smell again.

"Jake?"

Doug was staring at him, his hand reaching out for the keys that Jake still grasped.

Jake shook himself out of his dark trip down memory lane. He tossed the keys to Doug, who'd be driving the department's truck.

"Yeah, you're probably right. It's most likely gonna be just another Monday." His grip on the rifle tightened, darkening his fingernails and whitening his knuckles.

CHAPTER FOUR

"So, that's it?"

Sam leaned back into his seat, unfazed by the task assigned to him.

Marshall looked to Rob, Eliza, and Alex to see if there was anything he'd missed. After they nodded their heads in approval, he turned back to Sam. "Yeah...that's pretty much the whole deal. All we need is a way to get this—" he lifted the bag of pot, "—across the border without getting busted. And if you can pull it off, I don't think anyone here would be opposed to sharing a little bit of the wealth with you."

"Hey, if Sammy-boy can come through," Rob chimed in from the front seat, "then I think we could afford to throw more than just a *little* his way."

Sam brought his left hand to his chin, contemplating the proposal. All those seated in front of him stared, unblinking in anticipation. After ten seconds of silence, Alex couldn't stand it any longer.

"So, can you help us?"

The boy's eyes rose from the floor of the van.

"Well, if all you're looking for is a way to dodge the border patrol, then sure. I know a way. No sweat."

Sam's answer was greeted by a shared cheer that rocked

the frame of the vehicle. In her usual flirtatious manner, Alex planted a fat kiss on her palm and then pressed the hand to Sam's cheek. "You're the best! You just saved our asses big time."

Leigh brought her fingers to her mouth to conceal a smirk. Who knew what else Alex would've done in gratitude if Marshall wasn't sitting next to her? She wondered if anyone else noticed the lingering eye contact Alex offered Sam, or the way her eyebrow raised ever so slightly.

Leigh, of course, had grown quite accustomed to spotting this type of behavior from her roommate. What wasn't par for the course, however, was Sam's reaction. When Alex removed her hand, the boy looked away immediately to the window, as if the endless trees passing outside interested him far more. The initial connection Leigh felt towards this stranger was beginning to gain clarity. The fact that Sam didn't look twice at such typical "eye candy" further suggested a depth to him that surpassed the rest of her present company.

Leigh brushed a lock of hair from her forehead, summoning enough courage to look the handsome boy in the eyes. She still hadn't shaken that strange feeling of guilt that they might be leading Sam into more than he had bargained for

"You know," she said to him, "you don't have to do this if it's any trouble for you."

Sam flashed his teeth. "No trouble at all. Actually, it's really very simple. There's an un-posted hiking trail a little ways up that crosses over the border and reconnects to this same road. So all you have to do is walk your..." Sam hesitated, searching for the right word, "...*stuff* through the woods while someone takes your van across the checkpoint."

Eliza drummed her fingers on the dashboard in excitement. "Sounds pretty good!"

"Hell yeah, it does!" Marshall agreed.

Rob slowed the van to allow himself to look back at Marshall in the rearview mirror. "Don't get too excited, man. You're the one who's going to be driving the van across the border."

"Oh, really?" Marshall challenged.

"Yes, really. Ain't no way I'm parting ways with our score. Besides, you owe me and you know it."

Leigh expected Marshall to retort with some half-witted comeback but his response was merely a single word.

"Shit."

And then Leigh remembered: the first night they were in Montreal, they'd wasted no time getting drunk at the first pub they stumbled upon. Long after he'd lost count of the number of beers he'd emptied, Marshall excused himself to go take a piss. But instead of heading to the bathrooms in the back of the tavern, Marshall staggered outside, relieving himself against the side of the Peel Pub. Leigh was the only one to realize Marshall had yet to come back right before Alex discovered she had an unheard voicemail on her cell phone.

"They threw me in the drunk tank. Come bail me out."

Two hours later, it was Rob who had offered cash from his own wallet to get his tanked buddy back to the hotel, safe and sound. Leigh found it unusually bighearted of Rob to step up to the plate without a moment's hesitation—but now here he was, using the favor as leverage.

The world made sense again.

Marshall eyed his friend behind the steering wheel. "So you're saying if I do this...I won't owe you the money?"

"Like it never happened."

Marshall gritted his teeth, swallowed hard, and finally said, "Okay."

"Well, all right!" Rob punched the roof of the van, adding a high-pitched whoop. "Looks like I'll be taking a hike with my main man, Sam!"

"It's nothing," Sam said sheepishly. "You guys are taking me all the way to Burlington. It's the least I can do. In fact, I have something else for you if anyone is interested."

Leigh watched as Sam hoisted his backpack from the floor and placed it in his lap. He tugged the zipper open and reached his hand into the largest pocket A moment later he pulled out a plastic zip-locked bag filled with dark strips of dried meat.

Sam shook the bag and smiled. "Anyone hungry?"

Alex eyed the bag without attempting to hide her look of curiosity and disgust. "What is it?"

"It's jerky!"

Marshall put an arm around Alex and eyed the bag as well. "I don't know, dude. It doesn't look much like a Slim Jim to me."

"Oh this is much better than that factory packaged junk," Sam replied. "It's homemade." He looked from one passenger to another. "So, any takers?"

Marshall offered his most polite smile. "Uh, that's real nice of you, man, but I'm not really that hungry."

"And I'm a vegetarian," Alex piped in, lying through her teeth.

"I'm going to have to pass as well," Rob shouted to the back of the van. He nudged Eliza. "Don't have a taste for squirrel." Eliza tried to cover Rob's rude commentary by quickly following it up with, "Maybe later, Sam. After we've gotten back and blazed up. I'm sure I'll be craving it by then."

Sam shrugged as if to say "Whatever," but Leigh didn't fail to notice the subtle manner in which his eyes narrowed or how he adjusted himself in his seat. Leigh had paid enough attention in her psychology classes to know these were signifiers of discomfort, even possible feelings of dejection. She shook her head for the thousandth time that trip, once again disapproving of the group's collective behavior. She tapped Sam's shoulder.

"I guess I'll try a little piece."

Sam's gaze sprung from the floor and met hers, sending another surge of electricity down her spine and into every limb.

"Check out Leigh going for it!" Marshall teased. "Most adventurous thing we've seen you do this whole trip."

Leigh rolled her eyes and accepted the dried chunk of meat from Sam. The strip appeared harmless enough, a rich brown color that gave off a distinctively smoky, gamey fragrance. While the rest of the gang watched, Leigh took a timid nibble off the tip of the piece.

It took only three chews for her to decide the jerky was absolutely delicious.

"Wow!" she remarked, genuinely impressed with the meat's flavor. "Sam, you weren't kidding. This is really delicious."

Sam chuckled, most likely surprised by such a strong reaction. In any other case, Leigh would've worried her comments were coming off as blatant flirting, but she just couldn't help it now. It really was that good.

"You guys should really try this. It's probably the best jerky you'll ever taste."

"We said we're good," Rob shot back, speaking for everyone.

"Whatever." Leigh reached into the bag for another, larger piece. "Your loss."

A pothole sent a violent tremor through the van, jostling the jerky strip from Leigh's fingers. The jerky landed on the sliver of vinyl seat between her and Sam, and they both instinctually reached for the meat at the same time.

Their fingers connected momentarily. Leigh froze.

She looked up to find Sam doing the same, and their eyes locked awkwardly in a shared moment of stillness. His touch was delightfully warm; several degrees above her own chilled, air conditioning-exposed digits. She tried to say "sorry," or "excuse me," but found herself taking a deep breath and swallowing her words.

Sam removed his fingers from Leigh's and offered the "excuse me" that Leigh hadn't been able to. She could only shrug as if to say, "Don't worry about it," and brought the piece of jerky to her mouth. Mercifully, it seemed no one in the van had witnessed their moment, and for that, Leigh was eternally grateful.

The van continued along the winding dirt road that gradually straightened the further along they traveled. Once the turns had ceased altogether and the road became a long, flat lane, Rob pushed his foot down on the pedal hard enough for their speed to reach sixty-five miles per hour.

"Slow down," Eliza ordered her boyfriend. "Just because it's straight doesn't mean you have to turn this into a drag race."

Rob ignored her request and replied, "We're making good time. I want to get to that trail already."

"But we've already almost mowed down one person today. Are you going for two? Slow down!"

Leigh tuned out the remainder of the argument and concentrated on the scenery whipping by her window. It offered little variety: just trees, rocks, and bushes. She would've much rather been chatting with Sam and getting to know him better, but damn her incompetent brain, she just couldn't think of a topic that didn't seem forced or trite.

What about this weather? No way.

So, how do you like college? Yuck. It was a generic question she herself was sick of getting from about every member in her family tree.

It also didn't help that every other passenger in the van could eavesdrop to their heart's desire. At a loss, Leigh kept her eyes trained on the window.

Just as the monotony of the identical trunks and shrubs began to put her to sleep, a large square-shaped object emerged from the greenery. Leigh leaned closer to her window, squinting to make out the words on the faded billboard coming into view.

Its paint was washed out almost to the point of transparency. Unlike the modern advertisements Leigh had seen looming over the roads just outside of Montreal, this sign had obviously been standing here for many years. But even against its weather-ravaged wood, the billboard's cracked lettering was still legible.

Eat at the Spruce Moose Diner! Just two miles past the sawmill in Embry, VT!

The text was accompanied by a painting of a waitress who strongly resembled Lucille Ball. She stood in front the supposed mill with a plate of eggs, bacon, and toast held above her head. Three burly men in flannel shirts and suspenders gathered around her. Though she was sure the men were supposed to be attracted to the tantalizing breakfast, Leigh couldn't ignore an unfamiliar cold feeling that crept into her gut as she watched the billboard fly by.

Three men approaching a lone woman from behind. Surrounding her.

Hungry men.

"Hey!"

Lost in this strange reverie, Leigh jumped when Sam shouted over Marshall's mix CD blasting on the van's stereo.

"You better slow down a little," he called up to Rob. "The trail's right up here."

Rob leaned forward in his seat, squinting through the windshield. "I don't see anything."

"Just do what he says," Eliza said with a sigh, not bothering to open her eyes as she leaned her head against her window.

"See that white birch tree coming up on your right?" Sam pointed, though there was no way Rob could see the gesture. "That marks the opening."

Leigh leaned to look out past the dashboard and saw the landmark that Sam was pointing out. In the midst of a thick group of grayish-brown tree trunks, there was no way anyone could miss the white, papery bark of the birch.

"Yeah, okay," Rob muttered, pulling the van to the side of the road. "I see it now."

To Rob's credit, the van stopped perfectly in line with the white birch. Alex pulled the sliding door open and there it was: an unmarked but clearly identifiable path.

"Last stop," Rob said, mimicking a public bus driver. "Everybody out." He then turned around to Marshall and added, "Except for you, buddy. Your shift's just beginning."

"And mine." Alex swung a slender arm around Marshall's neck. "I wouldn't abandon my man."

Eliza opened her door and lifted up the bag of pot, shaking it tauntingly. "Not even for this?"

"On second thought…" Alex giggled at her own joke. "But seriously, you guys better go before I change my mind."

Among the discarded Jimmy Dean wrappers that had been that morning's gas station breakfast, Leigh found a couple bottles of water and few choice snacks. She loaded all the supplies into her backpack, but Sam insisted he carry the load. Rob, too, carried a pack, but his willingness to heft some weight was not a chivalrous gesture: his pack only contained the precious weed, a prize he demanded be kept securely on his own person.

Marshall climbed in behind the wheel and slammed the door. Leigh couldn't help but notice the aggression behind this action.

"So I just keep going straight on this?" he asked Sam.

"Yup. Just look for Miller's Road. That'll take you right to the border patrol. Once you get past them, just keep goin' 'till you see an old collapsed farmhouse. The trail comes out just past that."

Alex, who had moved into the front seat, playfully jabbed an elbow into her boyfriend's side. "Think you can handle that?"

"I think I got it" he said flatly.

Sam continued, "You'll most likely beat us there, so you'll probably have to wait a little while."

"Yeah," Rob said, jiggling his backpack, "we might take a little break."

Marshall grimaced. "You better not smoke any more than your share."

"Of course I won't."

Leigh knew Marshall had every reason to be concerned, and judging by his furrowed brow, she was pretty sure he didn't believe Rob either.

Eliza walked over and leaned on the driver's side mirror. "I thought you were supposed to get paranoid *after* you smoke, not before."

"I'm serious." Marshall's eyes matched his words, which had taken on an uncharacteristically edgy tone. "If half that bag is gone by the time we meet up, I'll be fuckin' pissed. You hear me?"

"Loud and clear, dude," said Rob. "We're just going to have a tiny toke to make the hike a little more tolerable, that's all. I promise."

Marshall turned his attention to Eliza. "Do me a favor? Make sure he keeps his word."

"Oh, don't worry, I will. We'll save the *real* party for when we get home. But for now, we'll have just a little sample to pass the time." Eliza blew the couple in the van a kiss. "Bye, kiddies! Enjoy your air conditioning; I know I'll be missing it in like two minutes. This bag is the only reason I'm not hitching a ride with you guys."

"How about you, Leigh?"

The mention of her name snapped Leigh's attention away from her nervous examination of the looming forest. She turned to see Rob shooting her a malicious grin.

"Is that your reason too?"

Leigh decided to ignore the question, refusing to give Rob the satisfaction of getting under her skin. There was no doubt in anyone's mind that Leigh had no interest in marijuana or any other drug. Still, she felt the blood rushing to her cheeks at Rob's teasing comment. Leigh couldn't deny that she chose to accompany the trio through the woods just to spend some more time with Sam.

"Okay guys," Alex said, buckling her seatbelt. "We're gonna get moving. See you in a bit."

Marshall leaned his head out and gave his best patronizing grin. "Enjoy your scenic nature walk!"

With that, the van was gone, tires spinning up pebbles as it disappeared into a cloud of dust.

Sam spun from the entrance of the trail to address the group. "Everyone ready?"

Leigh shrugged. "As ready as we'll ever be."

"All right, then. Let's do it."

They had just entered the trees, taking no more than three steps down the dirt path, when Eliza asked timidly, "There's nothing in these woods we should be concerned about, right?"

Rob slapped his forearm, grumbling, "Besides these mosquitoes?"

"I meant is there anything dangerous."

Sam, who led the line of four marching through the trees, stopped to look back at Eliza. "These woods? Heck, no. It's as safe as your own backyard."

The answer seemed good enough for Eliza, who nodded and continued on her way. Sam gave Leigh a reassuring smile before returning his attention to the uneven trail.

Leigh stared at the Major League Baseball emblem sewn into the back of Sam's cap as they trudged along. The part of her that had been hesitant about choosing not to go with Alex and Marshall in the van—the part that couldn't ignore the luxuries of a comfortable Rob-less ride—had completely dissipated. And all it took was one smile from a handsome guy.

Is that how easy you are? Asked Leigh's critical inner voice. *Is that all it takes for you to lose your head and make a poor decision? Maybe you're not as different from Alex as you thought.*

But then, instead of feeling yet another pang of regret, Leigh brightened.

Well then, maybe I'm not. Maybe I know how to relax and have a good time after all.

Just as she was starting to enjoy the self-assured feeling of empowerment, a flash of movement to Leigh's left ruined the moment. She stopped, examining the endless weave of branches and tree trunks that obscured her vision. Besides the greenery, there was nothing to be seen. Perhaps it had been a deer, now perfectly still and camouflaged by the undergrowth.

Eliza, who'd been paying attention to her own feet, bumped into Leigh's back.

"Why'd you stop? Is something wrong?"

Instead of causing alarm and making herself look just as much of a fish out of water as her friend, Leigh waved her hand and kept moving. "It was nothing, just thought I saw a squirrel or something."

But as she picked up her pace to catch up to Sam, Leigh's eyes kept darting to the surrounding evergreens, surprised at how shaken she was. Even if something was indeed watching them, it probably wasn't anything to be concerned about. It was just a frightened deer or another startled animal. It had to be.

CHAPTER FIVE

Dark clouds stretched across the afternoon sky. Had Marshall been back in San Diego, driving out to the beach for a full day of surfing, the blackening sky would've certainly turned his mood. But as it was, the worsening conditions were turning his previous scowl into a self-satisfied smile. By the time his friends reached the meeting point, they'd be drenched from the sudden downpour that was sure to be unleashed at any moment. Meanwhile, he'd be relaxing comfortably in the dry van, listening to the soothing sound of raindrops tapping the roof and the mellow rhythms of his Bob Marley album.

That is, of course, if they would ever going to find the turn they were looking for. If Sam's directions were correct, it seemed like he and Alex had been driving for far too long.

Alex craned her head to peer up through the windshield. "It looks like it's going to rain. Are you sure you didn't miss the turn?"

Marshall couldn't help but notice her choice to say "you" instead of "we," but he took a deep breath before replying.

"I'm sure, babe. Have you seen a Miller's Road yet?"

"No, but it feels like we've been driving for way longer than we should've been, and I don't want those guys to have to wait in the rain."

Marshall turned his head away to hide his sneer.

I guess that's where we disagree.

"I totally agree," he said, looking at his girlfriend. "But I guess this is what we get for taking directions from some backwoods hillbilly."

Though he was staring straight ahead to pay strict attention to the uneven dirt road, Marshall could feel Alex's menacing glare in response to his comment.

"Don't call Sam a hillbilly. It makes you sound like Rob."

Marshall nodded. She had him there.

"Just call him a….a local," Alex said, finishing her thought.

Marshall gritted his teeth. *Yeah, just a local. As if that's what you'd call him if he had buckteeth and a beer belly.* The thought suddenly spurred another. *As if you'd still call me your boyfriend if I had the same..*

"Well, for a local he sucks at giving directions. He made it sound so simple. But where the fuck is it?"

Alex shrugged. "You probably weren't paying attention and missed it. I think you should turn around."

His grip on the wheel tightened. Damn, she was pretty to look at—and incredible in bed—but it was times like these that made Marshall question if perhaps they weren't so different after all. There was no arguing that Alex was perpetually caught up on the outer appearance of people, but was he any better? If he was, why wasn't he chasing after girls with a little more going on upstairs? Someone who wasn't always so quick to deny all responsibility and pass blame to anyone she could within an arm's reach. Someone like Leigh.

Whoa. Where did that come from?

Marshall shook his shaggy head of hair, sending the surprising thought to the back of his mind where he could ignore it for the moment. In the meantime, he had an argument to engage in.

"You want me to backtrack so we can waste time looking for a sign we both somehow missed?" He didn't wait for an answer. "I don't think so."

"Then maybe we should call them."

Marshall didn't care for the increasingly self-righteous tone of her voice. This was their first moment alone during the trip outside of a bedroom, and look at the result: his impatience verse haughtiness. Not exactly indicative of a healthy relationship.

He sighed. "Do I really have to tell you there's no cell service out here?"

"So then what the fuck are we supposed to do?"

"I don't know!" Marshall shouted back, surprised at the volume of his own voice. He took a breath. Moments such as this made him thankful for having been brought up by a Buddhist stepfather. He'd picked up a few techniques that came in handy when attempting to conquer a massive wave— or preventing his emotions from getting the best of him in a heated conversation such as this one.

"We'll just keep driving, okay?" he said, as calmly as he could. And then couldn't help but add, "And hope that redneck was right."

Alex fell back into her seat, arms folded across her busty chest. "What,a brilliant plan."

No mantras or breathing techniques could help him this time. Marshall exploded.

"Why, thank you! And let me just say your genius ideas are *invaluable*. Thank God I have you here to—"

"Shut up and stop the car!"

Alex's shriek caught him completely off guard. He'd just been getting into a satisfying rant, but her sudden outburst stopped him dead.

"What?"

,Craning her neck to look behind them, she hollered: "Stop the fucking car! I saw something!"

"Okay, okay." Marshall stomped on the break, lurching both of their bodies forward. Fortunately, their seatbelts saved them from slamming into the dashboard. Marshall braced himself against the tirade that was sure to come from bringing the van to such an abrupt halt, but instead Alex ripped off her belt and bolted from the van.

"Hey!" he called after her. "Hold up! What did you see?"

When she failed to respond, Marshall reached down and unbuckled his own belt. *And to think if I hadn't left the west coast I could be hanging ten right now instead of wanting to hang myself.*

His door opened with a loud rusty creak, a telltale noise of Rob's neglect for his car. Despite the darkening sky, the temperature remained high, and a wave of humid heat enveloped Marshall as he stepped out. By the time he reached where Alex was wading through the tall grass at the side of the road, tiny beads of perspiration were already rolling down the back of his neck.

He watched as his girlfriend ducked down into the sea of swaying thistles. "What the *hell* are you doing?"

A second later, Alex emerged hefting a long, wooden post. At the top of the pole, a makeshift sign spelled out MILLER'S ROAD in crude, faded handwritten letters. Marshall stared in awe as Alex proudly held up her trophy. With a hand on her hip and another wrapped around the post as if it were a strip club pole, she resembled a model for the kind of calendar you might find in the office of a seedy garage. Marshall could see it now: *Twelve Months of Back Road Girls.*

"You can start kissing my ass at anytime," Alex said victoriously.

"Honey," Marshall said, his voice lowering, "I'd like to do way more than that to you right now. And there isn't a single person around to see."

Alex returned his hungry stare with her own seductive glance. But it unfortunately vanished the next instant, replaced by sobering reason. "When we get back, *maybe* I'll let you redeem yourself. But right now we don't have time." She let go of the sign, returning it to the engulfing weeds. "In the meantime, be sure to get that tongue of yours ready. It has a lot of work ahead of it."

"I'll start on my exercises," Marshall joked, extending a hand out to help Alex back onto the dirt road. With her palm securely in his grip, he yanked her forward, embracing her with a passionate opened-mouth kiss. Alex wasted no time invading his mouth, her tongue expertly wrestling his own. His hand found its way to her left breast, kneading the lovely flesh through her 36D-sized bra. But Alex started to push herself away from Marshall just as the pressure began to build in his groin,, despite how badly she clearly wanted him.

"Wait," she whispered between gasps of pleasure, "Let's not get into it. We have to get to the others."

Marshall sighed. "Yeah, I guess you're right." It wasn't easy releasing the girl from his fondling hands, but at least no one was around to notice the circus tent that had become of his pants. It dawned on him, however, that an embarrassing boner was the least of his concerns right now.

"So, you found the sign, that's great. But where's the road?"

Alex brushed her hair back, apparently not concerned. "It's obvious the sign's been cut down and thrown here. So that means we must have passed it."

Marshall's fists tightened when he realized he had to concede. "I guess without the sign we couldn't see the road through all this tall grass." He took a deep breath. "I guess we have to…go back."

Alex's hand slapped the right cheek of his ass. He flinched, feeling the sting of her hand through his jeans. "Just like I said." She licked his earlobe. "You know, you're lucky I don't have a dick or you'd be sucking it right now."

"Let's just go, okay?"

"I thought you'd never ask!"

The couple joined hands and started to walk back towards the van, all the bickering now a thing of the past. Swinging arms, Alex continued to tease him for being wrong while Marshall ignored her playful pestering and ruminated on the physically dependent state of their relationship.

We were at each other's throats only a minute ago. But one quick round of grab-ass and look at us: right as rain.

Was this really the extent of his capability to maintain a steady relationship? He swore he'd never end up like his parents—divorced, over their mutual selfish search to find the greatest sex on earth. With his mid-twenties right around the corner, Marshall had enough experience to know that sex never differed *that* greatly. If discovering a new bedroom trick here and there was all he needed, he wouldn't have been bothered by the one-dimensional personalities his partners always seemed to have. Moving away from home was supposed to have changed all that, a chance to find someone far from the empty-headed bimbos that followed him around the beach. But perhaps there are some things you *can't* get away from. Maybe shallowness isn't a product of poor nurturing. It could be genetic, like when the rotten genes that cause alcoholism jump from one generation to the next.

If that's the case, I'm fucked. No pun intended.

"What's wrong, honey?"

The concern in Alex's voice wrenched Marshall from the bowels of his grim daydream, his heart instantly warmed by the look of genuine concern in his girlfriend's face.

"Don't feel bad about missing the turn," she said, her slender arm snaking its way around his. "I made you feel bad, didn't I?" Her voice took on a babyish tone as she circled one finger across his chest.

"Nah, it's okay."

"I hope so. Because I'd be a mess without you. You know that, right?"

Marshall did not. In fact, this was one of the few times he'd seen her display true devotion.

"You're more to me than just a pair of dreamy eyes and a handsome face," she continued. "If that's all I wanted, I'd probably be dating Rob." She made a gagging noise. "God. Puke."

That was all Marshall needed to hear. His folks's marital troubles may have done a number on him, but as he lovingly stared at his girlfriend, he began to think that just maybe he had a shot at a meaningful, long term relationship....

This feeling lasted the entire walk back to van. Then, it disappeared, blown away by the summer breeze after one look at their lopsided vehicle.

"Alex," he muttered, "Please. Please tell me I'm not seeing this right."

She was silent. The van was tilted at a severe angle, the driver's side headlight drastically lower than the rest of the car's body. It didn't take a mechanic to realize that one of the front tires was as flat as flat can get.

This time, Marshall didn't bother taking a deep breath or repeating one of the soothing expressions his stepfather had passed down to him. Instead, his voice echoed against the tall trees and between the rolling green mountains.

"How the *fuck* did this happen?!"

Alex seemed to remain considerably calmer as she assessed the situation. To her, the answer seemed obvious enough. "You must have hit a sharp rock or something. These back roads are terrible."

Marshall ignored her theory and jogged over to the damaged wheel, which was leaking the last of its remaining air with a devastating hissing sound. Marshall immediately spotted the culprit glinting in the little sunlight that remained. With one vigorous tug, but Marshall was able to remove the object, ripping away some small chunks of rubber from the tire as well.

Alex was standing a few feet away near the vehicle's taillights. "What is it?"

Marshall slowly stood up, eyes glued to the thing resting in his palm. He walked over to Alex, grabbed her right wrist, and gently placed the cold, metal object in her hand.

It was a circular saw blade the size of a compact disc, the points of its jagged teeth digging into her fingers.

CHAPTER SIX

Beneath the canopy of the interweaving leaves and evergreen needles, Leigh hadn't noticed the rate at which the sun was fading until it had completely vanished behind an impenetrable wall of threatening gray clouds. Sam came to a dead stop ahead of her and looked up with a worried grimace.

"Uh oh," he said through gritted teeth. "Looks like we may get a little wet."

Leigh looked skyward as well. The atmosphere had become colorless.

Leigh frowned. "I hope you're right when you say 'a little.' By the looks of it, seems like may get drenched. How far do we have left to go?"

"It's still a little ways. We could get lucky, though. It may hold off."

Though the seemingly immortal pessimist who lived inside Leigh had her own thoughts on the subject, she was able to reply with a pretty convincing "Fingers crossed," before Eliza yelled from behind.

"You guys! Look at me!"

The couple turned to see Eliza holding up a digital camera to her eye. Leigh didn't have a chance to adjust her hair or even smile before she was blinded by a flash of white light.

"Oh, thanks Eliza," she said, trying to rub away the floating white dots that hovered in her vision. "I'm sure that will be a good one."

Rob, who had stopped to tie the laces of his black Converse, jogged up to Eliza's side and shook his head when he saw the camera in her hands. "I can't believe you brought that thing. Don't you already have enough embarrassing photos of us to put on Facebook?"

Eliza's retort was a point-blank flash right into his eyes. Rob blindly tried to snatch the pink camera from her grasp, but Eliza evaded his swipe with a quick sidestep, giggling the entire time.

"C'mon you guys," she said, backing up to a take a group shot of her three companions. "When else are we ever going to find ourselves smuggling pot through the woods? These are memories, people!" Her finger pressed down on the shutter button with an audible *click*. "Besides, it's so beautiful here!"

Sam nodded his head in agreement. "You guys did choose a good time to travel through this way, while the summer's still holding on."

"We didn't 'choose' anything," Rob muttered, taking the lead as he pushed his way in between Sam and Leigh. "Labor Day was just our last chance before school started."

Leigh let Rob walk ahead and didn't bothering commenting that he didn't know the way. Instead she turned to Sam and asked, "What day does your semester start?"

Sam hesitated, biting his lip. "Actually, JCV's fall semester is already in session. We began August 25th."

"So why were you home? Did you get Labor Day off?"

"Not exactly," Sam's voice lowered, "I'm at the end of serving a campus suspension."

Rob stopped in his tracks and spun a sneakered heel. "Hey, now!" Despite Sam's best effort to keep the comment between himself and Leigh, Rob's eavesdropping ears had picked up every word. "Things just got a little more interesting! All right, Sam, let's hear it."

Even in the dim light, Leigh could see the red blossoming in Sam's cheeks. "It's nothing, really," he said. But Leigh knew from experience that Rob wasn't about to let him off the hook that easy.

"Sam…"

Leigh stepped in front of him. "He obviously doesn't want to get into it. So let's just leave him alone."

"No, it's all right ." Sam pulled on the brim of his cap, a nonchalant gesture that Leigh couldn't help but notice helped conceal his eyes. "Let's just say I was defending the honor of a lady…and I may have gone a little too far."

Rob gave Sam a hard. approving slap on the back and shook him playfully. "Sammy! Kicking ass for the ladies! How chivalrous. Fuckin' Knights of the Round Table and shit."

"Ha," Sam gave a forced, unenthusiastic laugh. "No, it was nothing like that. Just a brief loss of control that I've paid dearly for."

Leigh gently placed a hand on Sam's shoulder. "I'm sorry."

He returned her gesture with a warm smile. "Thanks, but it's in the past. And believe me, I won't ever make the same mistake." He seemed momentarily lost in the troubling memory, but with a shake of his head pulled himself back. "Let's keeping going."

"Lead the way, Sir Sam," Rob said. Usually, Rob's sarcasm bothered Leigh to no end, but she found this comment quite comforting. All it took was one vague fight story to turn Sam into "one of the guys."

Leigh looked back down the trail to see that Eliza had wandered a little off the path to take a picture of two squirrels chasing each other up a tree. She circled the trunk, trying to catch the spastic rodents in a still frame.

"Eliza!" Leigh shouted. "Let's go!" Her loud voice froze the squirrels in their dance; they became statues at the threat of a nearby predator. It was just the moment Eliza was waiting for. With a quick zoom in on their furry faces, she was able to capture a succession of perfectly framed pictures.

The squirrels eventually finished their frenzied race up the tree and galloped off across the awning of tangled branches and leaves, leaving Eliza satisfied for having captured such a spontaneous moment. Snapping the cap back on her lens, she ran to catch up to her friends.

She reached Rob first and was just about to wrap her hands around his eyes and whisper "Guess who?" when he walked through and then let go a thin branch stretching out into the middle of the path. The branch whipped back at Eliza, lashing the flesh of her neck just below her jaw.

"Ow!" She shrieked as the scratch created a line of stinging pain that coursed across her skin.

Leigh twirled around at the sound of Eliza's cry. She saw her friend holding a hand to her neck and a mixture of hurt and anger welling in her eyes.

"Rob!" Eliza took a swing at her boyfriend. Her knuckles just brushed his collarbone. "Shit, that really hurt!"

"Damn." Even Rob seemed surprised at his own carelessness. "I'm sorry, babe. I had no idea you were behind me."

Eliza didn't seem at all impressed with Rob's apology. "You should be more careful!"

"It was an accident!"

After having witnessed quite a number of their previous fights, Leigh knew the bickering would only escalate if someone didn't intervene right away. Pushing Rob aside, Leigh approach Eliza and coaxed her to remove her hand from the wound. The cut was clean and very shallow-more of a long, red mark than an actual laceration.

"It looks fine," Leigh said, relieved. "It just scratched you is all."

"Still hurt," Eliza grumbled, returning her hand to the tender flesh.

"Is she okay?" Sam had made his way over to Leigh's side and inspected Eliza's neck.

"She's fine. I think we're good to go."

"Yeah," Eliza agreed, and with a hard jab to Rob's ribs added, "But I'm walking in front of you from now on!"

"Fine!"

Rob's voice was completely drowned out by a deafening rumble of thunder that erupted from above,.

Sam's shoulders sunk. "Here it comes."

As if Sam were a biblical prophet, the weather obeyed his proclamation in an instant. The sky opened and the rain began to fall, starting as a gentle trickle that became a steady downpour in mere seconds. Rob and Eliza's argument was already forgotten as everyone's soaked clothing began to stick to their bodies.

Under the dripping brim of his trucker's hat, Rob mumbled perhaps the first thing that Leigh had ever completely agreed with:

"This sucks."

The trees initially provided them protection from the downpour, but soon the small clusters of leaves provided by the ash and maple trees wasn't keeping them even remotely dry.

Leigh was just about to ask Sam if he had any ideas that might save them from walking the rest of the way in a thunderstorm when he spoke up and offered the drowning foursome a life raft.

"If you guys want, I know of a nearby deer camp we could hold out in till the rain passes."

Eliza stuffed her camera into the pocket of her jeans to protect it from water damage. "How nearby?"

Sam pointed to a bend in the trail several yards ahead. "It's coming right up on the trail. If we hurry, I think we can make it there before it *really* starts to come down."

"Then what are standing around here for?" The deafening percussion of of raindrops was making Rob's voice, like all of theirs, very hard to hear.

Leigh considered the tempting proposition but realized there might be one problem:

"What about the owners? They won't mind?"

As miserable as she was, Leigh had no desire to add trespassing to the day's itinerary. She was, after all, already involved with international drug smuggling, and one crime per day was more than enough.

But then Sam shook his head. "No, it's okay. They won't be there."

"How do you know that? Isn't it hunting season?"

"They're dead." Sam said, and nothing more.

"Well then," Eliza said, breaking the momentary silence that had followed the abrupt announcement of the owners' demise. "In that case, I'm in."

"You know I am," Rob added.

Leigh exchanged glances with her company, realizing that her vote was the only one remaining. She was already involved with drug smuggling. Did she want to add trespassing on top of that? But as more and more large, icy cold raindrops landed on Leigh's neck, she made up her mind.

"I suppose we don't have a choice. Alex and Marshall will just have to wait a little longer."

"Then let's get moving," Sam said, taking steps forward. "The worst of this downpour has yet to come."

The rest of the group followed, forming a single file line. Leigh brought up the rear, walking directly behind Eliza, who was now lightly raking her fingers horizontally across her fresh cut.

"I wouldn't touch that," Leigh warned. "You'll get it dirty."

Eliza stopped and turned to face Leigh, a look of excruciating discomfort distorting her face. "I know, but I can't help it," Eliza whined. "It really itches."

"Just hold on a few more minutes. I'll help you clean it when we get to this cabin, or whatever it is."

Eliza nodded and reluctantly removed her hand from her neck. But before she turned back to continue the hike, Leigh's head jerked, what she saw on her friend's skin causing her to do a double-take.

To Leigh's amazement, it looked as if the cut had already started to show signs of infection. The flesh surrounding the laceration was discolored, a few shades darker than the rest of Eliza's throat. But the abnormal coloration didn't at all resemble the usual pinkish hue of agitated tissue. Even red or purple splotching, though probably a call for concern, would've been less alarming: what Leigh saw was startling enough to draw her eyebrows up to her hairline leave her jaw hanging open.

Eliza's skin was tinted green. Green.

Leigh inhaled to say something about her peculiar observation, but decided to shut her mouth about it instead. It had only been a glance, and her perception of the color spectrum must be suffering as a result of the stormy skies, which were greenish in tone.

Satisfied with this logic, Leigh followed her three companions to the safe haven of a dry shelter, convinced she'd been mistaken.

CHAPTER SEVEN

Frigid water numbed all five of Marshall's toes as his sandaled foot fell into another rain-filled pothole. He and Alex trudged along in search of Miller's Road, their feet making wet, squishy noises with every step.

It was hard to believe how drastically the tables had turned on Marshall Thomas. It felt like only minutes ago that he had been basking in the celebration of having a van to shield him from the elements while Rob and the others miserably marched through the drenching, autumn rainstorm. Now here he was: on foot as well and probably getting even wetter than the rest of his friends since he didn't have any tree branches to provide protection from the falling rain. And damn it all to hell, they still had that weed, too. All he had was a girlfriend so furious she was making PMS look like a good mood.

She did have a right to be upset; Marshall could admit that much. After they'd discovered the circular saw blade—probably the same one that had been used to chop down the Miller's Road sign—Alex had initially reacted calmly.

"Well," she said, simply shrugging her shoulders as he tossed the round, jagged blade into the brush, "we can just put the spare on, right?"

That's when it got bad.

"Um…" Marshall didn't want to say what he was about to. He could already feel the storm about to break, and it wasn't from the dark clouds above. "Rob didn't pack the spare."

For a moment, Alex stared at him blankly as if he'd just spoken in a foreign language.

"What?"

Marshall's voice trailed off. His eyes drifted to the tops of the swaying trees. The horrible moment had come.

"He took it off to make room for the keg."

"You have *got* to be kidding!" Alex screamed, her voice booming above the rumbling thunder that had just arrived.

But it was true. Rob had removed the spare tire from the rear door of the van and instead used the harness to attach a keg of Molson he'd purchased while in Montreal. The spare had been left outside the brewing company headquarters on the St. Lawrence River after the conclusion of their booze-filled tour. The girls had been out shopping in the meanwhile, and Rob had bet Marshall that none of the ladies would notice the switch until they reached home.

"I CANNOT believe you agreed to that!" Alex yelled, even louder. She'd started in on the arm gestures, too.

"What! We agreed that if we got into any trouble we could just hire a mechanic and split the cost!"

Alex had now gone silent, eyes staring wide at Marshall and giving him the cold shoulder in order to convey her shock and disappointment. Marshall continued to rant anyway, not caring that she wouldn't yell back. "How we were supposed to know this was going to happen? A saw blade in the road? It's gotta be a one in a million chance!"

His girlfriend kicked a stone off the road. It rolled along the shoulder before falling off into some thick, long grass. She mumbled, "Well, isn't this just terrific? Fan-fucking-tastic."

Ever since dropping his friends off for their trek through the woods, Marshall's emotions had gone on what felt like the steepest rollercoaster ride known to man. One moment he was completely enamored by his current lover, and the next he didn't want anything to do with her. Well, maybe if he somehow got control of his feelings he could still enjoy the coaster's exhilarating drop that had to come when he and Alex made up.

"Look," he said, taking a deep breath and closing his eyes. "We'll just walk back the way we came, find Miller's Road, and get the border patrol to help us."

Alex twisted around to face him. Judging by the look on her face, she wasn't at all satisfied with this solution.

"Do you realize how long that's going to take?" She was still shouting, despite the soothing tone Marshall had switched to. "What about the rest of them?"

"What can I tell you? They're just going to have to wait for us instead of us waiting for them." A single raindrop landed in his mop of hair and found its way to his scalp. "Is that really so bad?"

Marshall got his answer just as a startling crack of thunder roared overheard, bringing with it several more of its fat, wet friends.

With her arms crossed at her chest, Alex stared at him through the sheet of falling drops, her hair already wet enough to stick to her forehead.

"Just so you know, I'm blaming this all on you when we see them."

She grabbed a sweatshirt from the van to hold above her head and stomped away.

After a moment of watching her leave him behind, Marshall muttered, "Whatever," and jogged to catch up.

Twenty minutes later, they still hadn't seen a single turnoff from the road, Miller or otherwise, and the rain was coming down much harder now than when they started.

"This is fucked."

Marshall's eyes shot up from the muddy ground at the sound of Alex's voice. They were her first words since leaving the van. "At least we know the others are getting soaked too," he mumbled, knowing there was nothing he could say that would remedy the situation. "Of course, they do have the weed... which I think we could both really use."

Alex came to a halt and turned to face him. Even in her horrific mood, Marshall couldn't help but be turned on by the way her damp tank top clung to her large, perfect breasts. He was surly going to take shit for this predicament for hours, maybe even days, after they found their way out, but hey, a free wet t-shirt contest wasn't such a bad consolation prize. Even if this particular competition had only one contestant, the image of Alex in a skintight top was all he needed.

"Do you have service yet?" she asked under the makeshift tent of her jacket. The covering blocked the rain that fell straight down, but did nothing when the wind picked up and blew the drops horizontally in a head-on assault. It was this type of rain that Marshall could thank for the spectacular view he had now.

Marshall whipped out his usually trusty smart phone from his pocket and was not surprised at all by what he saw. "I told you before, babe, we're not gonna get a signal here."

"Well, keep checking! You never know when you might stumble into a random patch of service."

"Listen." The cell dropped back into his pocket. "The only way we'd have a chance of getting even a single bar is if we climb high enough on one of these hills."

Marshall braced himself for another loud, senseless response, but was caught off guard when Alex's tone returned to one that was much more composed. "That actually doesn't sound like such a bad idea."

A laugh of sheer disbelief burst from his mouth. "Are you kidding me? It's a long shot at best."

"I know, but there's still a chance it could work."

"Not the way our luck has been going. Get real."

"Well I'm not going to let you walk away without trying." Alex's hands went to her hips. Marshall knew that look all too well. It was pretty much game over whenever she took this positoin. But despite the hip pose, he challenged her once more.

"Why do I have to be the one to go?"

Perhaps if she had chosen to strike his meaty bicep and not the vulnerable bones of his ribcage, Marshall would've been too impressed by the speed of her punch to actually notice the ache that came with it. But the spark of pain that radiated down his side from Eliza's sharp knuckles pretty much knocked him senseless. She hollered, "Because *you're* the one who took the spare tire off. Now, go!"

"Fuck!" Marshall took a quick step away from the hysterical girl. "Jesus, woman, for the last time, it was Rob!" He rubbed his sore rib and wondered if she knew what the repercussions for such a sucker punch was for men. "But if you really want to waste some more time, say no more. Maybe it'll give you some time to cool off and realize that this isn't my fault."

Marshall stormed away, feeling very satisfied with his final comment. He thought he heard her offer a weak retort of "Hurry up!" but ignored her fading voice as it vanished into the overpowering sound of the storm.

It only took a few steps off the road to breach the tree line. Marshall discovered a small clearing just past the pine-needled floor of the completely flat site where the ground took on an abrupt upward slope, although density of the trees prevented him from seeing how high the hill actually reached. Knowing it would probably not be tall enough, Marshall proceeded to ascend the bluff anyway, having no desire to spend any time searching for a higher peak. He just hoped Alex would be satisfied with a single try so that they could get back to searching for the cursed Miller's Road.

While the soft pine needles of the forest floor led him to believe the woods were considerably dryer than the exposed roadway, Marshall's first step up the steep hill proved just how wrong this theory was. His flimsy sandal slid across the slick surface of a tree root as if it were covered in oil.

"Whoa," Marshall blurted out as he caught his balance.

Slower than he would've liked to go, Marshall made his

way up the hill, planting every step carefully. The journey was turning out to be even less enjoyable than he'd predicted. Dark mud became packed under the nails of his exposed toes. A combination of sweat and rain streamed into his eyes. But worst of all were the drops falling from his shaggy bangs, each landing just above the bridge of his nose like a form of Chinese water torture. He'd always thought buzzcuts made guys look like army recruits, but now he found himself willing to give anything for a pair of clippers,

The terrain beneath his feet had become increasingly challenging the further up he traveled. The falling water ran down the hill's face, turning the slope into a mudslide. Luckily, some of the trees' low-hanging branches proved perfect handles to grip as Marshall used his strong arms to pull himself uphill.

It was one of these helpful branches that Marshall was holding onto for dear life when the yet another drop of water struck his forehead. Without thinking, he instinctually brushed his hair away, only realizing what a grave mistake he'd made the moment his hand left the sturdy tree limb. Without the strength of both of his hands supporting his weight, his feet slid out from underneath him and his body fell head first into the slimy, black earth.

He landed face down, unwillingly tasting the gritty flavor of soil and dead leaves Marshall's fingers clawed at the earth as he somersaulted backwards down the mountain, blindly reaching for anything that might slow his violent tumble. For several painful seconds, Marshall could see only trees, followed by the darkness of the wet ground.

Trees. Ground. Trees. Ground.

And then, thanks to nothing short of a miracle, his fingers caught hold of something jetting out from the mud. Something spongy yet firm that felt slimy under his cold hands.

Marshall took a moment to allow the world to stop spinning, then looked up at whatever it was he was grasping: a cluster of large, light green mushrooms. His hand tightly squeezed the slimy stems beneath their bulbous heads. It was remarkable how such a fragile-looking collection of fungi had somehow been strong enough to stop his fall and hold his weight.

Their roots must go pretty far down into the—

Marshall's thought broke off with the stems of the mushrooms as they silently tore from the earth and sent him rocketing down the hill once more. He continued to roll ass over end down the muddy slope, grunting loudly as the solid ground knocked the wind out of his lungs again and again.

Just when Marshall had resigned himself that the tumbling descent would go on forever, the back of his skull connected with the rock-hard trunk of a gargantuan oak tree.

Before he lost consciousness, Marshall groggily reached his hand to the back of his head and felt a warm, wet spot, numb beneath his touch. Something in his mind told him he was bleeding, but he wasn't able to process if that something to be concerned about. Meanwhile, a fuzzy, green blanket of spores enveloped his hand like an emerald woolen glove. But more than wool, this stuff itched like *hell*.

Then everything went black.

CHAPTER EIGHT

The door of the cabin slowly opened with a long, arthritic creak.

"After you," Sam said, gesturing for the rest of the party to proceed indoors.

When they had first arrived at the abandoned deer camp, Sam grabbed the front door's handle and, unsurprisingly, discovered that it was locked. Before anyone could mutter the slightest hint of a groan, he whipped out a Swiss Army knife from his pocket like a pirate brandishing his sword.

"Not a problem," he said, jamming the knife's blade between the doorjamb and the lock. It took him less than a minute to gain access, and just like that, the group had shelter from the storm.

Even Rob gave Sam kudos for his helpful skills, patting him on the back and saying, "Nice job, Sammy boy. So, how fast can you hotwire a car?"

Sam chuckled and closed the door behind him once everyone was inside. While Rob's comment had obviously been in jest, it did leave Leigh wondering where and how Sam had acquired such efficient lock-picking skills. So she decided to ask him.

"That was nothing," Sam simply replied. "It's not like these old cabin doors have a complicated locking mechanism. I think it's just something that anyone who carries a knife should know how to do."

Leigh nodded, though not completely satisfied with his answer. "Can anyone do it as fast as you? It just looked like you've had a lot of practice."

Sam shrugged. "Call it a perk of being a country boy, I guess. You should see me start a fire with two sticks and bundle of tinder. Then you'd be *really* impressed."

"Oh, I've seen that done on 'Man vs. Wild.'"

"Man vs. who?"

Leigh tried not to laugh but couldn't help it. "Never mind." Eliza tapped Sam on the shoulder.

"Is there a bathroom in this place?" She scratched at her neck as she asked the question.

Sam pointed towards the back of the cabin. "Check back there, the door next to the bedroom. But don't turn the faucet on yet. Let me see if I can get the generator going so the water pump will work." He re-opened the creaky door and vanished outside.

After watching him go, Leigh took a moment to examine the living room. She stood behind an old couch, its faded, light green upholstery spotted with numerous stains, yellow fluff bursting from the seams of several tears. In front of the couch sat an antique-looking coffee table, various men's magazines stacked on its scratched finish. On the other side of the table, an old cast iron woodstove sat against the far wall. Piles of gray ash and black soot surrounded its feet like darkened snowdrifts.

But of all the objects in the room, none commanded Leigh's attention more than the gun cabinet to her right. Though she didn't have the slightest interest in any sort of weaponry, her eyes were drawn to the impressive selection of firearms visible through the cabinet's glass doors. What stood out most of all were the bow and quiver that leaned against the cabinet's side. Whoever these hunters were, they seemed like they had been quite prepared for any hunting season to come their way.

"All right!" Rob's excited voice came from Leigh's left,

where the cabin's kitchen was located. She followed the sound to find Rob leaning over an open cooler filled with several cans and bottles of beer floating in water. Without any hesitation, Rob dunked his hand into the melted ice and retrieved a bottle of Labbatt Blue. "Anyone want a brew?"

Not waiting for a reply before flipping the cooler closed, Rob walked over to the kitchen counter. Placing the edge of the bottle's cap on the counter's ledge, Rob slammed the heel of his hand down onto the top. The maneuver, which Leigh was sure Rob practiced every day of the school year, successfully removed the cap, but left a noticeable scrape in the counter's surface.

Leigh sighed.

What?" Rob didn't even bother looking in her direction and took a long swig from the low-budget choice of college kids and rednecks alike. "Didn't you hear Sam? The owners are worm food. I doubt they'll give a shit about their table."

It was easy to see by Rob's furled brow just how confused he was to Leigh's response when she said, "You're right about that."

"So what's the problem."

Leigh pointed to the bottle in his hand. "Isn't that a twist-off?"

Rob looked at his drink, his eyes lingering on the bottle. It seemed his mind was struggling to come up with a witty retort, but when he looked back to Leigh, all he could say was, "Guess you're right." He walked past her without another word.

Leigh knew that if it had it been anyone else in their little squad, she wouldn't have received any satisfaction from such a little victory. In fact, if it were anyone else, she wouldn't have pointed out the mistake in the first place. But after his lewd behavior in Montreal, the least Rob deserved was to be taken down a few notches.

Now alone in the kitchen, Leigh walked over to examine a Polaroid picture hanging by a thumbtack above the sink. The photo showed two men clad in hunting gear and a tree-filled background. Both men wore similar clothing—army green t-shirts covered by orange vests—but their physical appearances varied drastically. One was noticeably overweight and looked a few years older than the other, a bushy, red beard concealing the lower half of his face. The other was a younger, leaner man, and with the exception of light stubble, had no facial hair. He did, however, brandish a barbwire tattoo on his right bicep, which both men flexed in a macho pose.

Giving into her curiosity, Leigh carefully removed the photograph so as not to damage the edges and turned it over in her hands. A caption had been written on the back:

Dale and Red, Spring Turkey Season.

Leigh turned the picture back around and chuckled. They apparently didn't see the irony of posing like fearless warriors even though their prey were harmless birds. Or maybe it was suppose to be in jest? It would certainly explain the huge smiles they shared.

But then she remembered what Sam had said before. These men, if they were indeed the owners of this cabin, were no longer smiling and never would again. They were dead.

"Okay, the water should be running now. Just try not to leave it on for too long at once." Sam had returned from starting the generator and was speaking to Eliza in the living room.

"Cool. I just want to clean the cut on my neck." The sound of a turning knob and a door slamming shut meant Eliza had disappeared into the bathroom.

Sam came into the kitchen, shaking rainwater from his cap. Rob, having already downed the first bottle of beer, was starting his second. Sam raised his hand in a passing gesture as Rob offered him one as well, and walked over to Leigh.

She pointed to the men in the photo. "Are these the owners?"

Sam's bit his lip and nodded. "Yes, they were Well, the younger-looking man on the left was. Dale Preston. It was left to him and his sister after his parents passed away. Least that's what the papers said." He extended a finger towards the bearded man. "That was his sister's husband. Something Hogan, I can't remember."

"Red," Leigh replied. Before he could inquire how she knew such a thing she added, "It's written on the back of the photo."

Sam rotated his arms backwards in a shoulder-popping stretch that reminded Leigh of the cabin's creaky front door. "Yeah, that's him."

A disgusting wet belch erupted from their right. Rob lazily slouched in a chair at the kitchen table, crushing the now empty can in his grip. For a guy from the suburbs, Leigh thought his uncultured mannerisms might fit in quite nicely around here. "How'd they die?" he asked between hiccups.

Sam's grimaced . "I suppose I wasn't being entirely accurate before. But I didn't want to have to explain the whole thing while we stood in the pouring rain and got soaked. Anyway, *died* isn't the best way to put it.

More like they disappeared."

Leigh slowly turned away from the photograph to see if he was kidding or not. By the look in his eyes, he wasn't. "Disappeared?" she echoed in disbelief.

"Crazy, right? Two veteran hunters, born and bred, spent their entire lives here. You'd never think they would both be swallowed by the forest like Hansel and Gretel. But last week they went into the woods for bow and arrow season and…" Sam trailed off, as if lost for words. He sighed. "…and never came out. Not a trace; no bodies, nothing."

Leigh was speechless. It was exactly like every horrible ghost story about the deep, dark woods she had ever heard. If Sam was trying to scare her, he was doing a terrific job. But the grave expression on his face said he was simply relaying the truth, or at least what he had heard.

"Well," Rob said, kicking his feet up onto the table, "That's not gonna happen to us. Because unlike those two poor sons of bitches, we got ourselves an expert guide to lead us out of these scary woods. Ain't that right, Sammy?"

Sam looked away into the corner of the room. "Yeah, sure."

But Rob continued, now speaking with a mock hillbilly

accent. "And if anyone tries to mess with our womens, my man Sir Sam is going to set them straight. I'll tell you what!"

"You're hilarious, Rob." Leigh shot Rob the dirtiest look she could muster but it didn't seem to have any effect; he just replied, "I know."

She turned to Sam. "If you care to join me, I'll be on the porch. I want to watch and see if the rain lets up." She then walked away, making sure to shove past Rob in the process.

God, Rob was such a dick!

But on the other hand, Leigh questioned if she would've had the courage to invite Sam out onto the privacy of the porch had Rob not been there to provoke her.

But that's just an excuse, isn't it? Something to hide yourself from the fact that maybe Sam just isn't that interested in you.

Leigh was considering naming her inner voice Ms. Benedict Arnold in honor of its turncoat ways. Supportive one minute, unmercifully crushing the next. Between her school studies of psychology and the time spent with her therapist, Leigh that one day she would be able to not only confront her demons, but destroy them. Instead, she was starting to seriously believe she was messed up beyond repair.

Leigh took at a seat in one of the two rocking chairs positioned under the roof's overhang that shielded the porch from rainfall. Shaking her head vigorously, she promised she'd analyze herself to pieces once she was back in the safe confines of her dorm room. She had to remember she was not alone, and the last thing she wanted was to be caught in an "Is something bothering you?" moment with anyone here.

Especially with Sam.

And there he was, invading her thoughts again. But if she were to stop and actually think about it, was he really the right match for her? From what she'd seen, he was just a knife-carrying, lock-picking, junior college student who kept up on the recent obituaries and beat people up to the point of suspension. When presented that way, Sam suddenly bore very little resemblance to the Prince Charming she'd been fantasizing about since she was a little girl.

Why, why did she have to overthink things so much? Her restless brain brought her excellent marks in school, but always seemed to bring more problems than it was worth. Though not a religious person by any means, there was one Bible passage that Leigh always appreciated for its undeniable truth:

He who increases knowledge, increases sorrow.

"Do you see something?"

The sound of Sam's voice practically made her jump out of her skin. Why hadn't that damn squeaky door given her a warning?

"Oh, um…no." She realized she had been staring unblinking into the surrounding forest for quite some time now. "I was just spacing out."

Sam took a seat in the chair next to hers. Out of her peripheral vision, she could see the boy staring at her. "Hey… Is something bothering you?" he said hesitantly, asking the question Leigh had hoped so badly that no one, especially him, would ask.

"I was just thinking about Marshall and Alex." Leigh was pleased at how easily the lie had automatically fallen from her lips. "I just hope they're having better luck than we are."

The wood of the porch rumbled along with the thundering skies under the sway of Sam's chair as he slowly rocked back and forth. "Hey, they're not the ones who have to trudge through the cold, wet woods, right?"

"That's true. But I just wish we could call them. Let them know we're okay."

Leigh turned to Sam and felt that same warm tremor she had experienced since he first boarded their van. Thanks to the "PSY230: "Advanced Social Psychology" course she'd taken sophomore year, Leigh knew to be cautious with first impressions. Those initial impressions could affect how you treat people you had just met, and that treatment would then affect the way they react to you in return. Her professor had called it, "self-fulfilling prophecies."

And yet, here she was, throwing all of those lessons out the window in spite of herself. Her therapist would've surely been pleased to see Leigh trusting her instincts and letting someone new inside. Professor Riker? Probably not.

Sam smiled. "I know. It's too bad phone lines don't run this far into the woods. But all they have to do is sit and wait for us. I'm sure we'll regroup soon enough.?"

"Yeah, okay," Leigh answered, thankful to her mouth for managing to form words. Why did she feel like a starstruck girl standing in the front row at a rock concert? Not wanting to lose face, Leigh straightened her shoulders and jerked herself from her dreamy state. "You're right, Sam," she said with conviction. "They'll be fine."

Leigh turned her head away so Sam wouldn't see the worry that was actually clouding her eyes. She hadn't thought of her two separated friends since it had started to rain, but now that she had, a frown strained the muscles of her mouth when she pictured their faces. Knowing they had the safety of the van would've soothed her nerves if not for having heard the mysterious fate of those two hunters. How had Sam put it?

Swallowed by the forest like Hansel and Gretel.

Leigh pretended to smack at a mosquito on her face, but was really slapping the ridiculous idea from her head. *She* was the one trekking through the wilderness on foot, not them. They were on a state-recognized road, safely making their way to the authorities. If anyone needed breadcrumbs to find their way out, it was most definitely Leigh and her team of rag-tag hikers.

CHAPTER NINE

Alex's watch told her that Marshall had been gone for more than twenty minutes, leaving her standing by herself in the pouring rain. She knew he was milking it on purpose as a way to get back at her, but this was getting ridiculous. In this unforgiving weather, a five-minute wait would've been sufficient punishment.

Punishment for what, exactly? Getting angry for my boyfriend's incredible stupidity?

It wasn't her fault they were stranded out in the middle of God-knows-where. If only they still had a spare! Cell service or not, a call to AAA wouldn't have been necessary for this one; even *she* knew how to change a flat tire.

Alex brushed a lock of wet hair from her eyes and peered into the trees, trying to catch a glimpse of her imbecile boyfriend.

Maybe that's unfair. You know he's intelligent.

And that was true, proven by both his decent grades and all those post-lovemaking talks, when she would listen for hours to his philosophical thoughts while wrapped in his arms. Of course, they were both usually high when he went on and on about things like religion and politics, but sober or not, those topics had never been a concern to any of her past boyfriends.

No, Marshall's problem was also one of his most likeable attributes: his willingness to please. In spite of her blinding anger, Alex still knew it had been Rob's idea to chuck the spare and make room for the keg. Marshall may have even tried to talk him out of it. But she knew her boyfriend, and all it took was Rob saying something like, "Come on man, just think of how stoked the girls will be when they see what we brought home!" Oh, she was stoked all right.

Alex inhaled a deep breath and released it with a soothing hum. She'd seen Marshall do this exercise plenty of times in the past and it always seemed to calm him down. But when the final wisp of air had left her lungs, she knew the method was as useless here as her cell phone. A deep breath wouldn't change the fact that she was soaking wet, shivering in the cold, and still waiting on a careless boyfriend who had yet to return.

"Careless," Alex said to herself through a long sigh. "That's just us, I guess." Though between the two of them, only Alex knew just how much trouble their free-spirited ways had brought them. Skipping class, getting high, and speeding in Marshall's Jeep Wrangler were harmless enough. Alex's secret abortion, however, was a different matter all together.

She was going to tell him—eventually. But the longer she stayed with the charming surfer from the West Coast, the more she feared that dropping this bomb would scare him away. It hadn't been easy lying to him when she said the reason for missing school was a bad case of mono, but she swore her intentions had always been good: to protect Marshall's feelings and save their relationship. But as she stood there, forgetting for a moment about the drops of water rolling down her neck, she began to realize that all her silence had accomplished was to transform a mostly physical relationship into something much worse. Instead of being based on sex, it was now based on a lie.

"God damn it, Marsh," Alex muttered, now cursing her boyfriend for both leaving her waiting and for playing his part in her unplanned pregnancy. "What's taking you so long?"

Fed up, Alex took a step off the road and into the long, wet grass that bordered the edge of the forest without thinking it through. If she could bear the hardships of an abortion, paying for the whole thing herself and never telling a soul, then she sure as shit was tough enough to go into some darks woods and drag her boyfriend out by his balls. It was time they had a little talk.

Alex pushed aside a low-hanging pine limb and entered the forest. She was pleasantly surprised to see that the trees weren't nearly as dense as she'd thought them to be. On the contrary, the bushy evergreen branches parted to reveal a circular clearing at the base of a fairly steep hill.

"Marshall!" Alex yelled, her voice bouncing off the endless tree trunks. "Can you hear me? Are you all right?"

She waited a moment and received no response. Had Marshall really climbed the entire hill to try to get a single bar of cell phone reception? If so, Alex would be quite impressed. He might be world-class surfer, but Marshall was far from a mountain man. A mixture of guilt and self-pride sluiced its way into Alex's mind. On one hand, she felt bad for sending her sandal-clad boyfriend into such an unfamiliar environment, but she also had to give herself props for being able to make a man bend to her will so drastically. After all, there was no way in hell any guy could've *ever* convinced her to brave such a hike.

But perhaps that was exactly what Marshall was trying to do.

"I swear to God, Marshall!" Alex shouted. "If you're doing this just so I'll come after you, it's not going to work!"

Still no response but the infinite patter of rain hitting the ground.

Alex inhaled as much air as her lungs could hold and screamed, "Marshall! Answer me, you bastard!"

Nothing.

"Marshall! Marsh—"

Her shouting ceased when she saw what stared at her only ten feet away. Its soulless gaze made the light peach fuzz on the back of her arms stand straight up, just like the fur on the creature's back. Over the heavy percussion of the falling rain she could just make out the low rumble of its growl.

"Oh my god…"

She was eye-to-eye with a rabid raccoon. Saliva dripped from its bared yellow teeth. Its glassy eyes, wide and black, bulged with insanity. The animal seemed to be looking through her, as if it could see the muscles and organs it craved.

Alex slowly shifted to her left foot, but the movement only provoked the mad beast into the swiping the air with its clawed paw. She gasped, frozen, her eyes locked on its infected incisors. One bite and this contagious madness would bury itself under her skin and tunnel its way into her central nervous system. A horrible cry shrieked from the raccoon's drooling mouth, raking Alex's eardrums.

It bore its fangs.

And charged.

Alex didn't make it a single foot before she tangled her ankle in the gnarly grasp of a tree root and was yanked to the ground. Her scream died as the solid ground knocked all of the air from her lungs. Dazed, she lifted her head to see a ball of mangled fur just inches from her face. She raised a frail arm to guard her head and neck, knowing that this pathetic attempt would offer little protection.

She squeezed her eyelids shut and braced for the pain.

But instead of feeling her flesh break beneath puncturing teeth, she heard the raccoon give a furious, startled screech.

Alex opened her eyes to see a long metal chain wrapped around the animal's throat like the leash of a common house pet. Her eyes followed its steel links to the hand of a man stepping out from behind the thick trunk of a nearby oak tree.

"Don't worry, little lady!" The skinny stranger in dirty mechanic's overalls parted his lips to reveal brown rotting teeth. He licked them ravenously.

"No need to be afraid of Cooney, here. I got him under control."

Alex pushed herself up into a sitting position, freezing again when the movement caused the raccoon to thrash and flail on its chain.

THE REMEDY

Her eyes darted back and forth between the beast and its gaunt, filthy owner. She couldn't decide who looked more threatening.

Another disturbing smile crossed the man's face as he loosened his grip on his pet's metal chain. The raccoon dashed forward another inch, prompting a terrified shriek from Alex's mouth, before being yanked back.

"Whoops!" The stranger bellowed, laughing at his own game. "Sorry about that, ma'am. I'm all thumbs today."

Alex's body quaked, tears now pouring from her eyes as she struggled to speak. "Please…"

The man threw up a hand to his ear. "What's that?"

"Please. Leave me alone."

"Ha!"

Alex winced as her captor coughed up a ball of viscous phlegm and spat it in her direction, the disgusting wad just barely missing her arm. He scratched his crotch and said, "Come on now. Don't be like that. Cooney here is *real* nice once he gets to know you."

He released the chain a little more.

"Stop!" Alex wailed, wiping away the salty tears that were clouding her vision. The raccoon continued to hiss and gnash its teeth so closely to her face that she could actually smell its rancid breath. "Please! Go away!"

"Go away?" The man's scratched his neck. "But we haven't even been formally introduced." Dirty fingers gripped the rim of his brown baseball cap and tugged it downward. "They call me Bugger, and it's a pleasure to make your acquaintance, miss… What might your name be?"

Alex didn't hear the question. She was too distracted by the snarling raccoon's yellow fangs. It hissed at her again and she scurried back, trying to distance herself from its snapping jaws. But when she felt her back brush the rough bark of a tree trunk, she knew she could go no farther. The trunk stretched from shoulder to shoulder, an obstacle far too wide to get around before the man and his best friend would be upon her.

She began to sob even harder, and an awful wet warmth began to spread across her groin.

The man who called himself Bugger shook his head. "Ah, now don't cry. You're too pretty to cry." His right eye twitched. "So pretty…"

He released the chain.

Alex, so overcome with fear and adrenaline, wasn't even aware that her hand clutched a short, thick tree branch until she was swinging it at the charging raccoon with all the left strength in her shaking body. Luckily, the makeshift weapon found its mark, slamming into the charging beast's skull with a sickening crunch. The raccoon released a short yelp before slumping to the ground, limp as an old teddy bear.

For a solitary second, both Alex and Bugger stared at the creature's still body.

And then Alex was on her feet, sprinting through the forest's tangle of bushes and branches, taking advantage of her captor's state of complete shock. But the distraction didn't last long; Alex could hear the booming voice of the raccoon's enraged owner as if he was speaking right into her ear.

"Hey! You killed Cooney! You fucking *bitch*!"

The scream was followed by accompanied by something even more terrifying: the pounding of Bugger's approaching footsteps. Alex, teary eyed and wailing, ran as fast as her boots would allow. Branches whipped at her face, cutting her cheeks and whipping past her eyes. She had no idea which direction she was heading; all she cared about was getting away from the psychopath chasing after her. He was closing the distance, expertly making his way through the thick underbrush with a native's knowledge of the terrain. Alex knew she wouldn't be able to keep up this game of cat-and-mouse for much longer.

Her only chance was to somehow double-back and try to make it to the road. She had a snowball's chance in hell that a car would drive by at that exact moment, but would the man be daring enough to continue his pursuit outside the cover of the woods? She prayed he wouldn't risk acquiring a witness to his sadistic mission and sink back into the trees, in search of another outsider to torment.

Where the fuck is the road?

The frantic question was ripped from Alex's mind when her boot slammed into a large, pointy rock jutting from the earth. Her stubbed toe sent her into a headfirst tumble, her face crashing to the dirt below. Teeth rattling and knees scraping the forest floor, Alex was already planting her hands to push herself up—

And that's when she saw it:

The hollow, rotten trunk of a fallen tree.

Remaining in her prone position, Alex crawled to the hollow log like a commando sneaking up on an enemy base. She just barely made it inside the rotten wood when Bugger sprinted into view. To her absolute panic, he stopped dead in his tracks.

"Oh, little *laaaady*!" He called in a singsong manner, his hands cupped around his mouth. "Where are *yoooouu*?"

He sniffed the air.

"I can smell your insides."

From within the fallen timber, Alex's entire body quivered so badly she feared she might quake the rotten wood to pieces. She clamped her mouth from screaming, her sweaty palm squeezing all the blood from her lips.

Something with many legs crawled across her bare calves.

Oh God…

A snap in the distance brought Bugger's eyes to the trees beyond her hiding place. In an instant he was gone, chasing after whatever had miraculously acted as bait just when she needed it.

Alex counted thirty seconds. And then ran.

Although she couldn't hear him, it didn't mean he wasn't right on her heels, quietly toying with her before striking her down with a razor-sharp machete or something equally terrifying. But Alex didn't dare turn and look as she sprinted into the endless forest, not even feeling the sting of the pricker bushes that stuck to her legs. She did, however, feel a growing pressure in her exhausted lungs, her legs turning to jelly, and cramps jabbing into her sides.

The world was beginning to spin. The ground and sky were coming together in a dizzy dance. She was going into shock.

But then, through her blurred vision, Alex saw that the trees up ahead grew further apart. She had almost made it to the clearing, and the thought of what that meant gave her a boost of strength and numbed her incapacitating pain. The road would be just past the clearing, and with it, her best chance at escape.

A burst of optimism fueled her pumping legs, and the hint of appeared on her face.

But like the fleeting thing it is, all hope vanished with her next step.

Her left leg snapped as it left the ground, taking the rest of her body with it. Disorientation swallowed her world as Alex flew above the forest floor, dangling upside down from the branch of a towering pine tree. When was done bouncing her up and down like a rag doll, Alex achingly lifted her head to discover the loop of a snare trap tightly wrapped around her ankle. Abdominals cramping as she attempted an impossible crunch, Alex groaned in an effort to grab the out-of-reach knot.

A pain as sharp as a dagger ripped through her lower back, and she could do nothing to stop her core muscles from releasing their tension. Her body unbent itself with a pathetic whimper of defeat, and her arms flew beneath her.

She just did not possess the strength.

The tears began to flow.

Alex cried in silence, not even possessing the strength of spirit to bawl with vigor. She swayed back and forth in the air, listening to her weight creak the overhead branch and the birds sing a cruel celebration of the lightening rainfall.

Then she heard a sound.
Bugger stood below, chuckling with delight.
"Well, what do we have here?"
He rubbed his hands together in childish delight.
"Fresh meat."

CHAPTER TEN

It's starting to clear up.

Weirdly enough, that was Marshall's first thought as his eyes slowly opened to the thinning clouds above. The black had lightened to a soft gray, and the sky was beginning to peek through in brilliant blue strips.

This observation on the weather was immediately followed by a second thought:

My fucking head!

The back of Marshall's cranium throbbed in a slow, excruciating rhythm. Using the two fingers of his right hand, he gingerly prodded his hair, which was crusty with dried blood. By gritting his teeth and taking long, difficult breaths through his nostrils, Marshall examined the wound. It felt roughly the size of a quarter, but not deep enough to reach the bone. He knew that he needed to seek medical attention as soon as possible, but the bleeding had stopped and he was starting to regain his bearings. As long as he didn't trip and knock his noggin a second time, Marshall was hopeful he'd be able to reach help before passing out again.

The depleted battery of his cell phone made it impossible to know how long he'd been unconscious. But judging from the drastically changed weather, it must have been a considerable length of time. He thought about checking the surrounding area for Alex in case she had come looking for him, but quickly changed his mind. She'd been beyond pissed when she sent him on this treacherous errand, and probably hadn't even bothered waiting for him to return. She was most likely flirting with a border patrolman by now, while her boyfriend nearly killed himself to fulfill her wishes.

"Fuck it," Marshall grumbled as he took his first shaky step forward. He'd go directly back to the road; if Alex wasn't there, he'd jump off that bridge when he got to it. For now, he had his hands full trying to navigate the remainder of the hill without his blurred vision bringing him down. This trip was not going to be easy.

As if to prove that point, the slick carpet of wet leaves under Marshall's right foot suddenly slid forward and sent Marshall's arms shooting out to both sides. Fortunately, an ash trunk to his left provided the handle he needed to keep himself afoot. Marshall cursed at himself for his carelessness. He couldn't afford to let another breaking branch or unearthed plant send him somersaulting to his second crash landing.

Marshall turned his head towards his hand pressed against the trunk—

—and opened his mouth in a silent scream.

His hand was gone.

At first, Marshall thought he'd somehow sunk his extremity into a mound of tree growing fungi without noticing. But when he tried to wiggle his fingers and the pile of green fungus moved, bile rose in his throat with a dreadful realization:

The horrendous growth was growing *on* his hand.

Marshall slowly reached out to gingerly touch the green, fuzzy mass that had once been his hand. He brushed the edge of a mushroom that grew from his index finger knuckle. A tingle tickled his nerves.

No...

The mushroom wasn't growing on his skin,

It *was* his skin.

Marshall's turned and vomited sour, white foam into a patch of drooping ferns at his feet. He stood there hunched over, dry heaving until he was able to take a deep breath without gagging.

Though his brain still felt as it were swimming laps around the inside of his skull, Marshall took a deep breath through his nose and tried to settle his nerves. If his father's meditation techniques were ever going to work, Marshall prayed they would now. At least his hand wasn't burning like before. Through the dark murk of his hazy memory, Marshall could recall how it had felt as it were on fire seconds before he lost consciousness.

"Okay, man," Marshall whispered to himself, trying not to hyperventilate. "Keep it together and find some help."

Trying to not even glance at his infected-beyond-recognition hand, Marshall started to jog down the last slope of the hill. He knew he was going faster than he probably should have in his condition, but the injury to his head had become the least of his concerns. As a surfer, he'd knocked his skull around plenty of times before, giant waves throwing him against both the ocean floor and his own board. A few stitches were nothing—a hand made of penicillin was something else.

The ground finally leveled out under his feet and Marshall breathed a sigh of relief. The clearing was just ahead and then, thank God, the road. Once his first foot hit the road's gravel, Marshall would run as fast as his throbbing head would allow. Maybe he'd even send Alex ahead so she could reach help faster. That is, if Alex was even still there waiting for him. Marshall now found himself actually hoping she'd gone ahead and already made it to the border. Pushing branches away with his good hand, Marshall fantasized about reaching the road and being greeted by a patrolman's cruiser. But no matter how he did it, Marshall had to find someone to help him—and fast. It might've been his own imagination, but he swore he could feel the fungus spreading upward to his forearm; just past his shell bracelet was beginning to itch.

Marshall, however, did not feel the burning irritation for long. When a final spruce branch swept past his eyes to reveal the clearing, all concerns for his own well-being vanished.

Alex dangled upside down by one leg from a gargantuan pine tree.

"Alex!"

It was only when he reached the area directly underneath her that Marshall realized he had no idea how he was going to get her down. Alex's raspy snoring instantly reminded him of the time his buddy T.J. was launched from his moped while not wearing a helmet. Marshall came upon his friend to find him taking long, gurgling breaths through his open mouth. Alex was making the exact same noise now.

Marshall looked up at his girlfriend. "Alex?" he said. "Can you hear me? Come on, wake up!"

Still, she didn't respond.

A gnarly stick lay a few feet to Marshall's right. He retrieved the limb and reached up to gently prod Alex's shoulder.

"Come on, baby girl. Wake up for me."

No response.

"Alex!" Marshall screamed. "Wake up!" He poked the stick into her cheek.

Her eyes fluttered open.

"Ugh," she moaned groggily, her pupils rolling in her sockets. It was impossible to know the extent of her injuries, but Marshall smiled all the same. She was awake, and that's all that mattered. They were probably both suffering from concussions, but now at least Alex could help Marshall figure out a way for her to escape and get the hell out of these godforsaken woods.

"There we go," Marshall soothingly whispered as Alex awoke. 'It's okay, baby. I'm here." Try as he might to maintain this calm charade for Alex's benefit, he could not keep his panic bay. "What THE FUCK happened to you?"

Marshall scanned his eyes upward to examine her body and discovered the mangled condition of her ensnared leg. It was obviously broken, and Marshall grimaced at the complications that was sure to bring to their escape.

Alex coughed and winced in pain, jolting her out of her daze. After blinking several times, her eyes finally landed on her boyfriend, a wave of recognition washing over her face.

"Ma…Marshall?"

"Yeah, it's me." Marshall looked up and tried to regain his worry-free smile.

"Marshall?"

Orientation and short-term memory were always the last thing to return to a recent victim of head trauma. Marshall could remember how T.J. had asked, "What day is it?" about fifteen times once he had come to.

"Yes, honey. It's me, Marshall. I'm right here." He was compulsively nodding his head in an effort to reassure her.

"Marshall!"

Just as Marshall watched Alex's narrow eyes pop open like a jack-in-the-box, a tremendous force slammed into his knees and sent his feet flaying out from underneath him. In that single moment of hang-time, Marshall felt just like the goons he'd laughed at so many times as a kid in *Home Alone*. But there was no nostalgia when he slammed facedown into the dirt and felt his kneecap nearly shatter under his body weight.

Marshall inhaled to scream but a blow to his ribcage pushed all the oxygen from his lungs with an excruciating snap. Every shallow breath that followed was like a red-hot poker being thrust into his side.

Unable to move and hardly able to breathe, Marshall could do nothing to defend himself from his unknown assailant. Something wet landed on the back of his neck. He assumed it must be his own blood dripping from whatever blunt object had battered him. But when a hard kick to his gut rolled him onto his back, he realized the falling drops were Alex's tears.

Another splashed on his cheek.

"Leave him alone!" Alex wailed, as helpless as her boyfriend. Her plea was returned with the most sadistic, high-pitched laugh Marshall had ever heard.

The broad heel of a muddy boot pressed down against his throat. Through fading vision, Marshall squinted to see a gaunt man in mechanic's overalls standing over him and bearing his brown teeth in a rotten grin. Over his shoulder rested a long walking stick with a large, solid knob on the end, like an Irishman's shillelagh. A dark splotch of dried blood stained the cane, and Marshall knew he wasn't the first to feel its bone crushing power.

The man pressed his boot down harder, temporarily blocking off Marshall's windpipe.

"Stop it!" Alex screamed from above. "You're killing him!"

The man looked up and guffawed at the girl above him dangling like a worm on a hook. "Killing him?" The man asked with a crooked smile. "Nah. We just havin' a lil' fun. That's all." The foot gave from Marshall's throat just as the world was beginning to turn black. Through spots and stars, his vision slowly began to return.

The man turned his head back down towards his victim on the ground. "But I guess you're right, little lady," he said. "This really isn't the time to be playing games. This pretty boy needs help." With that, the man reached behind his back and retrieved a round, rusty object that instantly chilled the sweat dripping from Marshall's brow.

A circular saw blade.

"It was you," Marshall whimpered.

The man shrugged and moved his foot from Marshall's neck to his forearm just above the fungal hand. With his hand securely pinned to the ground, Marshall squeezed his eyes shut and heard the man say, "Now don't move, you hear?"

A second later, Marshall heard an airy whir buzz by his ear. A flash of sharp pain ignited his wrist, as sudden and quick as a spark of static electricity. And then it was gone, everything below his forearm now completely numb. He could still feel the rest of his arm, but it was strange. Different.

It felt lighter.

"There." The man crossed his arms at his chest in triumph. "Good as new."

Marshall knew what he would see when he unclenched his eyes. Regardless, that did not stifle the surprise of seeing a blood-spurting stump where his hand had once been. Though shock was temporarily sparing him from the intense pain that was sure to arrive at any moment, the gruesome image of his own severed limb was horrific enough on its own. He could see his sliced bone protruding from the bloody stub, the streak of white so bright against the arterial blood that almost seemed to glow.

And yet, Marshall did not feel the slightest compulsion to scream. In a churning ocean of dizziness and shock, a soothing wave of relief immersed him like a warm bath. Removing his hand was like extracting a tick or a leech from your flesh—you'd let someone crush a burning cigarette into your leg in order to get it off.

"I don't care, just get it off!" you'd shout. "Just get it off! Get it off!"

And now it was off.

Marshall's eyes drifted from his oozing stump to the redneck surgeon who had performed the operation.

"Thank you," he muttered, the corners of his mouth pulling up in a perverted smile.

The man threw his head back, releasing a loud, excited hoot. "My pleasure, boy!"

Above, Alex had gone into a comatose state, staring straight ahead while a constant tremor vibrated her body.

It was the last thing Marshall saw before he lapsed into darkness.

The last sound he heard was the man's laugher echoing throughout the towering evergreens.

CHAPTER ELEVEN

Leigh had been so lost in her own thoughts that she hadn't noticed how slow the patter of the rain had become until Sam said, "You hear that? It's finally letting up."

Looking out into the damp trees and undergrowth, she could see that Sam was correct. The rain had slowed to a gentle drizzle and the clouds above were breaking apart.

"I guess we should go tell Rob and Eliza," she said before her mouth opened in a jaw-stretching yawn. "Now we can get back to the nice, warm van. After the day we've had, I could use a nap."

Just as Leigh grabbed each armrest of the rocking chair and prepared to push herself up, Sam placed a hand on hers.

"Wait," he said.

"What?"

Sam glanced away, his cheeks flushing. "I wanted to ask you something."

Leigh smiled, amused by his timidity. ""Okay, shoot."

His foot rolled a twig back and forth across the ripples of the porch's old wood. "I, uh, noticed all your friends are dating each other. But why didn't your, um…boyfriend…come with you on your trip?"

"Well, I think the answer would be pretty obvious," Leigh said with a little laugh. "I don't have a boyfriend."

"Really?" The shock in Sam's voice sounded sincere. "I find that hard to believe."

"I guess that's because you don't really know me."

"What's that supposed to mean?"

Leigh hesitated when she realized what she was about to say had never been shared with anyone since she began college. Not even Alex knew the part of Leigh's past that she was about to reveal. This, of course, raised the question, "Why share it with *this* guy?" Maybe it was because of the indescribable connection to him she had felt the moment he took a seat beside her in the van. Maybe it was because of the way her usual defense mechanisms, pessimism and cynicism, had failed to diminish her attraction to him. They had never failed her before.

Whatever the reason, it did present the perfect opportunity to put her therapist's theories to the test. If fear was really just "false events appearing real," then maybe it was time to embrace her counselor's alternative acronym:

Face Everything And Rejoice.

Besides, a near perfect stranger was just as good a candidate as she was ever going to get. At least she knew Sam went to a different school, so there was no chance of him spreading rumors around her campus.

"I haven't been in a relationship since high school." Leigh blurted out the fact before she could talk herself out of it. Sam nodded, seemingly unimpressed, but that came as no surprise. That had been the easy part.

"That's cool," Sam said, shrugging. "I know a bunch of people like that. I mean, just because you're in college doesn't guarantee you'll find Mr. or Ms. Right sitting next to you in class." It was hard not to notice the authenticity in Sam's voice. "Besides, most college kids are animals. I don't care what school you go to."

Leigh released a long sigh. "Yeah, that's definitely true. And it sure would make a great excuse."

Sam's eyebrow rose. "But?"

The moment of truth had arrived.

"But in my case, that's not the truth. That last relationship I mentioned, the one in high school…" Leigh inhaled a deep breath. "It was with one of my teachers."

She threw her hands up with an exaggerated shrug as if to say, "What can you do?" But she knew the gesture must have looked as artificial as it felt, doing nothing to convince Sam that it was no big deal.

Sam's reaction, however, was difficult to judge, his expression one of neither repulsion nor support. When he spoke, it was a single simple word.

"Huh."

Well, it was out. But strangely, the load which Leigh had assumed would be instantly lifted with the spoken words had yet to slide off her shoulders: there was still more to confess.

"He was my civics teacher, Mr. Hudson. Jerry. He didn't molest me or anything, if that's what you're thinking. I was eighteen and he was only twenty-eight. I won't tell you how it started; it's not important. What does matter is that people found out. My friends, my mom. Christ, by the end the entire town knew. But the first to know was my older brother, Dennis."

She paused for Sam to comment, but he remained silent, listening.

"Dennis had graduated two years before me but stayed in our town to work and raise money for college. Our father died when we were kids, and my mom wanted to pay for his education, but Dennis insisted he'd pay his own way. Said she'd struggled enough raising us on her own, so now he'd take care of himself. Anyway, when Dennis found out about what was going on, he drove straight from his job at the power company to the high school, saw Jerry walking to his car, and attacked him."

"Whoa."

Leigh nodded her head, staring into the trees. "As you can imagine, it really hit the fan after that. When Dennis was questioned after his arrest, he told the authorities everything. But since I'd been of legal age, the court dismissed the case."

Sam coughed and cleared his throat. "He must have lost his job though."

"Of course," Leigh said, finding she needed to take a breath before her next sentence. "But so did Dennis. And to this day he still hasn't applied for school. My mom ended up moving away, too. She couldn't stay with all the shame hanging over our family's head. She lives in upstate New York now."

Leigh ran a finger along the bottom of her eye to discard the unshed tears that were threatening to leak out. After saying it loud and hearing the horrible story with her own ears, she began to realize how artificial her own self-assurance really was. She wasn't a loner because of her priorities or being misunderstood.

She was just fucked up.

"So," Leigh said, shaking her head clear of heavy memories, "bookworm or not, that is why I do not have boyfriend." She then turned to Sam and forced a smile. "The end."

Sam shook his head in disbelief. "Wow. Well, hey. Ask a question, get an answer, right?"

Leigh lifted her gaze from her shoes to see Sam's expression was one of total bafflement. For reasons she didn't understand, his raised eyebrows and half-mouthed smile initiated a sneak attack of boisterous laughter that erupted from her mouth.

Even when she turned away, she could still see Sam staring at her in disbelief from the corner of her eye.

"What's so funny?" he said, now chuckling himself.

Leigh threw her hands up. "Not a thing. Or hell, maybe all of it is." Upon saying the words, Leigh realized they may have held more truth than she intended. The story of her past had never come close to conjuring a humorous response, but Sam's company had changed something.

Indeed it was history that could never be changed, but it was not her present. A rainy afternoon alone with an attractive and kind-hearted guy—that was the here and now. Maybe that didn't completely justify turning her sob story into a laugh fest…

The hell with it.

Sometimes laughing is the only thing you can do. You just need to find somebody to laugh with.

Again, Leigh traced the side of her finger along the bottom of her eye, mentally addressing how quickly and drastically the reason for her tears had changed. Her vision cleared, Leigh lowered her hand just in time to spot a blur of movement in the trees beyond Sam's shoulder.

Sam saw her smile fall away and asked, "What is it?"

"I think I just saw something in the woods."

"Like an animal, you mean?"

Leigh squinted, looking into the thick brush but couldn't make out the shape she'd just spotted moving between the ferns and thorn bushes. "Maybe," she muttered, getting up from her chair and approaching the porch's railing. "But I'm not sure. It could've been a person."

"A person?" Sam was now also on his feet and had joined Leigh by her side. "What, just taking a stroll through the middle of the woods during a rainstorm?"

"Well isn't that what we were doing?"

Sam smirked. "Good point."

The two stared out into the thick gathering of trees and undergrowth, but besides lilting from raindrops, the plants remained still.

"Hello?" Leigh flinched at the abruptness and volume of Sam's voice. His call did not receive an answer.

You're sure the owners aren't around anymore?" Leigh asked.

"Yes, I'm positive. Besides, even if I was wrong and it *was* one of them, why would they be hiding?"

"I'm probably just seeing things," Leigh admitted. She wasn't exactly at full alert while telling her traumatic story.

"Yeah, you most likely were." Sam turned around and walked to the porch's steps. Without another word he descended them and began walking towards the forest.

Leigh called after him. "Whoa! Where are you going?"

"I just want to have a quick look." Sam's voice had lowered to almost a whisper. "I want to make sure it's not some kids looking to break into this place and use it as a party house. And if it is, I'm gonna give them a scare so they think twice about coming back."

"Why?" Leigh found herself speaking lower too, though it was more from following Sam's lead than actual concern. "Does it really matter? I mean, we basically did just that."

"Exactly." Sam gave her a wink. "We got to protect our turf. If we let others move in, where we will hold our reunion next year?"

When Leigh smiled, she knew it wasn't in response to Sam's joke. It was the thought of seeing him again.

"Hold on, I'll go with you."

Sam threw his arm outward to wave her back. "You better stay here, just in case."

"No." Leigh's hands went directly to her hips. "I'm not afraid of bunch of teenagers. Believe me, I can be quite the bitch when I want to be."

A smile spread across Sam's face from ear to ear. "All right, then. Let's go. But keep quiet."

As quietly as she could, Leigh made her way down the stairs to Sam's side. Together, the two entered into the trees, taking slow, deliberate steps. The damp ground made it easier to remain silent since they did not have to worry about the loud crunching of dry leaves or twigs. The only real challenge was refraining from violently swatting at the mosquitoes that whined in their ears.

They walked about fifty feet from the cabin's porch and discovered nothing. It seemed Leigh had been mistaken. It had likely been an animal that scampered away just as quickly as it appeared.

"I guess it was nothing," said Sam.

Leigh turned her eyes down, embarrassed. "Sorry. My eyes must have been playing tricks on me."

"You don't need to apologize," Sam replied, bending down to tie his shoe. "I'm glad you were wrong. It's a relief to know no one's been messing with this place." He finished his knot and straightened himself back up. "Okay, I'm ready. Let's head back and get the others."

"Sounds…"

The word to come next from Leigh's mouth would've been "good." Instead, a distinctly human moan filled their ears, causing the hair on the back of Leigh's arms to stand straight up.

"*Uuuggghh…*"

"*Shh*!" Sam hushed. "What the hell was that?"

Leigh's eyes darted in all directions as she tried to figure out where the sound was coming from. "I heard it too. It's close."

A second groan, painfully drawn out and wet with phlegm, pinpointed the noise's origin behind a large, moss-covered log.

"There!" Leigh pointed to the fallen tree. The log was dark with wetness and age, its wood soft and covered with growths. Among the patches of rich, furry moss grew some scattered mushrooms, all a sickly yellow-green. This was to be expected; the rotten log made a perfect environment for fungus to develop.

What wasn't as likely was that one of the mushrooms could move on its own, lifting up and slithering forward an inch.

"Holy fuck!" Sam jumped just as far back as Leigh. "Did you see that?"

Leigh was too focused on the creeping fungi to give an answer. She was so overcome with shock that it took her a few seconds to realize what exactly they were looking at.

The growth wasn't connected to the wood at all. What moved in their direction was a human hand, struggling to pull up the body that was emerging from behind the log.

Two years ago, on a rainy Sunday afternoon, Leigh had taken a much-needed break from writing a research paper to channel-surf for awhile. Since she and Alex had only sprung for basic cable in their room, her choices for daytime programming were limited to soap operas and educational shows on the

Discovery Channel. Leigh had opted for the latter and fallen upon a fascinating documentary about a man in Indonesia who suffered from the strangest disease Leigh had ever seen. Warts had enveloped most of the man's body, making his hands and feet look more like plant-life than human flesh. Long, banana-shaped warts dangled from his fingers and toes like roots. The growths were so severe that the locals of his small town called him "The Tree Man." Leigh had never seen anything like him—

Until now.

As improbable as it was, it seemed that the Tree Man had come to pay a visit to the forests of Vermont. Only this was man was Caucasian, or at least he had been at one point; the sparse patches of uninfected skin that dotted his body proved as much.

Christ. He looks like a moldy piece of bread.

The man got half of his torso over the log and collapsed against it. Using what little strength he must have left, he looked up at the two college and students and whispered a gurgling, desperate plea.

"Heclp meesh."

Sam, who had taken a guard-like position between Leigh and the ill stranger, looked back to her. "What did he say?"

"He said, 'Help me.'" Leigh struggled to compose herself against an overpowering wave of nausea. "Whatever that is all over him must be in his throat also."

"Shit," Leigh heard Sam say under his breath. Cautiously, he knelt down to speak to the man at eye level. "What happened to you, man?"

Instead of answering the question, the Tree Man lifted his arm and extended what was left of his open hand towards Sam. The arm rose slowly as if it were supporting fifty pound weights. Through fuzz-covered lips, the man whispered,

"Pleeeassh…"

With his arm outstretched, Leigh could see the entire length of his mold-covered bicep. Something on his limb caught her eye. It was darker than the rest of the green fungus, traced along a solitary strip of untouched skin. Stepping forward carefully, Leigh knelt down to get a better look at the marking.

"No, Leigh!" Sam grabbed her arm. "Don't get near him. Whatever he has might be contagious." Leigh obeyed Sam's order, but only because she was already close enough to identify the mark.

A tattoo—barbed wire—wrapped around the man's upper arm.

It was one of the men from the photo in the kitchen.

"Sam! This is the owner of the deer camp!"

"Oh my God." The words ran from his lips like a bubbling stream. "Dale? Dale Preston?"

The man slowly nodded his head up and down. Keeping her eyes trained on the green-carpeted mass of man, Leigh asked, "You know him?"

"Not personally, but he's a local."

"Well, we have to help him. And fast."

"I know." He turned to Dale. "Just stay right there, okay Dale? Don't move. We're going to get help." He grabbed Leigh's sleeve and pulled her several steps back.

"All right," he said, staring deep into her eyes. "I think one of us should stay with him to try to keep him calm while the other gets Rob and Eliza to help find something to carry him with. Touching him ourselves is definitely out of the question."

Leigh nodded. "I agree. But what about a phone?"

"No good. Your cell won't work out here and there aren't any phone lines that run to the house. Most hunters who have camps out here spring for satellite phones or they rely on walkie-talkies."

"Well, maybe there's one of those lying around."

Try as she might to think proactively and portray a sense of optimism, there was no ignoring the scream that was slowly crawling up the back of her throat.

Sam threw a quick glance at Dale, who was breathing with great difficulty. "I didn't see one before, but we can look. Now, are you okay staying with him or do you want me to?"

"No, I can do it." Leigh pulled her shoulders back to illustrate confidence. "You'll probably be able to find your way around the cabin better than I would. And Rob will act faster if it's you who asks him to help. He seems to already like you more than he's ever cared for me."

Her voice came out as shaky as an 8.0 earthquake, Leigh laughed in an attempt to conceal the tremors. It came out weak and terribly artificial, but Sam smiled all the same.

"Okay," he said. "I'll be fast. And I'll send Eliza out to help you."

Leigh returned the smile. "Thanks."

There it was again. Even with a dying man covered in a disgusting, flesh-eating fungus just a few feet away, an intimate second of silence somehow found its way between the young pair.

Sensing the immense inappropriateness of their moment, Leigh snapped out of it. "I'll be fine. Go!"

Sam said nothing more and left. Leigh watched him turn and jog back to the cabin, feeling surprisingly calm despite the direness of their situation. Of course, she'd give anything for a phone to call 911, or a vehicle with room for five and four-wheel drive. But for what they had to work with, it was a good plan.

And let's not forget. Sam's here.

Sam was a fast thinker and even quicker to act, two traits that the rest of her company didn't exactly have Under his leadership, they would figure out a way to drag poor Dale Preston out of the woods to get the help he so desperately needed.

Everything would be okay.

Leigh released a strong, self-assuring breath.

From within the cabin's walls, Eliza screamed.

CHAPTER
TWELVE

Rob collapsed backwards onto the bottom mattress of the musty bunk bed in the bedroom's corner. Eliza spied on him through a crack in the bedroom's door, watching her boyfriend rifle through the drawer of the small nightstand. The scratch on her neck still itched, but she found the irritation easier to ignore while distracted by her little peepshow. Besides, she didn't want to risk the noise any scratching might make, afraid it would reveal her presence.

Finding only a dog-eared issue of *Guns & Ammo* and a discarded pack of Skoal, Rob slammed the drawer shut, unsatisfied. Placing his arms under his head, he stared up at the bottom of the upper bunk, boredom painted across his face.

"Fuckin' rain," he mumbled to himself. "Let up already."

Eliza had to bite her finger to stifle the laughter building within her. She knew it would be any moment now that Rob would figure out something to do to pass the time. Truth be told, she was both surprised and impressed it had taken him this long to indulge in one of his favorite pastimes.

Wait for it....

His hand traveled down his thigh, scratching what was probably a bug bite received during their miserable trek though the woods. As his fingers dug into the flesh under his baggy, oversized jeans, something bulging in his pocket pushed out into view. It was a pack of Zig Zag rolling papers. It fell from his pocket to the hardwood floor. He bent down retrieved the carton, flipping it over to examine the bearded man logo.

As if on cue, Rob's eye's widened with the opening of his mouth. There was no mistaking the thought behind the expression:

Oh, shit! That's right. What the hell am I waiting for?

Eliza's grin widened. It was a good question.

In one deft movement, Rob sprang up into a sitting position. Eliza winced when it looked like Rob was going to slam his head on the upper bunk's support bar, but he kept his neck bent just enough to avoid injury. Like a starving castaway who'd caught his first fish, Rob ravenously snatched his backpack and tore open the zipper.

The look on his face when he discovered the empty bag was nothing less than priceless.

"What the *fuck*?" Rob shouted, as if the bag it would provide any answers. "You've got to be kidding me!" The bag hit the floor, its zipper scratching the old wood. Through gritted teeth, Eliza could hear Rob grumble, "Marshall. You son of a—"

"Looking for this?"

Eliza threw the bathroom door open and held the coveted bag of weed between two pinched fingers. Now that the jig was up, she finally let go of the torrent of laugher she'd been bottling up inside. Rob did not join in.

"You bitch," he said, placing a hand on his chest. "You just gave me a heart attack. Very funny."

Eliza chucked the weed at Rob's head. His hand whipped up just in time to prevent the it from smacking him in the face. "*I* thought so," she sneered. "And don't call me a bitch."

Rob carefully opened the plastic bag. "Well, then, don't play mean tricks on me for no reason."

"No reason, huh?"

"What are you talking about?" Rob wasn't even looking in Eliza's direction, too preoccupied with removing a paper from the pack of Zig Zags and beginning construction on a perfectly rolled joint.

"Let's just say I've learned to never leave you alone for a *second* with anything you could fuck. Including my friends."

That comment brought Rob's eyes away from his work, precious weed fluttering like snow to the floor. "Aw, shit!" He quickly placed the joint on the nightstand. "Now look what you made me do."

"Oh I see," Eliza turned away from him and crossed her arms. "Instead of apologizing you're just going to try and change the subject. Nice."

She could tell the exaggeration in Rob's sigh was intentional. He pushed up the brim of his trucker's cap up so she could see his eyes. "Listen, babe, if this is about something I did on this trip, I don't remember. Okay? It's called blackout drunk. I know you've experienced it yourself. So can we just let it go?"

Eliza hesitated. Her anger still burned, but it was becoming rapidly apparent that further arguing wouldn't do any good at all. Whether or not Rob was telling the truth, his excuse was infallible. And at least she had been witness to how much he drank, which was certainly enough to cause a considerable degree of memory loss. Still, he hadn't apologized, nor promised it wouldn't happen again. What if Eliza wasn't around to catch him next time?

"Well, if you can't handle your alcohol then you should watch how much you drink." A self-satisfied smirk planted itself on her face. She knew Rob would receive the comment as an insult, but due to his own excuse, he couldn't argue. Instead, he could only look away and mutter, "Okay, mom."

With a final lick of the rolling paper, Rob sealed the joint and stuck it between his lips as he patted his pockets in search of a lighter. In a flash, Eliza darted forward, plucked the joint from his mouth, and retreated back.

"Hey!" Rob lashed out for the joint but missed. "Give me that!"

Eliza teasingly held out the joint in front of Rob's face, but whenever he would grab for it, she'd jerk it away just in time. "I'm your mom, right?" she said, taking righteous pleasure in her taunt. "And what mom wants her son smoking drugs? We're gonna flush this down the toilet, young man." She made a move towards the bathroom door.

Rob's eyes narrowed. "You wouldn't."

"You don't think so?"

"No way. You want it as much as I do."

"True." Eliza's voice became abruptly solemn. "But not as much as I want an apology."

The joint vanished from her fingers into her closed fist.

"Okay, okay!" Rob threw his hands up. "I'm sorry! I'll control myself from now on, you have my word. Can I have the joint now, *please?*"

Eliza leered at her begging boyfriend. "I don't know." She drew closer, straddling his thigh. "Maybe Mom needs to give you a spanking first."

"Hmm," Rob said, bringing his face closer to hers. Still holding the joint, Eliza's wrapped her arms around his neck and her lips closed on his. Her tongue darted into the warm cavern of his mouth, sending electrical shivers throughout her entire body. Charged by lust, Eliza jammed their mouths together even harder while crawling on top of him. It didn't take long for the deep kiss to harden the bulge in Rob's pants and push a welcome pressure between her legs.

Eliza pulled back and inhaled deeply. A long string of saliva stretched its way between their parting lips.

"What about the others?" Rob whispered.

Alex shook her head. "Don't worry about it. I think they went for a walk."

Rob smiled and lowered his head to nibble her long, slender neck. He stopped when he realized her flesh was entirely concealed in cloth.

"Baby," Rob said, stepping back and putting a sudden stop on their steamy make-out session. Eliza's eyes, which had been squeezed shut in ecstasy, popped open. Her boyfriend stared at her with an inquisitively raised brow. "What are you wearing?"

Distracted by her prank and the foreplay, Eliza had completely forgotten she'd changed into the plum-colored turtleneck that was many sizes too large for her.

"Oh yeah," she said, touching her fingers to her neck. "I found this in one of the dressers. I thought it would feel nice to wear something dry for awhile."

"I see," Rob said with no enthusiasm behind his words. "But even if it feels nice, it looks pretty stupid on you."

Her fist hit Rob's shoulder before she even knew she was throwing the punch. "Fuck you!" Sometimes the insensitiveness of her boyfriend could be downright unbelievable. Her arms folded across her chest. "You're the one who's fucking stupid."

"Damn, girl!" Rob said, hooking a finger from each hand into the belt loops of her pants and pulling her forward. "There's no need for that kind of language." His eyelids lowered in a sly expression. "All I'm saying is that maybe you should take it off."

His tongue traced the outline of her upper lip. Eliza shivered, feeling herself become increasingly moist. She stared into his gorgeous brown eyes. "Oh, you think so?"

His hand squeezed the left cheek of her ass. "I do."

Her palms went to his shoulders, pushing him back onto the bottom bunk. "And do you think we should get you out of your wet clothes, too?"

"Good idea."

Eliza grabbed the bottom of Rob's t-shirt, first ripping off his damp denim vest and then eagerly pulling it up over his head. Eliza took a moment to admire his sculpted pecs and abdomen.

He can be an asshole, sometimes. But damn. Damn. Damn! What a body.

Leaning over him as he lay on his back, she moaned as his hands kneaded her breasts through her shirt and bra. Eliza had always been secretly jealous of her sister's larger cup size, but she still had something to flaunt up top. And even if Alex had been blessed with the 36 D's, it was Eliza who had gotten the supermodel legs. Compared to Alex's stumps, Eliza's had the stature of an Amazonian—a fact that hadn't gone unnoticed by the guy writing beneath her.

"Your turn, baby," Rob whispered, gently tugging on the bottom of Eliza's loose fitting turtleneck.

Eliza reached down and grabbed a handful of the material. She drew the shirt upward, bending her spine to allow the garment enough room to come overhead. For a brief moment, she could see only purple darkness as the cloth pulled over her eyes, tiny cracks of static electricity snapping in her ears.

After a deliberately slow ascent in the sexiest manner she could, Eliza pulled the turtleneck from her head and her boyfriend returned to her view.

But Rob didn't look turned on like she had expected he would at the sight of her firm, sexy body. His eyeballs were stretched open to the limits of their sockets, and his jaw hung open in a frozen state of shock.

No, not shock.

Horror.

"What the *fuck*?" Rob screamed. He grabbed Eliza's waist and flung her to the side, showing no concern when her head slammed into the wall. A heavy thump rocked Eliza's vision as Rob scrambled out from underneath her, crawling away the moment his body hit the floor.

"Rob!" Eliza's tear ducts were already at work. She held a shaking hand to her throbbing head, baffled by her boyfriend's terrified reaction. "What the fuck are you doing?" she yelled.

Rob opened his mouth to answer, but instead putrid contents from the depths of his bowels came sputtering forth. He pressed his fingers directly to his lips, trying in vain to dam the acidic liquid that was spraying onto the quilted rug under his feet. But the vomit was mostly beer, so it flowed like water between his teeth.

By the time Eliza realized Rob was fleeing from the bedroom, he was already at the door, slamming it behind him.

"Hey!" Eliza shouted, jumping to her feet and racing to the door. The knob wouldn't turn an inch. "What the hell are you doing?" Her fists pounded on the door, shaking the wood in its frame, but Rob would not respond.

"*Rob!*" She was bawling now, a steady stream of tears rolling down her cheeks. "I'm scared. Please...open the door."

There was still no answer.

Eliza was just about to punish the door with another barrage of fists when she glanced at the mirror above the bureau directly to her right.

At first, she refused to believe she was looking at her own reflection. But after ten seconds of breathless staring, she couldn't deny the sickening reality any longer.

A thick blanket of green, fuzzy mold covered her entire throat and extended across to her left shoulder. Eliza watched the fungus sprouting from the gash on her neck, tendrils reaching out like ivy.

Eliza screamed, her fingernails clawing at her neck. Somewhere inside her head, a voice pleaded with herself to not tear out her own throat.

CHAPTER
THIRTEEN

An image of the cabin, with its covered porch and hand crafted rocking chairs, illuminated across the inner projection screen of Jake's mind. More than once had he pondered the origin of such random thoughts, memories that weren't conjured by any sensual trigger. Sometimes it felt like the human mind was a broadcast tower picking up signals from satellites we couldn't see.

"Did you check on Red's cabin last week like I asked you to?"

Jake asked the question while he drove and ate, far from the first time he had to multitask during his lunch. Doug sat next to him in the truck, also enjoying his midday meal.

Through a mouthful of turkey sandwich, Doug answered, "Yeah. The place looked fine. No signs of a break-in or any trespassing."

Though this was the answer Jake was hoping to hear, for some reason he could not get the abandoned cabin out of his head.

"Maybe today we should swing by again."

Doug rolled an empty plastic baggie into a ball and tossed in on the floor. "Why? I mean, I was just there. I'm telling ya, it was all good."

"Yeah," Jake said, his voice trailing off. He knew Doug was right. The Hogan cabin was quite a ways into the woods and going all the way up there would take a considerable chunk out of their schedule. It definitely wasn't worth committing them to such a cumbersome task just because of some weird feeling. "Forget I mentioned it."

Doug nodded in agreement and reached for the volume knob to turn up Crosby, Stills, and Nash over the patter of rainfall. Jake wanted to comment on Doug's flawless memorization of the lyrics, but bit his tongue until the song came to a finish.

"Didn't realize you were into the classics," Jake said, reaching into the Coleman lunchbox situated between them. "It's nice to see a young person showing some respect for the greats."

He tossed a pack of peanut butter crackers at Doug who caught them and said, "You talk like you're in your fifties. You're barely ten years older than me and it's the only kind of music I can find on your iPod."

Jake laughed through a mouthful of granola bar. "True, but I always think of myself as a rare breed. I've just come to expect all kids your age to listen to, I don't know…Eminem, or Green Day or what have you."

"Nah, man," Doug said, waving his hand. "Fuck that noise. Give me Neil Young, Van Morrison, or Cat Stevens any day over that shit."

Jake smiled. "Good to know."

Their bodies bounced in unison over a bump in the road, bringing a beat of silence that ended the conversation. Doug took the opportunity to change the subject.

"So," he said, eying his partner who was balancing the steering wheel with one knee while eating a spoonful of raspberry yogurt. "I gotta know, man. Did you ever have to take someone down? Phil made it sound like you did."

Jake swallowed his mouthful and took a decisive glance at his younger colleague. It was not a story Jake enjoyed telling, but as he stared at Doug's solemn expression, he knew it would be best to explain. It would only serve the rookie well if a similar situation were to ever arise.

"Yes," he said. "It's true. I had to shoot a man, once. Only time I've ever fired a weapon at another human being, but I had no choice." He threw the spoon back into the box and closed the lid. "Still, I regret it. And I always will."

He could feel Doug's unwavering eyes staring at the side of his head. "So what happened?" he asked.

Jake inhaled a deep breath. "Believe it or not, it was during my first outing with Phil. We started out like any usual day— doing the rounds, shootin' the shit. Pretty much like we are now. But then we parked for lunch."

He paused to toss an old, brown-spotted banana peel out the window. It disappeared into a blur of passing ferns.

"So we're sitting there enjoying our lunch—since Phil doesn't like to eat and drive at the same time—when Phil gets out to take a leak. So he goes jogging out into the woods so we won't have to smell it while we eat. And I'm sitting in the truck by myself, listening to some tunes—when my radio goes off."

"Phil?" Doug didn't miss a beat.

"Yeah. Walkie-talkie practically explodes with Phil's voice telling me to grab the rifle and get out the fuck out here. So I spill half a thermos of chicken noodle soup on myself, yank the rifle free, and start sprinting blindly into the trees. I don't get but fifty feet from the truck when I see it."

"See what?"

Jake had to chuckle at Doug's childlike anticipation. The rookie ranger was like a Cub scout listening to a campfire ghost story. Jake did his best to turn the laugh into a dry-throated cough and continued.

"It was like I'd walked onto the set of a 1980s slasher movie. First thing I saw was a body slouched over a bloody tree stump—head split completely open. Then somewhere from my left I heard Phil screaming '*Wait*,' over and over. So I run towards his voice and I'm yelling, 'Phil! Answer me!' and all that. Only took me a second and there he was, lying on his back. His left eye was completely swollen and bruised. But before I could ask him what the fuck happened, Phil's starts pointing and yelling, 'Behind you! Behind you!'"

Jake took a moment to loosen his death grip on the wheel. His fingers were beginning to fall asleep, blood loss tingling down past his knuckles.

"I didn't even think. I just pulled the trigger and watched a big, burly man drop the axe he had raised above his head. The guy took about three steps back, took a look at the hole in his chest, and fell to the ground. Dead."

Doug released a lungful of air and shook his head. "Holy shit," he whispered, unable to say anything more.

Jake nodded. "Holy shit is right. Guy was just about to put an axe in Phil's head before I came along—just like he did with that poor son of a bitch on the tree stump. If I had hesitated for a second longer, both of us would've probably been found floating face down in Emerald Lake."

"So who was the guy?" Doug asked.

"A guy named Murray Dobson. He wasn't from around here—just some drifter who turned out to have quite the police record. In fact, after the cops ran his name through the computer, it said he was currently wanted on suspicion of armed robbery and assault. And he'd been missing for some time. Everyone figured he must have been en route to Canada, walking through the woods so he wouldn't be caught. The man with the split head was Seymour Cedar, a local lumberjack who worked at the saw mill for years before they shut down. The way the cops pieced it together, Dobson came upon Seymour while he was out chopping some firewood. He got the jump on him, took his axe out, and that was that."

Doug grimaced. "Poor son of a bitch."

"You got that right." Jake sighed. "He and his wife had just had their second child when he died. Everyone felt so bad for his widow that when she insisted she and her kids stay on the family land, no one had the nerve to persuade her otherwise. Nevermind that she was now raising two children on her own, without any modern amenities. Besides, I don't think she had anywhere else to go. But I'll be damned if she didn't prove everyone wrong when she somehow raised those two kids without any running water or electricity."

"You mean they're still there?" Doug sounded as incredulous. "Shit, how do you like that? No way I would've stayed out there after they closed the mill and shut down all the power in the area. No friggin' way."

An orange blur at the side of the road caught Jake's eye as they rounded a turn. He turned to look out his window just in time to see a fox retreating back into the trees. A baby woodchuck hung limp from its jaws, its small body still bleeding from fresh wounds. Another life claimed by the natural order of the forest.

"Well," Jake said as the fox vanished in his side mirror, "that makes two of us."

CHAPTER
FOURTEEN

For a moment, Leigh and Sam could only stare at each other. Sam finally broke their shared trance by quietly asking, "Was that…Eliza?"

Leigh ignored the question as she sprinted past Sam towards the front door of the cabin, the shill scream still echoing in her ears. All concerns about Dale's horrible condition instantly vanished, replaced by worry for her friend.

Practically ripping the front door off its hinges, Leigh burst through the threshold, frantically scanning the room for Eliza. Instead she found Rob sitting on the floor, his back against a bedroom door. His face had turned bone white.

"Rob?" Leigh asked, bewilderment in voice. "What are you doing?"

Rob leaned against the door that shook behind him every time Eliza's fist connected with desperate fury. "It's Eliza," he said, gasping for air. "She's covered in something."

Sam stepped forward. "A fungus?"

"Yeah, exactly!" Rob's wide eyes instantly narrowed with suspicion. "Wait—how did you know that?"

Before Sam could reply, Leigh said, "There's a hunter out in the woods. He's completely covered. We think he's dying."

"Rob, you didn't touch her, did you?" Sam's words came out fast in a frantic, high-pitched voice.

"No." Rob patted his arms and neck as if he hadn't considered this possibility. "At least, I don't think so. I got out as fast as I could and trapped her inside."

Leigh looked at the door. It did not appear to have been tampered with. "How did you do that?"

Rob pointed to the space between the doorframe and the handle. "I pennied the door. Thank God I had some change in my pocket."

Leaning closer, Leigh could see the edge of a penny sticking out from the wood. She had seen the trick done many times at school; a common prank to perform on one's roommate. The coin was used as a wedge that kept the deadbolt in place.

Rob turned towards the door and spoke a little louder. "I don't want her coming anywhere *near* me!"

A muffled shout of protest came from behind the door. Although it was impossible to decipher what exactly she was saying, there was no doubting the panic in her screams. Eliza was losing it.

"Shut up!" Rob yelled back.

Leigh took a careful step towards him. "Listen, Rob, you need to calm down."

"Fuck that!" Rob's eyes grew wide. "What we need to do is get help! Right now!"

Leigh was just about to repeat her order for Rob to get his shit together when Sam spoke up behind her. "He's right. And I think I know who can help us."

Leigh turned, surprised. "Who?"

Sam alternated between looking at Leigh and Rob as he spoke. "There's a ranger outpost not far from here. A ranger should be on duty, but if not, we can at least call someone for help."

Another cry erupted from behind the bedroom door, though this time it was considerably weaker, filled less with anger and more with fear.

Rob clapped his hands together. "Sounds good to me! Let's get out of here."

A wave of disgust washed over Leigh as she witnessed how easy it was for Rob to tune out Eliza's helpless wails.

"No."

The sternness of Leigh's voice surprised even herself.

Rob stared at her incredulously. "What?"

"You're going to stay here. Sam and I will go and try to get a hold of Marshall and Alex."

Leigh's lower back tensed as Rob took a step towards her. His eyes burned like lit matches in response to Leigh's demands. "Why should *I* stay here?"

Slightly shaken, Leigh stood her ground.

"Someone has to stay with Eliza," she said.

"So why can't that be you?" Rob countered.

"Listen, asshole!" Leigh surprised herself again. "You're supposed to be her boyfriend. Fucking act like it for once!"

It seemed Leigh was not the only one shocked by the reserves of anger she had stored beneath her timid demeanor. Rob stood speechless before her, the two of them now staring each other down silently. For a moment, the only noise was Eliza's dampened sobbing coming from within the bedroom.

Sam stepped forward. "We really don't have time for this."

Leigh had nearly forgotten Sam. It was nice to finally hear a voice that actually sounded in control.

Rob threw his hands up as he turned away. "Fine! Fuck me, I'll stay with Eliza. But I'm not letting her out of that room."

Leigh nodded. "Right, I don't think you should. Not until we know exactly what we're dealing with."

"And what about this guy who's creeping around outside?" Rob motioned towards the window. "What are we going to do about him?"

"He didn't look like he'll be going anywhere soon," said Sam. But just in case, lock the door behind us when we leave. We don't need him spreading whatever he's got in here, too."

"Look, just stay inside and try to keep Eliza calm," Leigh said, exhaling the last of her anger. She placed a comforting hand on Rob's bicep. "We'll be right back."

Leigh looked sympathetically into Rob's eyes, and for a second, he looked vulnerable.

He sighed. "All right. Just hurry, please. And for Christ's sake, be careful."

With a hand on the knob of the front door, Sam addressed Rob. "We will be. And we'll be as quick as we can. I don't know how much time that guy out there has left."

Sam opened the door and gestured for Leigh to exit.

She took a deep breath. "Right. Let's go."

The two exited, Leigh in the lead, but she slowed to let Sam pass. She then immediately knelt down and began fussing with her shoelaces.

"I'm right behind you," she said. "I just need to tie my shoe."

"Okay," Sam said, bounding down the porch steps in a single leap. "I'm going to go check on Dale one last time before we head to the station."

As he turned and started trudging through the thick ferns in Dale's direction, Leigh finished tying her shoe and snuck towards the cabin's window. While she didn't think Rob would do anything to harm her friend, she had to be certain he was thinking clearly. The last thing any of them needed was for Rob to do something stupid.

Being cautious not to be seen from her spying position, Leigh carefully raised her head high enough to see into the cabin's living room. Rob stood at the bedroom door, his ear pressed against the wood.

"Eliza?" he asked. Leigh was glad to hear a level of gentleness with the question, but was disappointed when he did not receive a reply.

"How you doing in there?"

Silence.

Rob backed away from the door and shrugged his shoulders.

"All right then," he said nonchalantly. "I'm gonna get myself a beer." He walked away and vanished into the kitchen.

While not completely satisfied with what she had seen, it was enough to allow Leigh to sneak away from the window. Rob seemed to have gotten a hold of himself, and maybe a little beer would help to further calm his nerves. But knowing Rob, she and Sam would have to hurry before one harmless beer became one too many. She didn't know if they could handle drunken hostility on top of everything else.

Rushing down the porch steps, Leigh didn't take long to spot Sam's back amidst the ferns. He did not turn when he heard Leigh approaching, but kept his hands on his hips while staring out into the surrounding forest.

Leigh slowed as she approached his side.

"Okay, I'm all set. How's Dale doing?"

Sam did not look at her when he replied, "I don't know."

"What do you mean?"

Sam pointed to the log they had left the hunter resting upon.

Dale was nowhere to be seen.

CHAPTER FIFTEEN

Alex was standing on a beach. She didn't know where the beach was or how she had gotten there. All she knew was that she could see Marshall in the distance on his surfboard, expertly riding the waves. She called out to him and he smiled back, giving quick wave before falling into the pipe of another rising crest. She wanted him to come to her so she yelled again. But he was too intent on riding the endless waves that rising and falling around him.

I'll just have to go to him.

Alex took her first step into the water, surprised at the warmth of the ocean waters. The temperature of the sea rose as she waded deeper into the foaming, hot waves, but for some reason she was oblivious to the danger of angry torrents.

"Marshall!" she yelled, trying to get her boyfriend's attention. Finally, Marshall looked in her direction and threw his arms up for her to stop. Despite the deafening crashes of the churning water, Alex could hear his voice as if he was speaking directly into her ear.

"What are you doing, babe?" he whispered. "You shouldn't be coming out here in your condition."

My condition?

Alex looked down at her belly and realized she was swollen with pregnancy.

Breathless, she looked back up just in time to see Marshall's smiling face before he was pulverized by a gigantic tidal wave that swallowed him whole.

"No!" Alex cried out as she dived headfirst into the waves. She couldn't see a thing. The water had become a deep red, thick and heavy. She was floating in an ocean of blood.

Suddenly, something squeezed her ankle and began to pull. Alex assumed a shark had latched its jaws around her foot, but then realized rather than being pulled downward, she was flying up and out of the bloody sea until she hung upside down above the crimson waves, suspended by a rope that reached forever upward into the sky.

"Well look at that." The voice came from the shore, which seemed miles and miles away. Standing on the black sands was the creature from her worst nightmares: a man dressed in dirty overalls and a baseball cap. In his arms, a newborn boy cried for his mother.

"He looks just like his daddy."

Helplessly dangling by a rope from the heavens, Alex watched in horror as Bugger lifted the child by one stubby leg and raise it above his mouth. His jaw unhinged like that of a snake, stretching far beyond the capacity of a normal human being. Bugger let go of the baby's ankle and it disappeared into the black hole of his maw, sliding down his throat in one powerful motion.

Bugger slapped his belly and belched. His black eyes looked right into Alex's and he said, "Tastes just like his daddy, too."

Before Alex could scream, the rope holding her leg snapped, and she plunged into the sea of blood.

Alex jolted awake just as she was about to hit the surface, screaming through something jammed in her mouth. From the taste alone, she could tell it was a dry, filthy rag, its sour material stretching across her tongue. The open forest where she had lost consciousness no longer surrounded her, though she was still suspended in the air. Only now she hung by her hands tied together above her head, the other end of the rope fastened around a dangling meat hook.

The darkness enveloping her new environment made it difficult to see, but she could tell she was in a basement. That was for sure. A single lantern burned atop a nearby table, casting light onto the floor, a pungent, dark soil surrounded by four stone walls. A staircase along the opposite wall led up to first floor, dim light seeping through the cracks between the planks of the wooden ceiling. Strapped to or hanging from the walls were various hunting tools: rifles, bear traps, snares, and shotguns. But even more disturbing than the firearms and traps were the numerous cutting instruments strewn about the room—a cleaver, a hacksaw, a Bowie knife, and a mammoth chainsaw.

And that smell...

The air was thick and hot, filled with the scent of rotten meat and mildew. Rancid humidity entered her nostrils and threatened to induce vomiting. Alex resisted the urge to throw up and concentrated on an aspect of the room she had failed to notice at first:

A narrow, vertical strip of light shone through the space between the doors of a storm cellar entrance to her immediate right. If Alex could wriggle her wrists free from the metal talon above her, freedom would only be a few steps away.

She looked up at the rope, balling her hands into fists. She took a deep breath—

THRACK!

Alex startled at the sound, her whole body twitching like a hooked worm. A door had been thrown open on the floor above.

Thump. Thump. Thump.

Someone, or something, was coming down the stairs.

Something big.

Quakes of fear racked her entire body as she trembled and watched a looming shape slowly descend the creaky, wooden steps. Hot tears rolled their way down her cheeks; even after everything she had been through, Alex found herself more afraid than ever before when the unknown behemoth stepped into the dim light of the low burning lantern.

A face that had once belonged to an auburn-colored bear concealed its own. She could hear him breathing under the mask; heavy breaths escaping between the bear's yellowed teeth. The headdress must have been treated by a master taxidermist, as the bear's fur was in perfect condition. So were its teeth, frozen in a snarl baring lengthy, sharp incisors.

Alex tried to ask her captor what she was doing here but through the filthy cloth in her mouth she could emit only a muffled garbled, moan. The stranger seemed intrigued with Alex's form and cocked his head to one side like a curious puppy. As Alex began to sob, the masked man strode toward her, unsheathing a large tanning knife from his belt.

Alex's sobs turned to frantic squeals at the sight of the blade. As the man came closer, she desperately tried to shake the knot loose from the meat hook above her, but the rope wouldn't budge. Her leg connected with the brute's thick thigh as she flailed, and the man grunted in response. When Alex tried to kick him again, the giant caught her by the ankle and squeezed. The incredible strength of his grasp squeezed the breath from her lungs; her eyes widened at the intense pain from his grip. He released her leg, relieving her of the enormous pressure, but was now approaching her exposed neck.

Alex squeezed her eyes shut and held her breath, waiting for the knife's edge that would slit her throat and end her life— but then the storm shelter doors ripped open with a crack.

"Grizzly!"

The voice echoed against the stone walls of the basement.. The knife was no longer pressed against her throat, and the giant bear man was standing like a soldier at attention. A long sigh of relief escaped her nostrils, but her breath caught again when she saw who stood at the top of the steps.

It was Bugger: the demon of her nightmares and reality. An unconscious body hung limp, draped over his shoulders. The body had shaggy hair and a drooping shark-tooth necklace: it was Marshall.

"What do you think you're doing?" Bugger made his way down the steps, yelling at his companion as he went. Grizzly said nothing in reply, but motioned to Alex with his knife.

Bugger reached a dusty wooden table and slammed Marshall's body down on top of it. "Oh, no! Don't you even *think* of touching that one! Not yet!"

Although much smaller than his partner, Bugger pushed Grizzly away with a mighty shove to his chest. Grizzly cowered, intimidated by the smaller man for some incomprehensible reason.

"Just get away from her!" Bugger yelled. "We're not carving her up until I say so."

Grizzly grunted.

"Because!" Bugger's fingers were dug into Alex's jaw, yanking her face closer to his. "For reasons you wouldn't understand."

The hillbilly's cracked lips parted to reveal his rotten teeth that he licked with a rancid tongue. Alex squeezed her eyes shut and wished that Grizzly had killed her when he had the chance. Fortunately, Bugger released his grip and did not stick his vile tongue in her mouth like she feared he might. Instead, he took three powerful strides towards Grizzly and jabbed a finger into the larger man's chest.

"Now. If you really want to make yourself useful then you can get to work on this one here." He pointed at Marshall's unconscious body, then turned and winked at Alex.

"Don't worry, darlin'. I'm not gonna let anyone hurt you."

Alex turned away from Bugger's sadistic smile, her eyes filling with tears. Not knowing where to look to escape this nightmarish scene, she focused on Marshall, who actually looked peaceful in his blacked out state. She tried to block out everything else and only think about that wonderful mop of hair she'd once run her fingers through. Or the toned, bronzed arms she'd clung to as they walked across campus. Those days seemed to be a lifetime ago. How could they be the same people who were now being held captive in a dank basement by a bunch of psychos? Things weren't supposed to be like this. They were supposed to be finishing school, going to parties and having fun. Just last month they were cruising around Champlain on a rented jet boat. She remembered how Marshall wished Vermont had seashore so he could find some decent waves...

The daydream collapsed with the reappearance of Grizzly, who now stood directly behind Marshall's head. In his hands he gripped a large double-bladed ax. Grizzly raised it high above his head and Alex shut her eyes, knowing what was to come.

She braced herself for the sound of metal slicing flesh and bone.

"Alex?"

She slowly opened one eye.

Marshall looked at her through groggy, half-open eyes. He seemed completely oblivious to where he was or that an ax-wielding psychopath towered above him. His eyes showed no fear, but rather puzzled amusement as to why his girlfriend was hung up like a coat in a closet. A crooked half smile pulled up one side of his mouth.

"What's going on?"

The smile remained on his face even after his head fell to the dirt floor and rolled past her feet. Blood shot from the stump of his neck like an opened fire hydrant, spraying everything that lined the opposite wall. Bugger jumped as the hot liquid splashed the back of his neck.

"God damnit!" he shouted, leaping out of the way of the bloody torrent. Meanwhile, Marshall's heels rattled the wood of the table in a spastic, postmortem dance. Alex watched in morbid fascination, watching her boyfriend's execution as if it were a scene in a slapstick comedy. When she began to laugh from behind the fabric in her mouth, she knew her sanity had finally snapped.

Bugger reached for a handkerchief and wiped the blood from his neck and face. It smeared across his skin and stubbly facial hair. "Make a bigger mess, why don't you?" he said, punching Grizzly in his huge bicep and snatching the ax from his hands. "Give me that! You can't do anything right, can you?"

Meanwhile, Marshall's legs continued to twitch on the table, heels clattering against the wood.

"Just let me do this," Bugger said, removing a blood-crusted meat cleaver wedged into the side of the table. "You just get back out there and keep hunting."

Grizzly grunted and threw his arms up. Somehow understanding Grizzly's secret language, Bugger tensed his neck and replied through gritted teeth. "Why? I'll tell you why."

He pointed a finger directly at Alex's chest and grinned.

"She's got friends."

Without another sound, Grizzly turned and paced over to the storm shelter doors. Grabbing a shotgun resting by the exit, he took the stairs in two giant steps, slammed the doors shut, and disappeared into the darkening evening. Bugger watched him go before returning his attention to Marshall's decapitated body. He offered Alex one last creepy smile before bringing the cleaver down into Marshall's left thigh. Even though Alex clenched her eyes shut, she could still hear everything below Marshall's knee fall to the floor and land in a puddle of coagulating blood.

There was nothing funny about her situation anymore; Alex guessed her mind hadn't completely snapped after all. Her only chance for mercy was to lose consciousness. She wanted to drown in that ocean of blood and never return.

CHAPTER SIXTEEN

Thankfully, the walk to the ranger outpost was much shorter than Leigh had expected. After a mere twenty minutes trudging across the soggy forest floor, a cabin, slightly smaller than the one they'd left Rob and Eliza in, came into view. It was designed in the same style as their previous shelter, but this structure boasted a dark green aluminum roof that looked rather new. A reddish brown US Department of Agriculture sign rested to the left of the front door; this simple symbol of authority brought Leigh instant comfort.

Less comforting, however, was the absence of any vehicles parked in front of the building.

"Damn," Sam mumbled under his breath, apparently noticing the same thing. "No ATVs. That's not a good sign."

Leigh nodded her head but didn't say anything in return. No need to add another voice to their mutal mounting despair—the cabin's darkened windows was enough.

Sam pressed his face against the glass. The sky was now almost as dark as the room within and Leigh knew Sam wouldn't be able to see much. She regretted that they hadn't thought to bring along flashlights.

"I don't see anybody," Sam said.

"So what do we do now? Head back?"

Sam offered her a hopeful smile. "Not yet." He headed for the front door, leaving her several paces behind. When Leigh caught up, she found him jiggling the doorknob, another look of complete disappointment overtaking his face.

"Shit!" It had yet to occur to Leigh just how softly they had been speaking to each other until Sam shouted the frustrated obscenity. "It was a long shot, but I was really hoping they didn't lock this. I guess I shouldn't be surprised with all the equipment they must keep in there."

A pinprick brought Leigh's hand smacking down on her right knee. Another mosquito, bringing the total number of bug bites collected on her skin to a causal thousand or so.

"Well, can't you just work your magic like before?" Leigh tried to ignore the bump she could already feel irritating her skin. "I didn't think locks were any match for you and your knife."

Sam threw a sarcastic smile and a glare that could only mean "very funny," but it was quickly replaced with seriousness.

"This isn't some flimsy little pin I can slide back like at the other cabin. These guys secured this place pretty well." Sam pointed to a round, metallic disc that surrounded the keyhole. "That's a bolt lock. I'd need something way better than my pocket knife to get through it."

"Then I guess that's that." Leigh turned, assuming Sam was right behind her. She'd already taken several paces away from the cabin when the sound of shattering glass stopped her in her tracks.

He didn't.

Leigh turned around, knowing exactly what she was about to see: Sam stood sheepishly next to a broken window.

He did.

"What the fuck, Sam?"

Sam shrugged his shoulders and grinned. "I found something better than my pocket knife." He carefully reached through the jagged broken glass and found the window's latch. Once unlocked, he pushed the window up and waved his hand through the open portal.

"Ladies first."

Leigh was fully aware just how childish it was to be turned on by such a cliché "bad boy" act. And yet, that's exactly what was happening as she took Sam's hand and carefully made her way through broken the window. She'd been attracted to her new friend since they had first met, that much she could admit to herself. But before it had felt like a somekind of deep, strange connection. Now it was purely lust. Leigh could give a shit about like minds and soul mates at a time like this. She just wanted to jump the country boy's bones.

And all it took was a little breaking and entering.

Leigh wondered if she'd ever again be able to justify looking down on Eliza for dating someone like Rob. You could suppress carnal desires for a long time, sure, but fighting primal instinct was a battle you'd always lose, eventually—and Leigh was losing it right now.

And it felt good.

"All right." Sam's voice was directly in her ear. "Let's see if we can find the light switch."

Feeling along the wall, Leigh had to catch herself from falling face first when she stubbed her foot on something round and hard. She didn't need light to know that it was the stone Sam had chucked through the window pane.

Something square shaped and smooth slid its way under her fingers. A protrusion jutted out from the square, pointing down towards the floor.

"I found it!" Leigh announced. Her excitement was quickly extinguished when several vigorous flicks upwards and down accomplished nothing.

In the darkness, she heard Sam sigh with disappoint at the sound of the ineffective switch. "Damn it. Power's not on."

"You think there's a generator or something?"

"Could be one outside, maybe around back." Sam marched across the room, making his way back to the window.

Leigh flinched at the loud thump paired with a painful *umph!* that came after Sam's fourth step.

"You okay?" Even in light of their urgent situation, Leigh had to cover a laugh.

"Yeah," Sam groaned. "I just walked right into a table. Something landed on my foot. Hey, wait…" he trailed off as he reached down to retrieve the object. After a beat of silence, he shouted once again, this time in joy rather than disappointment or frustration.

"Yes! I found the radio! It was the mic that hit my foot. Give me a second. I'll see if I can find the power switch."

After a series of shuffling noises and the metallic snaps of switches, a dim green light illuminated the area surrounding the table as well as Sam's face. His teeth eerily reflected the light as he smiled at the backlit dials that springing to life. Leigh had to smile too when she heard the comforting sound of static and knew they were in business.

"Thank God it's battery-powered," Sam said, taking a seat behind the radio. "Okay, while I try to reach someone, why don't you try to find us a flashlight or something?"

"What about the generator?"

Sam shook his head. "Finding it and getting it running would be a waste of time. We don't need it. If you can't find anything, that's okay. I think I can manage with what I got here."

"Well, let me see what I can find."

While the radio offered very little light, even its dim illumination seemed to double her visibility in the lightless cabin. In one corner of the room,she could make out a short stack of two or three cardboard boxes.

Grabbing the top box, she lugged it over to the swath of green light that bathed the floor around the radio's table. Amazed to discover another little miracle, Leigh opened the flaps to see not only a book of matches resting on top, but the faded red stick of a flare right beside it.

"Oh, thank you," she said, not exactly sure to whom she was speaking. Leigh picked up the flare and held it between her teeth while she retrieved the matches and broke one off.

The sandy scrape of the match scratching the flint was the most satisfying sound Leigh had ever heard. And the single flame from the match warmed her like a bonfire.

Leigh dropped the book of matches and pulled the flare from the grip of her teeth.

She was just about to light the end when a cold hand grabbed her wrist.

"*Ahh!*"

Leigh screamed and dropped the flare but managed to keep a hold on the match. She jerked her head back to see Sam standing behind her, still holding her wrist in a death grip. When their eyes met, he finally let go.

"What the hell are you doing?" Leigh said as she tried to regain her breath.

Sam released her wrist and took a step back. "Look at what you were about to light."

He reached down and picked up the flare from the wooden floor. He brought it up into the lit match's small glow, rotating it in his fingers until thick, capital letters came into view. Just before Leigh shook the match to avoid burning her fingers, she caught a glimpse of the faded letters:

DYNAMITE.

"Oh my god! I almost killed us." Leigh could feel the blood rushing to her face. "Why the hell would they have dynamite just lying around?"

"My guess would be to remove tree stumps." Sam ducked down to the box and began rummaging around. "I'm not sure."

His sentence ended with a loud *crack*, and a dim blue light appeared in his hands. Leigh watched as the light's intensity grew and took the shape of a rod.

"Here," Sam said, handing her the glow stick. "I'll trade you."

Leigh accepted it and silently wished she had seen the pile of glow sticks resting at the bottom of the box herself. Leigh handed over her "flare," which Sam shoved in his back pocket.

"I'll hang onto this," he said grinning. "Just to be safe."

Leigh looked to the floor, ashamed.

"I'm just teasing, Leigh."

"I know. But you got us in here, got the radio working, and then found us some light. Me? I almost blew us up. So sue me if I feel like an asshole. I can't help it. You must think I'm retarded."

Sam cracked himself another glow stick. "First of all, I threw a rock through a window, flicked a switch, and dug to the bottom of a cardboard box. Wow, that's so impressive. And for the record, I don't think you're retarded. I think you're—"

Leigh looked into Sam's eyes. He paused.

"—really cool."

"Cool?" she replied, and burst out laughing.

Jesus Christ. Maybe I really am a ditz.

But Sam seemed to be the one who felt embarrassed. "What can I say? No one ever accused me of being suave."

"You could've fooled me."

"Oh really? Then I guess I'd better do this before you wise up."

While he came in fast, his kiss was soft and gentle. It took Leigh a moment to register what was happening, but as she felt his lips caressing hers, reality hit her in all of its thrilling ecstasy. Though they had consumed it hours ago, Sam's breath still smelled of jerky, but Leigh didn't care. She figured the same taste was lingering in her own mouth, and Sam didn't seem to notice.

As Leigh gave into the surge of pleasure coursing through her body, she shut her eyes to savor the sensuous moment. But it was not darkness that Leigh saw behind her closed eyelids.

It was Eliza—cowering, crying, and begging for help.

Leigh's eyes popped open. She threw her palms into Sam's shoulders and pushed. He threw his hands up.

"Sorry," he said. "I'm sorry. I shouldn't have done that."

Leigh waved her hand. "No, it's okay. It's just—"

Sam cut her off. "We should get on the radio."

"Right."

It was all Leigh could say.

Sam turned away and walked over to the radio, leaving

Leigh standing there, trying to control the electric current running through her body.

God, what is wrong with me? What the hell was I just doing?

Taking a deep breath, Leigh could feel her head reattaching itself to her shoulders.

Okay, time to return to Earth. Your friend needs you.

A moment later, Sam was wearing the radio's headphones and repeating into the microphone, "Can anyone hear me?" and "We need help, please respond." She felt uncomfortable just standing around and doing nothing, so Leigh decided to check out the remaining space of the room. Perhaps she could find something useful this time, preferably something that wouldn't blow them to kingdom come.

Using the glow stick as a torch, Leigh approached the wall to her right and examined the bulletin boards covering the walls. Most of the papers pinned to the boards were pamphlets and advisory messages that covered a myriad of topics: forest fire threat levels, warnings not to bring in outside firewood, a memo concerning a migrating beetle species that could bring severe damage to local tree life—none of the information seemed particularly helpful to their current situation.

Then Leigh came to another bulletin board, this one encased in glass. It seemed that while the other boards were for news and messages, this one was being used as a gallery. Several four-by-six photographs of different rangers were pinned across the board, cameos of men performing different occupational tasks. A humorous postcard lay crooked in the bottom corner that depicted a bunch of sheep blocking a tractor: a "Vermont traffic jam"

But what really caught Leigh's attention was a series of old newspaper clippings arranged in chronological order. Although the paper was yellowed and the ink had slightly faded, Leigh was still able to make out the capitalized headlines and black-and-white photos that accompanied each one. The first article read:

DISEASED TREES CREATE PRODUCTION DELAYS AT SAW MILL.

These words rested on top of a picture of a group of grumpy-looking mill workers who stood with their arms folded across their chests. They all stared down at a fallen tree, completely covered in moss.

Leigh read the next article headline.

MYSTERIOUS DISEASE THREATENS PERMANENT MILL CLOSURE.

This time, a dead white-tailed deer lay at the feet of a mill worker, its tongue hanging from its mouth. Spread across its entire body, including its eyes, were patches of of fungus. The mill worker standing above it wore a white surgical mask and long rubber gloves.

The final clipping was the worst of all.

SAW MILL CLOSES DUE TO WILDLIFE EPIDEMIC.

The accompanying picture was similar to the last but for a a single, drastic, difference: instead of a dead animal, a man now lay on the ground; his condition looked almost identical to that of the dying hunter they'd stumbled upon in the woods earlier. Leigh had to look away when she noticed the fungus growing out of the man's nostril. Furry mucus.

"Damn it!"

Leigh practically jumped out of her skin at the sound of Sam's cursing loudly. She turned to see him tearing the headphones from his ears and throwing them at the radio's frequency display.

"I can't get anyone to respond."

Leigh took one final glance at the horrific picture and then walked over to Sam's side. "Did you try more than one frequency?"

"I tried a few," Sam said. "But this note says what frequency is the ranger headquarters. And no one is picking up."

"Well, it's getting pretty late. Maybe they all went home."

"Maybe," Sam grumbled as he pushed his chair back and stood up. "I guess all we can do now is turn on the emergency distress signal." He pointed to a switch labeled as such. After giving it a flip, a series of beeps began to sound on repeat.

"Morse code," Sam said to himself.

Leigh listened to the string of beeps. "Do you know what it's saying? Is it S.O.S.?"

Sam shrugged his shoulders. "No clue. But it doesn't really matter. It could be ordering us a Big Mac and large fries, but the important thing is that someone hears it eventually. I'm sure they'll send someone to investigate when they finally get back."

"So what now? Do you think we should wait?"

Sam removed his Expos cap and wiped his brow. It was hard to know for sure what was making him sweat, the Indian summer night or the tense state of current affairs. Or maybe he was still hot and bothered from what had occurred a few moments ago. Leigh was beginning to feel a little warm herself just thinking about Sam's tongue running along the backside of her upper lip.

"No." For a second, Leigh thought Sam had somehow read her thoughts and was denying her wish to relive their necking session. "We don't know how long it'll take them to respond, and I don't feel right about leaving Rob and Eliza all by themselves for too long."

"You're right." Leigh blinked a few times to shake the steamy memories still fixated in her brain. "So how about we leave a note for whoever comes here next? Tell them to come to the cabin and bring help?"

"Good idea. Let's find a pen."

It didn't take long to find a writing instrument, as well as a discarded weather advisory report. Sam turned the piece of scrap paper over and scribbled their location and a request for help.

"There, it's done."

"Great," Leigh said, walking towards the door. "Then let's get out of here."

Sam didn't follow her and instead walked over to the stack of cardboard boxes. "Okay, just let me see if I can find some flashlights. It's getting pitch black out there."

Leigh went to unlock the front door. She brought the glow stick towards the latch that had previously caused them so much trouble.

Just as the bolt slid out of the lock with a *click*, the door flew open, coming within centimeters of slamming Leigh's nose. Her startled scream was cut short when she realized who was standing in the doorway.

"Rob!" Leigh gave him her most incredulous stare. "What the fuck?"

"Sorry," Rob said. His voice shook, his eyes locked for some reason on Sam. "I didn't mean to scare you."

Sam stood up from his kneeling position by the stack of boxes. He gripped a flashlight in each hand, one the large lantern type and the other a long metal kind usually used by highway troopers. "How'd you find us?" he asked, walking over to join them.

Rob stared at him. "I saw the direction you guys headed and spotted the light coming from the cabin as I got close. I figured it had to be you."

"But what the hell are you doing here? You're supposed to be keeping an eye on Eliza!" Even though Leigh was yelling in anger, Rob still wouldn't look away from Sam.

"It doesn't matter," Rob said in an eerily calm voice. It was as if he was trying his hardest to contain his anger from erupting. "She'll be fine."

"What are you talking about? She's really sick!" Leigh jabbed his shoulder. "You know what? Forget it. Just get out of the way. We're going back now."

Rob slammed the door shut before she could take another step. "Not just yet."

"Rob…" Leigh was doing her best to remain cool and collected. "What are you doing? Let me go."

"Just shut up and listen to me for a minute, okay?" Rob removed his hand from the door but remained standing in front of it. "After you guys left I wanted to clear my head, so I grabbed a beer and sat down on the couch. And as I sat there and tried to sort out everything that's been going on, I got to thinking. All of this just doesn't add up."

Leigh shook her head. "What do you mean?"

"I mean this son of a bitch right here!"

Rob pointed his index finger at Sam's chest like a deadly weapon. The explosion he'd been suppressing was finally coming forth.

Sam brought his arms up as if to physically shield himself from the accusation. "Whoa! I don't know what you're—"

Rob didn't let him finish. "Shut up, asshole! And stay right where you are."

Leigh took a step sideways and placed herself between the two men. "Rob, you're acting crazy. You really need to calm down."

"No! I don't need to calm down. You need to *think*!"

"About what?"

"About how this guy led us through a forest infected with whatever is killing my girlfriend right now."

Rob's finger shook as it pointed, his hand and arm trembling with rage. In the most soothing voice she could muster, Leigh attempted to assuage his panic.

"Now Rob, how was Sam supposed to know that was going to happen?"

"Jesus Christ, Leigh!" It was obvious her calming tone was to no effect. "The guy is *from* here! He said it himself."

"Hey, man, that's not what I said!" Sam took a careful step forward. "I grew up *near* here, okay?"

"Bullshit!" Rob shouted, spittle flying from his mouth. "And didn't I say to shut your fucking mouth?"

"But I'm telling you, I had no idea! And I'm sorry about all this but I'm trying to help."

Rob opened his mouth to yell again; Leigh spoke first. "Sam…"

But when she looked at him now, she suddenly saw something… different Before, she had seen a boyishly cute guy with a shy demeanor that mirrored her own. She had seen a fellow outsider, someone eager to help if only to gain some friends. But now…

Now she saw a complete stranger. Someone who carried a knife and knew how to use it. Someone who didn't hesitate to break windows. And someone who her friends had blindly let lead them into the woods. It was true: without Sam, Eliza would never have contracted the disease that was now killing her.

Leigh walked over to the glass-encased bulletin board. She opened the case and removed the old newspaper clipping, the final one with the deceased mill worker covered in fungus. She held the article up in Sam's face.

"Are you telling us that you really had *no idea* about this?"

Sam stared at the disturbing picture and then looked uneasily at Leigh and Rob.

"I did know about what happened at the saw mill."

Rob's breath was as loud as a steam engine. "You son of a—"

"But this happened *years* ago!" Sam snatched the article from Leigh's fingers and flipped it around so they could see it. "There hasn't been a single case of this disease reported in my entire lifetime."

Rob tried to push Leigh back but she held her arm up to block him.

"Stay cool, Rob."

"But he knew!" Rob stomped his foot like a frustrated bull. "Come on, Leigh. You're supposed to be the smart one. So for fuck's sake, think about it. He was going to get us all infected, wait for us to end up like Eliza, ditch us, and take all of our shit. The guy's a drifter, probably does it all the time."

"That's bullshit." Sam no longer sounded desperate or afraid. His voice was now sharp with anger. "I don't have to listen to this."

"What, can't explain yourself?" Rob gave a disdainful snort. "Big surprise. You're going to pay for this, shithead."

"That's enough, Rob." Leigh turned her back on Sam to get in Rob's face. "You've made your point. I get it. Let's just get back to the camp and deal with this there. I want to get back to Eliza right now."

"And this guy's coming with us?"

"We don't know our way out." Leigh motioned to Sam.

"And he does. We need him."

Rob looked over Leigh's head to the guy behind her. "I don't like this."

Leigh reached out and tenderly squeezed Rob's shoulder. "I know you don't. But you trust me, right?"

Just like when they had left the cabin, Leigh spotted that same vulnerability that she would had never guessed Rob was capable of. Rob took a breath. "Yeah. I do," he said.

"Then can we go?"

"Fine." Rob took a step towards Sam. "But I'm keeping him in front of me, where I can see him, the entire way back."

Sam nodded in defeat. "That's okay with me."

Rob spat at his shoes. "I didn't ask if it was."

Leigh started to say something but decided to let it go. She hoped that Rob could hold himself back from physically attacking Sam, at least for the time being. She accepted the lantern from Sam, purposely avoiding eye contact, and made her way into the night.

As they walked in silence through the dark forest, twigs snapping underfoot, Leigh considered the insight Rob had brought with him to the ranger outpost. Though she wouldn't deny that his suspicions were justified, it didn't mean he was necessarily right about Sam. It could all easily be a misunderstanding.

Still, she wished she had some water to wash away the flavor of jerky that lingered from their kiss. All she could taste was that meat.

CHAPTER SEVENTEEN

The night shift for forest insects had officially begun. A cacophony of chirping crickets radiated through the trees, the sound of thousands of bug conversations. The noise comforted Leigh as she, Rob, and Sam approached the deer camp's front porch. It reminded her that some things at least were still functioning normally in the crazy nightmare that had become her life. Whatever this disease was, eating away at anyone unfortunate enough to come in contact with it, at least it didn't seem to affect the creepy crawlies socializing in the dirt and buzzing through the air.

The inside of the cabin, however, was dead silent. Leigh didn't know if that was a good sign or a bad one, since it meant Eliza had finally stopped screaming and crying. Either she'd gotten a grip and was patiently waiting for her friends to return—or she'd taken a turn for the worse. Leigh's pounding heartbeat echoed in her ears she approached the bedroom door.

Rob walked past her and gave a gentle knock. "Eliza?" he asked, with an uncharacteristic softness to his voice. There was no answer.

Leigh turned around to face Sam. "I think you should wait here."

His eyes and the corners of his mouth dropped in unison.

"So you really don't trust me either."

Goosebumps rose on the back of Leigh's neck when she saw the coldness in Sam's eyes. Leigh still didn't know exactly how to answer that question, so she did her best to dodge it.

"It's not about that. Somebody should keep an eye on the window. That hunter has to be out there somewhere. We should help him if we can."

Sam stared, unblinking. She turned away and Sam finally said, "Okay. Go check on your friend."

Without another word, Leigh returned to Rob's side by the closed door.

"She's not answering?" she asked.

Rob put his ear to the door. "No. I don't hear anything."

"Then let's just go in."

"She's probably just asleep." Though he tried to say it with conviction, the edge to his voice proved he didn't believe his own words.

Leigh rapped on the wood. "Eliza, it's Leigh. Are you awake?"

There was no response.

Leigh sighed. "That's it. I'm going in." She grabbed the knob and pushed, but only got the door opened an inch before Rob slammed it shut.

"Wait."

Leigh flinched. "Wait for what?"

Rob's breath had become very heavy. "Are we sure we want to go in there? We don't know how contagious…"

Leigh didn't let him finish. "Oh, Jesus Christ Rob, move!" With a fierce shove, she pushed him out of her way and nearly fell through the threshold of the bedroom as the door swung open.

The instant she saw the green, festering clump of mold that stuck out of the top of the plaid wool blanket, Leigh assumed Dale had snuck into Eliza's bed, like a diseased Goldilocks. But soon she recognized the long, black hair fanned across the pillows, sprouting from the top of the lumpy mass of fuzz. Although mushroom-like growths concealed both of her eyes, this pile of decay was indeed one of Leigh's closest friends; formerly known as Eliza.

Leigh's scream hurt her own ears.

Rob came out from behind the door and slammed into Leigh's shoulder, knocking her to the floor. He gave a breathless gasp

"Oh my God," he moaned.

Rob recoiled at the awful sight, tripping over his own heels as he awkwardly backpedaled towards the door. In a desperate attempt to save himself from falling on his back, Rob grabbed onto a handful of blankets at the corner of the bed. The quilts did nothing to stop his fall as pulled them to the floor.

Leigh looked to the blanketless bed.

The fungus-engulfed stump that had been Eliza's head, neck, and shoulders were the only parts that remained of her body. Everything below her collarbone had been removed, leaving only a blood soaked mattress behind. It appeared the amputation had been performed by a brutal series of hatchet chops, evident from the ragged, severed flesh that hung in strings from the leftover remains.

Rob and Leigh stood frozen in silence, the dripping blood seeping its way between the cracks in the bedroom's floorboards the only sound

And then came a guttural belch as Rob doubled over and vomited only a few inches from Leigh's shoes.

Rob's heaving snapped Leigh out of her terrified trance. Pivoting on the ball of her foot, Leigh dashed past the still gagging Rob back into the living room.

Sam stood at the window, staring blankly into the night. Hadn't her screaming alarmed him at all?

"We need to get out here," Leigh said, yanking on the cuff of Sam's shirt. "Now!"

Sam ignored both her, bringing a finger to his lips.

"Shhh!" He pointed out the window to something in the darkness. Before she could react to what she was seeing, Rob came crashing into the living room, his eyes targeting Sam as if there was a bullseye painted on his forehead.

"I'm going to fucking *kill* you!"

Rob started to advance towards Sam, but somehow Leigh managed to tackle him to the floor. In her crouched position by the window, she had just enough leverage that when she grabbed Rob's legs, the sudden slam into the back of his knees brought him flailing to the floor once again.

"What are you doing?" Rob shouted as he tried to wrestle away from Leigh. "Let go of me!"

"Shut up and stay down!" she ordered. "Sam didn't do that to Eliza. He was with us."

Rob eyes narrowed. "Then who did?"

Leigh slowly and carefully lifted herself from Rob's back but made sure to stay below the bottom pane of the window. With a hand on top of Rob's head to make sure he did the same, Leigh guided his gaze towards a hulking figure dragging a large, canvas bag away from the cabin.

"Holy shit! Is that a fucking bear?"

Sam sighed. "Yeah. And it's wearing a shirt and carrying a bag."

"Hey fuck you," Rob replied. "I only saw his mask at first, okay?" Rob returned his eyes to the window. "Who do you think he is?"

"Maybe a hunter. That could be a deer in that bag." Even as Leigh spoke the words she knew how pathetically optimistic she sounded. When a seven-foot tall giant wearing a bear head as a mask is outside your door, the time for optimism is over.

"Yeah, maybe Dick's Sporting Goods sells bear heads next to their fishing rods," Sam mocked.

In the flickering light of the stranger's torch, Leigh could see two things that disturbed her even more than his choice of headwear: a large ax strapped to his back, and a dark, dripping splotch on the bottom of the bag.

"It doesn't look like he's coming this way," Sam said, actually pointing out something not only hopeful but true.

Leigh nodded. "No, he's definitely walking into the woods. So let's just wait for him to go away and then get the hell out of here."

"But what if he's taking the same trail?" Sam asked. "We could run right into him."

"No we won't. We're going back to the road."

Now that the spotty illumination from the man's torch had vanished into the darkness of the trees, Leigh felt it safe enough to return to her feet. Sam followed her lead and grabbed her arm. "You want to go back?"

"That's right. We're going back to the main road to find help."

Sam slapped his forehead, a gesture Leigh had previously only seen in old Donald Duck cartoons and corny family sitcoms. "Do you know how long that will take?" His voice contained only a hint of restraint left. "I called for help. They should be here any minute."

"Then you can stay here if you want." Leigh realized she was using a tone she usually only reserved for conversations with Rob. "But the two of us are going back. Right?"

Rob didn't answer.

Leigh looked around the empty living room. He wasn't there. "Rob?"

The wish Leigh had been dreaming for all semester had finally been granted, at the worst time imaginable.

Rob had vanished into thin air.

"Rob? Where'd you go?" Leigh tried to ask the question as loudly as she could while keeping her voice below a shout.

Sam tapped her on the shoulder and pointed out the window. "There he is."

Sure enough, Rob was sneaking away like an army commando stalking an enemy. In one hand he gripped a club-shaped branch, keeping the makeshift weapon ready at his side. An arrow-filled quiver hung on one shoulder and a bow on the other crisscrossed his back. In his other hand he gripped a flashlight, but he had yet to turn it on, probably in fear he might attract the attention of his prey.

Had the situation not been so dire, Leigh might've laughed at what she was seeing. It was like watching a poor man's remake of *First Blood* or *Predator*, with a skinny, wannabe punk rocker who made just as much sense being cast as John Rambo as Ashton Kutcher.

"I don't believe it," Sam muttered. "He's going after him. He's completely lost it."

"Come on!" Leigh raced across the living room to the cabin's front door. As she passed the gun cabinet, a quick glance confirmed what she knew she'd see: the cabinet was open and missing its only bow and arrow set. Rob must have chosen this weapon knowing the rifles were devoid of ammo.

Sam still stood at the window, watching Rob as if he really were a character on a movie screen. While Leigh could sympathize with the feeling, she needed her companion to kick it into gear. Time had never been more of the essence.

"Move, Sam! We have to catch him before he gets himself killed." She grabbed the remaining flashlight from the coffee table in the center of the room.

"Should I bring one of these?" Sam motioned towards the firearms in the cabinet.

"They don't have any bullets, remember? And we don't have time to look for any."

Sam reached up and retrieved a handgun resting on a shelf above the rifles. The gun was black and had a peculiarly large barrel. He opened the chamber, smiled, and closed it.

"Then I'll bring this."

"What is it?"

"It looks like a tranquilizer gun. It's got a dart in it."

Leigh didn't know what a couple of rugged hunters who decorated their cabin with mounted deer heads would want with a non-lethal firearm, but she didn't have time to ponder the question.

"Great. Now let's go!" She tore open the door and fled outside. She was already at the bottom of the porch steps and jogging into the trees when she heard Sam say, "Hey! Wait for me!"

She forced herself to stop by a rough-barked maple tree. A

moment later, Sam came running up, holding the tranquilizer gun with both hands like an extra from *Starsky and Hutch*.

"All right," he said, slightly out of breath. Leigh figured it was from the tension of the moment and not the brief sprint from the cabin. "Let's do this."

Leigh took a step forward, then hesitated. She looked back at Sam, and in the gentlest voice she could muster, asked, "Can we switch?" She offered the flashlight towards him.

Sam raised an eyebrow. "What for?"

"I just don't think it would be a good idea for you to be holding a weapon when we catch up to Rob. I know it's stupid, but I think we can both agree that he's pretty on edge with you. I just don't want to give him another reason to freak out."

Sam looked down at the gun in his hand. With reluctance, he finally turned the gun around and extended it towards Leigh, handle first.

"Yeah, you're right. That's probably a good idea. Here."

Leigh accepted the weapon and handed him the flashlight.

"Okay," he said. "Now are you ready to catch up with your asshole friend?"

Intentionally keeping a few steps behind him, Leigh sighed with relief that he'd handed over the gun without a fight. Of course, that wasn't the real reason she wanted to be the one with the weapon. And as they made haste, Leigh was also thankful for the totality of the night's darkness. It disguised where Leigh was pointing the gun:

Directly at the center of Sam's back.

CHAPTER
EIGHTEEN

Jake had told both Doug and himself that the reason he was accompanying the rookie ranger to Maple Ridge Station was simple boredom. "What else do I have to do?" he said when Doug realized he'd forgotten the keys to his truck at the outpost. But as they navigated their ATVs along the narrow trail through the woods, the vehicles' solo headlights the only source of light to illuminate their way, Jake could not ignore the truth any longer. He was taking this lengthy trip through the cold, dark forest for a single purpose: to delay returning to an empty apartment and put off another long, lonely night. Even if his only alternative was traveling out to the middle of nowhere with a smart-ass rookie, tonight he'd take it. It seemed better than a Hungry Man dinner and prerecorded shows on the DVR.

If this is my only option for any sort of company, what the hell am I still doing here?

It wasn't the first time Jake had asked himself the question. The lack of prospects in Embry, VT was only magnified when he happened to venture to a more populated areas like Portland, places where seeing a pretty, single girl in a bar wasn't just a once-in-a-lifetime occurrence. Jake knew he had to get out of here someday—and someday soon, to be precise. While in his thirties, the bachelor still had a chance. There was time to raise some hell on earth with a sexy demoness. He just had to find her. And he doubted she was hiding somewhere out here behind an oak tree.

Jake forced himself to concentrate on keeping his wheels on the dimly lit path. He could start prioritizing his life tomorrow. For now, it was best to simply enjoy the brisk but comfortable coolness of a temperate autumn night and be thankful for the freedom his occupation afforded him every day. He'd rather be tearing along in a grown-up toy with a buddy leading the way than stuck in bumper-to-bumper traffic on his commute home from another nine-to-five cubicle sentence. So yes, companionship was valuable for sure, but freedom…

Freedom was priceless.

All the same, when Doug had realized he'd left his keys at the station, Jake was grateful for an excuse to avoid heading straight home, as he usually did.

"Ah, shit!" Doug had said, padding his pockets and feeling nothing. "Damn it all to hell, I left my keys at Maple Ridge."

Jake had been halfway to the headquarters' front door, just about to say goodnight to Phil and punch out.

"You sure they're not inside?" Jake motioned to the building.

"Yeah, I'm sure. I remember I threw them on the table after I unlocked the door. Totally spaced that I left them behind since, you know, I drove a four-wheeler up there."

Jake nodded. "Of course. Well just give me a second and I'll take the trip with you."

"You don't have to do that. Go home already." Doug was making his way to an ATV.

"No, wait for me," Jake turned and jogged to the door. "I want to, it's a nice night. Just let me give Phil the head's up and we'll shoot right up there."

Doug swung his leg over the seat of a dark red ATV and straddled the transport like a cowboy on horseback. "Suit yourself. Just hurry up. I want to get home for *South Park*."

"Oh, in that case I'll radio for a chopper!"

Jake could hear Doug chuckle at his remark as he swung the door open. Phil was shutting off the office lights and reaching for for his coat.

"Another day, another donut," Phil said, snagging the last remaining donut hole from a cardboard carton sitting by the coffee machine. He crumpled the container and chucked it in the wastebasket. Through a mouthful of dough he said, "I'll see you tomorrow."

"Sure thing, Phil. Doug and I are just gonna shoot up to Maple and grab his keys. Chucklehead outside left them there this morning."

Phil looked at him curiously.

"You're going too?"

"Yeah, just gonna tag along and make sure the jackass doesn't leave his head there this time."

Phil finished pulling his coat over his shoulders. "Seems like an awful lot of trouble, Jake. Why don't I just give him a ride home and he can get them in the morning?"

Jake pulled open the top drawer of the cabinets that sat to the left of the entrance. As expected, he was able to locate a Maglite among various pens, screwdrivers, and other miscellaneous items strewn about the junk drawer. He clicked it on to test the batteries. Satisfied with its power, Jake made his way back to the door.

"Yeah, pointless for me to go too, but what can I say? I guess I must be really bored. You can lock the door behind me. I'll see ya."

Phil mumbled something that resembled "um," but got cut off as the door swung closed behind Jake, who got only three steps away from the building when he remembered an important question. Jake threw Doug a "one second" gesture with his finger and darted back inside.

"Hey, Phil." Phil still stood by the coat hangers, his eyes staring into space, looking as if he were drowning in a sea of troubling thoughts. The elder ranger flinched at the sound of Jake's voice and snapped out of his trance. Jake couldn't help but notice how much older Phil's eyes looked than the last time he had noticed them.

"Were there any messages today? Calls, radio activity, whatever?"

Phil stared at Jake, apparently thinking very hard about a question that should've been an easy, instant answer.

Man, he must have had a long day. Thank God that cast comes off tomorrow.

Phil finally cleared his throat and spoke.

"Nope. Not a thing."

The forest became deathly quiet the moment Jake turned off the ignition of his ATV. Doug was already waiting for him when he arrived, the younger ranger pulling the key ring connected to the zip cord from his belt. Jake left his vehicle running so its headlight would make Doug's task of unlocking the door easier, but once the key had click opened the lock, Jake killed the engine, leaving the rangers in total silence and darkness.

Doug's flashlight ignited from inside the cabin.

"Hold on," Jake yelled, swinging his leg around from its straddled position on the ATV's seat. "I'll get the generator going."

Doug shone the light on himself so that Jake could see the thumb's up sign he was flashing through the window.

Jake laughed and returned one of his own. As he trotted carefully around the corner of the cabin, using his flashlight to avoid tripping on a stone or tree root, Jake realized that the newest member of their team was growing on him. Sure, Doug still had a lot to learn about protocol and routine, but he was naturally a team player. The woods of Northeast Vermont may not contain drug dealers and gang members, but having a partner watching his back was just as important to

Jake as it would be to a New York City cop. The forest had its own dangers, and trekking through them with a certified dumbass was just as dangerous as flying solo, if not more so. But fortunately, Doug was proving to have a good enough head on his shoulders. He'd come into his own soon enough and prove to be just as valuable as Phil. Not to mention, he was funny as hell.

The generator was nothing remarkable—just a standard diesel engine, rusted from the humidity and requiring a few more tugs than it should have to get it started these days. Shining his light over the gas gauge, Jake grimaced when he saw how low the fuel level was. Before they locked up and returned to the headquarters, they would have to remember to refill the tank. Doug should've checked it this morning.

Another time, Jake would remind Doug of his duties. For now, there was surely enough gas for the brief amount of time the two were going to spend in the cabin.

After a few vigorous yanks of the ignition cord and a couple muttered curse words, Jake finally got the old generator to turn over. The noise of the rumbling engine roared through the quiet night, drowning out the steady drone of the night's chirping insects. Any slumbering beast nearby would surely be disturbed now, grumbling as they trudged away in search of another bed.

The light above Jake's head flickered, and then radiated a steady, bright light. Mission accomplished.

Jake clicked off his flashlight and made his way to the outpost's front door. Upon entering the building, several things immediately struck him as odd.

First, two of the cardboard boxes of supplies that were usually stacked neatly in the corner had been dragged into the center of the room and left open.

Next, although Phil had said that all had been quiet tonight, the distress beacon of the outpost's radio had been activated, beeping and blinking along.

Lastly, Doug stood at the table that supported the radio with a hand-scribbled note between his fingers.

"Now what the hell is going on here?"

Doug shrugged. "Well, the keys aren't the only thing I found. Check this out."

Jake accepted the note from Doug and gestured to the open boxes. "Did you leave these out this morning?"

"Just read the note."

The sigh that escaped Jake's lips could be heard over the noise of the generator. Without even looking at the message in his hands, Jake knew it was going to be a long night.

"Yep," he mumbled. "Looks like we've got some people who need help."

Doug nodded enthusiastically. "It would explain who activated the radio." He sounded like a bored security guard who'd finally stumbled upon some action. Jake was thankful he'd decided to tag along with Doug; he wouldn't have wanted him to discover this alone. Zeal could get a guy in trouble without a more experienced partner watching his back.

"All right," Jake said, squeezing the bridge of his nose and massaging little circles with his fingers. ""So according to this note we've got a hiker who's sick and can't make it out of the woods on foot. We'll head over to their location and check it out. If possible, we'll give 'em a ride out. If not, we'll radio in some assistance. Sound good?"

Doug grinned. "Hell yeah."

Oh boy.

"Okay, then. Chuck these boxes back in the corner, turn off the radio, and wait for me by the four-wheelers."

"Where are you going?" Doug was already closing up one of the boxes and sliding it along the floor.

He turned back to Doug and with a deadpan face said, "To turn off the generator."

Doug winced. "Oh yeah, of course. Sorry."

"Just kill that radio, huh? I'll see you outside." Jake exited, sighing yet again.

A cloud of mosquitoes and moths had collected around the dangling light above the generator. Judging by the direction this night was taking, Jake knew his own sleep schedule was probably going to match up with that of these bugs.

What was I saying about freedom?

In reality, Jake was as much of a slave to his occupation as anyone in a cubicle. So maybe he didn't answer to a beer-bellied boss in a three-piece suit. He answered to clueless, foolish tourists in over their heads. And all he had to look forward to when it was all done was a microwavable meal of turkey medallions and mashed potatoes.

His fingers searching the backside of the generator for the off-switch, Jake found himself hoping that he and Doug would be able to wrap this all up nicely tonight and then toast a job well done over a glass of Purdy's fresh squeezed orange juice tomorrow morning. That is, if he could just find this damn switch…

Something round and cold touched the backside of his neck, freezing him in his awkward squatting position.

"Leave it running, Jake."

Phil?

Jake peered over his shoulder to indeed discover his more senior coworker standing behind him. Even more surprising was the rifle he had aimed right behind Jake's left ear.

"Now stand up, nice and slow." Phil was speaking loud enough to be heard over the rumble of the generator, but his tone was as cool and as casual as could be.

"Uh, what are you doing Phil?" Jake slowly straightened his legs and stood up to look him directly in the eyes.

"Where's Doug?" Phil didn't even seem to hear Jake's last question.

"He's in front, waiting at the ATVs. Man, I didn't even hear you drive up."

"I parked a little ways out and hiked the rest of the way."

"On your busted foot? Jesus, Phil, you mind explaining what the fuck is—"

Phil pushed the barrel of the rifle underneath Jake's chin and applied enough force to cut into his skin.

"Never mind that. Just tell Doug to go on ahead without you."

Jake squinted "*What?*"

"Tell him you're gonna refuel the generator and you'll be right behind him."

"For God's sake, Phil, what did I do? You don't think I'm messing around with your wife, do you? Is that it?

Phil pushed the barrel upward into Jake's throat hard enough to choke him. "Tell him!"

After a brief bout of coughing caused by the chokehold had passed, Jake yelled, "Doug? Doug!"

A moment later, a voice rose over the generator's roar. "Yeah?"

"Get on your horse and start heading for those hikers. I'll be right behind you."

"Really?"

Jake's eyes never left Phil's as he spoke. "Yeah, I just need to check something here. But we shouldn't keep those people waiting any longer if they're really in trouble. So go, I'm two steps behind you. Just keep your radio on, okay?"

There was a pause and then, "If that's what you want."

"I'll catch up. Now go!"

Doug didn't reply, but soon after came sound of his ATV starting and the growl of its engine fading as he drove away. The generator was now the only noise Jake could hear. He still had no clue what Phil was up to, but was relieved that he'd sent Doug away. Whether Phil was drunk or not, Jake didn't think that the older man would actually hurt him. But Doug and his smart mouth would've been a different matter.

"All right, Phil, he's gone." Jake forced his voice to maintain a calm, even tone. "It's just us now. So how about you lower the gun and tell me what's bothering you. Okay?"

Phil cleared his throat and spat a phlegmy wad on the dried leaves at his feet. "Not yet. We're going inside first. So turn around and walk, slowly, to the front door."

"Yeah, sure, Phil. You got it. But, you know, the gun's not necessary."

As he turned away from Phil's face, Jake took a deep breath through his nose in an effort to smell any sort of liquor on Phil's' breath. The test came out clean. Whatever reason Phil had to take Jake at gunpoint, he was doing it dead sober. And this frightened Jake even more.

Once inside the cabin, Phil commanded Jake to grab the chair resting at the radio desk and place it in the center of the room.

"Now sit down and reach your hands behind the back of the chair."

"Phil—"

"Now!"

Jake did as he was told. He heard Phil clear his throat.

"I'm going to tie your hands together now. Please Jake, I'm begging you, don't move. God knows I do not want to shoot you. But I swear I'll do it if you make me."

Jake frowned. "I don't believe this, Phil. What the fuck are you doing?"

The volume of Jake's voice increased with every word. Fright and confusion was quickly being replaced by the anger of betrayal. Phil remained silent as he finished tying Jake's hands.

"There," Phil said, ensuring the rope was tight with a final, hard pull. He came back around and placed a second chair in front of Jake. He took a seat and the two now faced each other. Removing his hat and resting the rifle across his lap, Phil leaned forward to his immobilized coworker.

"Now—" Phil's tone returned to his normal, day-to-day friendly pitch. The cold, demanding voice that had been directing Jake at gunpoint instantly vanished the moment Phil took his seat. With the same warm smile that greeted Jake at the start of every work day, Phil simply said, "Let's talk."

CHAPTER NINETEEN

It wasn't easy following Rob through the thick forest without the use of a flashlight. But despite stumbling whenever a rock or tree root snagged their feet, the two continued in darkness and resisted the urge to click it on. A beam of light would have given away their position, and as long as they could see Rob's torch ahead, they wouldn't lose their way.

Leigh wished she could shout loud enough for Rob to hear without alerting his prey. The sole of her foot slipped off another rock jutting from the earth, once again twisting her ankle. Had it not been for Sam walking mere inches in front of her, Leigh would've certainly suffered a debilitating sprain by now. But reaching out and grabbing Sam's shoulder saved her yet again, providing just enough support to prevent all of her weight from coming down on her angled foot.

"You okay?" Sam whispered, halting for a moment.

Leigh nodded. "Yeah," she whispered back. "Just hit another damn rock. I can't see a thing."

"Me neither."

Leigh felt a jolt when Sam's cool hand found her fingers and grasped them.

"Hold on," he said. His lips were centimeters from Leigh's

ear. "I'll help you up this knoll."

The killer in the bear mask had almost reached the top of a rising hill and was about to vanish over its crest. They would have to hurry if they didn't want to lose him and Rob. Leigh supposed they could always retreat to the cabin if that were to happen, but would they be capable of finding their way back at this point? Leigh wondered how Rob was keeping up his pursuit so well, blind as they were to the unstable ground.

"We're almost there," Sam said, hoisting her up over a slippery, moss-covered mound. "Just dig your feet in and don't let go."

Leigh did as Sam suggested, jamming her toes into the moist ground. It wasn't easy to maintain her balance with one hand gripping Sam and the other holding the tranquilizer gun, but Sam was able to pull her up with one strong tug.

"Thanks," she whispered. She could just barely see his eyes reflecting the dim moonlight above.

Sam returned her gaze, seemingly hypnotized. But just as she started to feel a spark of *something* again, Sam jerked his head to the left.

"Look!" he said, pointing downhill.

A cabin, far more dilapidated than the one they had come from, sat at the bottom of the knoll. Its roof was missing several shingles, its walls were blackened from wood rot. Though the structure looked like it would collapse at any second, the warm, orange light coming from the dirty windows proved it was still inhabited.

Leigh spotted the cabin just in time to see the man in the bear mask enter the front door, and a moment later, Rob emerge from behind a tree. He sprinted forward and disappeared behind a corner of the house.

"Did you see him?" Leigh whispered, pointing in Rob's direction. "He's getting way too close that place. He's going to get caught for sure."

Sam squinted, peering between the trunks of the pair of ash trees that concealed them. "Yeah," he said tensely. "All right, I'll go get Rob. You wait here."

Leigh flinched with surprise. "Wait, what?"

"Don't worry," Sam reassured. "I'll keep my distance from the windows."

"But Rob might not listen to you!" Leigh strained to keep her voice quiet.

Sam brushed away her hand that gripped his arm. "I'll make him listen, okay? I'm not sending you near that house. So don't move!"

Before Leigh could argue, Sam was gone, heading down the knoll to the cabin. "Shit!" Leigh whispered to herself as she watched Sam scurry around the side of the house like a secret agent. Unfortunately he'd forgotten their only weapon: the tranquilizer gun.

Jesus, is all this really happening?

Leigh pressed her hand against the trunk of a tree to support herself as the world began to spin. Fighting back nausea, she took a long, slow breath and closed her eyes.

Just then, the man in the bear mask came sprinting out the door, tripping on his own two feet. Terror gripped Leigh's heart.

He's heading right for me!

But then, a much smaller man came bursting out the cabin, yelling at the top of his lungs.

"Who said you could touch this!?" He screamed at the bear man, who cowered at his feet.

The smaller man gripped a pink backpack. Even from a distance, Leigh could make out the fuzzy-haired troll keychain dangling from the pack's front pouch zipper.

Her bones turned to ice.

That's Alex's.

"What'd I tell you before?" The smaller man shook the backpack shook as he shouted. "The one in the cellar is mine! You hear?"

The bear mask frantically nodded up and down.

"Good." The man holding the pack spat a mouthful of saliva behind him. "Now go inside and help Ma make supper."

The bear man crawled timidly to his feet and shuffled by his partner, who kicked him as he passed and then followed him inside. Leigh had a new piece of horrifying knowledge to keep her company.

These maniacs had captured Alex and were keeping her in the cellar. Even if Sam returned this instant with Rob in tow, they couldn't just walk away. Where was Sam, anyway?

Maybe he and Rob were just hiding out, waiting for the right moment to escape undetected. While that seemed likely, it still didn't help Alex any. But maybe they were already sneaking Alex out of the basement. Maybe they'd already freed her from her restraints and were about to reunite with Leigh and get away.

Leigh's surge of optimism collapsed when she noticed the storm shelter doors at the side of the cabin. They were shut. From this vantage point, she could see both the front door and the large cellar doors, and neither had been breached. Wherever Sam and Rob were, they certainly weren't helping Alex.

And I'm just standing here.

Without letting another doubt enter her consciousness, Leigh began to carefully tread down the knoll toward the cabin. The voices inside Leigh's mind screamed at her, *What are you doing? Go back! Go back!* but Leigh ignored them. Adrenaline was her only co-pilot now, pumping through her bloodstream and pushing her forward, one determined step at a time.

If they see me, I'll run. I'll run and lead them away so that my friends can make a break for it. Rob and Sam will follow. They'll help me. I can do this. I can do this. I can do this.

Leigh reached the doors and lifted the latch to the cellar as quietly as she could. Thankfully, the rust-caked hinges didn't squeak when she opened the wooden door and rested it on the ground. She glanced up at the four-panel window above her, but the grime covering the glass made it impossible to see anything inside. However, that also meant that the men inside couldn't see her, either. Reassured, Leigh descended the stone stairs into the basement.

A single flickering lantern hung from a wooden beam on the ceiling. The psychopaths clearly came and went from the basement frequently enough to not bother extinguishing the light. Leigh would have to hurry if she wanted to make it out undetected.

Easier said than done.

The clutter in the cellar was that of a hoarder's. Miscellaneous items were scattered in every nook and cranny, and the only items that seemed to have a designated place were the hunting tools hanging on the walls, and the various cutting instruments arranged neatly on a nearby table. Leigh looked around at the other stuff in the room.

A crate of wallets.

A box of cell phones.

Shoes. Sunglasses. Hats.

It was like a thrift store run by the local butcher.

But Alex was no where in sight.

The floorboards squeaked as feet shuffled overhead, accompanied by the muffled voices of the cabin's inhabitants. Leigh mustered just enough courage to whisper a shaky, barely audible call.

"Alex? Are you in here?" There was no reply. Leigh could feel the weight of tears collecting in the corner of her eyes. "C'mon girl, answer me."

Something wet and slick brought Leigh's foot shooting out in front of her. She clenched her teeth and her arms shot out to the sides, desperately trying to maintain her balance. In her desperate maneuver to stay upright, Leigh's hand collided loudly with the swinging, squeaky lantern.

Leigh reached to still the swinging lantern, and held her breath as she listened to the men above her. When their voices didn't rise or stop in mid-sentence, Leigh slowly released the air she was holding and lowered her gaze from the ceiling.

In front of her was the blood of Marshall's mutilated body darkening its wood surface.

Leigh slammed a hand to her mouth in order to conceal the scream threatening to breach her lips.

If not for the shell necklace and clothes that still adorned what was left of his body, Leigh might've not even known this was her college friend; his head had been completely severed and removed. All that remained was a blood-covered torso, both arms and legs reduced to bleeding stumps. A red-stained cleaver wedged into the table's side told Leigh the whole story.

Marshall had been sectioned and quartered like a grade-A beef.

So, which part is the brisket?

If not for the hand still clamped to her mouth, the cellar would've erupted with Leigh's maniacal giggle. She realized she had to preserve her sanity. Just back away and pretend the chopped-up body isn't really her friend, just a piece of uncooked meat. Just like one of those hanging hunks that Sylvester Stallone trained with in the *Rocky* movies.

Leigh had taken just four steps backwards when she bumped into something that swayed with her collision.

The object kicked her in the back of the knee.

Turning on toes still slick with blood, Leigh spun around.

Alex hung from a meat hook suspended from the ceiling; a rope connecting her wrists like handcuffs had been slung over the hook. A burlap sack had been placed over head, but the long strings of blonde hair peeking out from the bottom were a dead giveaway.

"Alex!" Leigh whispered as she grabbed the top of the bag and pulled. It was indeed her friend, but a slab of duct tape had been placed over her mouth. Alex seemed barely conscious, her head hanging limply. Her captors had removed her shirt and bra, leaving her topless.

As gently as she could, Leigh tugged on the strip of tape, pulling it across her friend's lips until it finally came off. "Alex? Can you hear me?" Leigh shook her shoulder. "Come on, wake up!"

Leigh held Alex's chin and shook her head vigorously; the motion luckily proved enough to rouse her.

The instant her eyes fluttered open, Leigh spotted the muscles in her jaw widening in preparation for an ear-piercing scream. Leigh slammed her hand over Alex's mouth.

"*Shh!*" Leigh commanded, bringing a finger of her other hand to her mouth. "Alex, it's me. It's Leigh. I'm going to take my hand from your mouth but you can't scream. Okay?"

Tears leaked from the corners of Alex's squeezed-shut eyes as she nodded in agreement. Leigh slowly moved her palm away from Alex's lips, who began taking in short gasps of breath.

"Leigh…" Alex moaned, her eyes barely able to roll up and meet Leigh's. Leigh grimaced at how weak her friend sounded and silently prayed that she'd be able to walk out of here without too much help.

"Yeah, it's me," Leigh reassured her while trying to undo the knots that bound her to the hook. "It's okay now. I'm gonna get you down and we'll get out of here."

The knots proved far too tight for Leigh's trembling fingers to untie, so she instead braced Alex around the waist and raised her until the rope lifted from the hook. After carefully placing Alex on her feet and making sure she could support herself, Leigh reluctantly went back to the butcher's block to retrieve the cleaver stuck in its side.

It's just a piece of meat.

It took some twisting and a hard pull, but Leigh was able to remove the cleaver without looking directly at her roommate's mutilated boyfriend. She'd have to try to prevent Alex from seeing the mess lest a blood-curling scream be the end of them both. Leigh turned the lantern away from the table and towards the shivering girl, leaving Marshall's remains shrouded in shadow.

The sharp edge of the cleaver sliced cleanly through the rope and succeeded in freeing Alex's wrists. Leigh whipped her head around and grabbed a dirty old wool blanket.

"Here," Leigh said, throwing the blanket over Alex's shoulders. "Now hold my hand and be as quiet as you can, okay? We're not going to run. If we run they'll hear us."

Alex nodded. Leigh cradled her close to her chest, guarding her face from the gruesome remains of Marshall as they passed. Alex trembled in her arms, dangerously close to collapsing to the floor, but somehow managed to maintain her footing as they shuffled towards the exit. After a few shaky steps, Marshall was behind them and the hard part was over. All they had to do now was get up the stairs and into the night.

Something upstairs hit the floor with a loud *clang*, shaking the ceiling above them.

"Hold on," Leigh whispered, stopping her friend from going any further.

"Damnit, Grizzly!" the man shouted. "Look at the mess you've made now!"

There was an indecipherable groaning noise in reply, but what the man said next froze the blood in Leigh's veins.

"I don't care. Just clean it up. I'm going to go downstairs to visit my special friend."

Leigh grabbed Alex's shoulders and made her friend look her directly in the eyes.

"Alex, listen to me. I want you to go up those stairs and stay as low as you can. You got me? Stay really, really low."

Alex was shaking so badly now she was almost convulsing. "Leigh," she mumbled hysterically. "I can't."

"Yes you *can*!" Leigh shook her hard. "It's just a few steps. And once you hit the trees, you start running. Run and don't stop. Understand? Do not stop running. I'll be right behind you."

Alex inhaled to mutter another protest, but Leigh was already pushing her towards the door.

"Go!" Leigh whispered, grabbing the bottom of her own shirt and pulling it over her head; the next moment Leigh saw her friend already climbing the storm door steps.

Above her, the door leading from the kitchen to the basement steps swung open.

"That better be all fixed up by the time I get back up here!"

The final scolding bought Leigh just enough time to snap off her bra and throw both it and her shirt underneath the butcher's table. The bundle of clothes had landed in a puddle of congealing blood, but Leigh didn't think about that as she grabbed the burlap sack that had covered Alex's face.

The steps leading down from upstairs creaked under the man's weight as he began his descent.

Pulling the sack over her own head, Leigh tried her best to conceal any strands of her dark hair that risked sticking out the bottom. Just as the sack came over her eyes, she spotted a pair of dirty work boots touch down on the final steps of the staircase.

Her sight completely obscured, Leigh shot her hands upward and, on tiptoes, felt for the hook.

It wasn't there.

Please God. PLEASE…

Something hard and cold grazed her fingertips. She'd found it. Leigh immediately sprang up and gripped the thick hook with both hands, suspending herself above the ground. Just as her feet had left the floor, she heard:

"There she is."

There was no way to know if the dim light of the single lantern would reveal the fact that the man's captive was no longer bound by the wrists. Leigh's heart slammed against the inside of her chest, pounding harder than it'd ever had before., She was surprised she hadn't gone into cardiac arrest.

Youth, however, was on her side, and she was going to use all her strength to kick the man square in the balls once he came close enough. But there was no way this ruse was going to work for long. Even if Leigh had succeeded in hiding all of her dark hair, her breasts were noticeably smaller than Alex's. And considering she'd found Alex nearly naked, Leigh had the sickening suspicion that this man was very familiar with Alex's body.

"Did you miss me?" the man asked as he crept closer. Leigh fought to control her breathing under the mask to feign unconsciousness.

The man was mere inches away now, but still not close enough for Leigh to land a solid blow. And even with Marshall's slaughtered corpse rotting just a few feet away, she could smell his stench.

The rubber soles of his work boots made an abrupt scuff on the basement's dirt floor. Through the sack, Leigh could feel the man staring at her, stopped in his tracks by his own puzzlement.

"Huh," he mumbled, and Leigh knew exactly what he was examining. Her lesser bust had given her away just as she had predicted, which meant it was time for her foot to meet the family jewels.

Leigh bit her lip.

Wake up time, you fuck.

"I think we gotta feed you some more, girl!"

Leigh remained motionless.

"I mean, don't get me wrong. I like my bitches skinny, but you're starting to thin out in the one place where I like a woman to have some weight."

If his hand hadn't found her breast so quickly, Leigh would've flinched at the man's touch. Before she knew it, the man was kneading her right breast, flicking her stiff nipple between his fingers.

"Ooh, look at you. You like that, don't you?"

Leigh squeezed her eyes shut and tried to block out the violation. She clenched the hook above her and tried to focus on the fact that her guise was working. As long as he didn't remove the burlap sack…

A disgusted groan uncontrollably escaped her mouth when the man's tongue traced a circle around her areola.

Oh shit…

"I *knew* you were awake," the man said, before returning his mouth to her nipple. Even though he sucked painfully hard, sometimes grinding her nipple with his teeth, Leigh knew she could take it if she just concentrated on something else.

Think about something else.

BE somewhere else.

It was easier thought than done. Leigh attempted to focus on keeping her grip on the hook above her, directing all her attention to the cold metal in her tight grasp. She concentrated on the grooves of the scratches in its surface, the flaky rust between her fingers, her own sweat …

But she couldn't escape hard, agonizing reality when the man's hand began to slide from her breast to the center of her stomach, and didn't stop there. His hand continued downward, sliding across her perspiration, its fingertips reaching the button of her pants.

No.

This she could not take.

This rapist's crotch was about to be hit by the force of a rocket launch.

Another loud crash rattled the ceiling above them.

"What the fuck?" the man shouted, removing both his hands and his mouth from Leigh's body. "What'd you do now?"

The man put his face right up next to the sack.

"I'll be back soon."

He quickly turned and marched away, footsteps shaking the stairs as he returned to the kitchen. The moment Leigh heard the door slam shut, she released her cramped fingers from the hook and fell to the basement floor. She yanked the bag from her head just in time to avoid vomiting inside of it. She puked as quietly as she could through the violent heaving racking her body,

When her gagging had finally subsided, Leigh retrieved her shirt from underneath the butcher's table. It was damp with blood, but it offered welcome concealment.

Navigating the cellar was far easier now than it had been when she first entered. Upon passing Marshall's body for the last time, Leigh snatched the shark tooth of his shell necklace and pulled, snapping it from the bloody stump where his neck had been. Alex might be thankful to have this one day. Necklace in hand, Leigh went up the storm door stairs, making sure to stay low.

She remained low, just below the line of the cabin's windows, as she snuck her way towards the corner of the structure. There was nothing more she wanted in the world than to run away as fast as her legs would allow, but she had to check for Sam and Rob one last time. If her stomach-turning experience in the cellar had been good for anything, it at least meant that her friends still hadn't been discovered. It was looking as though the two guys had gotten away on their own, maybe planning to double back and retrieve Leigh from her hiding spot.

Leigh knew she'd have to hustle if she ever wanted to catch up with Alex. She'd told her to run at full speed, but in this darkness and in these thick woods, Leigh knew her pace wouldn't be too difficult to catch. Once Leigh reached the corner of the cabin that both Sam and Rob had disappeared behind, she'd see if they were there.

It may have been a solid plan, but it fell apart the moment she turned the corner.

With his back to her, Sam was squatted over something on the ground. Overjoyed to finally have found find him, Leigh rushed forward.

When Leigh's saw what he was crouched over, her hand shot to her mouth again, her teeth raking the soft flesh of her knuckles.

Dead eyes stared at her from behind Sam's leg.

Eyes that belonged to Alex.

"Sam?" Leigh whispered.

Sam turned at the sound of Leigh's voice. A large, ragged wound bled from the top of Alex's skull, her blonde hair sticking together in clumps from where the blood ran down across her face. Even more frightening than the sight of her bludgeoned, murdered friend, was the club-like branch in Sam's grasp, its jagged tip dripping with fresh blood.

Sam stood up. "Leigh!"

"Oh god," Leigh moaned, her eyes refusing to look away from the bloody club.

Sam opened his mouth to say more but Leigh didn't wait for the words. She pivoted on the ball of her right foot to turn and run into the forest, but was at once blocked by someone's broad chest. A chest clad in a denim vest covered in punk band patches.

Rob caught her by the biceps of her arms, steadying her so that she didn't fall over. The bow and quiver taken from their cabin still hung from his shoulder.

"Are you okay?" he asked, staring her in the eyes.

Leigh concentrated only on his eyes in order to catch her breath. "Rob," she gasped, "you were right. Sam's with them. He killed Alex."

From behind her, Leigh heard Sam say, "I found her like this!" She turned to see Sam take a step towards them, which provoked Rob to grab the tranquilizer gun from Leigh's back pocket.

"Stop," Rob said, pointing the barrel of the gun at Sam's face.

Leigh took a step behind Rob so that he blocked the path between her and Sam. Speaking directly into Rob's ear she said, "Don't listen to him. The other two are inside. It had to be Sam. Look, he's holding the weapon he killed her with." Leigh pointed at the bulky branch in Sam's hand. Sam looked at the club incredulously, as if he hadn't even been aware he was holding it until now.

"No!" Sam said, dropping the stick. "No, wait a second." Sam took another step forward.

The dart hit him in the neck, directly below the lobe of his left ear. Sam stumbled backwards, crying out in pain.

Leigh grabbed Rob's shoulder, furiously shaking him. "Jesus Christ, Rob! They'll hear him!" But the tranquilizer already began to take effect, quieting Sam's screams to a gentle moan. As Leigh watched him slowly stagger and lose his orientation, something else suddenly caught her eye.

Now that Sam had fallen to the ground, Leigh could for

once see the entirety of Alex's corpse. Embedded in the thigh of her right leg was an arrow with red feather fletching.

As Leigh turned to face Rob, she shivered knowing what she was about to see.

The arrows sticking out of Rob's quiver shared the same fletching.

"Rob?"

He smiled. "Goodnight, Leigh."

Leigh only caught a quick glimpse of the butt of the tranquilizer gun as Rob slammed it into the bridge of her nose.

And then all was black.

CHAPTER
TWENTY

The knots restraining Jake's wrists would not be undone by mere twisting and wriggling, that was for sure. On several occasions, Phil had shared stories of his younger days in the Navy, expanding his horizons as he traveled around the world. One of several skills he'd picked up during his time on military vessels was the practiced art of knot tying. And while Jake didn't know the name of the particular style that bound his hands, he assumed it must be the first choice of kidnappers everywhere. The tightness pinching his skin proved that Phil's talent with a rope hadn't faded with age.

"Damn, Phil," Jake said, smirking at the man who sat across from him. "You've still got it. I can't move an inch."

Phil smiled as if greeting his grandkids. "Tying knots is like riding a bike. Once you learn how, you never forget."

Jake jerked his arms upward with all his strength. And though the wooden chair lifted from the floor and returned with a loud *thump*, his hands remained frozen behind him. "Yup," he said, shrugging his shoulders. "I'd have to be Houdini to get out of this. I bet the Navy misses you. And I bet they wondered why you chose to live and work hundreds of miles from a single drop of sea water."

Phil's rifle rested on his crossed legs. He removed his hat and hung it from the gun's barrel's like a multi-functional coat hook. "You're probably right about that. But what can I say? I had my fill of the ocean. I figured I'd see what mysteries the land had to offer."

Jake locked eyes with his captor. "You ever consider becoming an astronaut? There's a lot of fucking mystery in space, Phil."

If Phil's smile had been made of wood, it would've thudded when it fell to the floor.

"Speaking of mystery, you want fill me in now why I'm tied to this chair?"

The old man's nostrils whistled as he inhaled a deep breath in effort to control his emotions. With absolutely no way to defend himself, Jake had decided the time for calm, placating banter was over. Either Phil was going to shoot him or not, and all Jake could do was wait and see which he chose. In the meantime, he could at least try to get some much desired answers.

Phil ran a hand down to his injured ankle, rubbing the cast as if he could actually feel the massage through the plaster. "I can't wait to get this damn thing off," he whispered. The sentence seemed more addressed to himself than to Jake. "It really makes me feel my age. God, I've been in this town for so long."

He looked at Jake. "I grew up in Embry. You knew that right?"

Phil didn't wait for Jake's answer.

"Yeah, I'm sure I must have told you before. Well, consider this a little refresher."

He cleared his throat.

"I spent the first eighteen years of life here, and the only time I left was when I graduated high school and joined the Navy. Back in those days, the saw mill was our town's number one source of income. And though you wouldn't believe it now, that sucker had the highest productivity in the entire Northeast."

Jake squirmed, unsurprisingly to no avail. "Yes, I know all this, Phil."

The elder ranger shook his head. "Impatient—just like when we go fishing. You should work on that while you're still young. It only gets harder to change as you get older.

"But where was I? Oh right, I went and joined the Navy, leaving my home a thriving lumber town. I didn't have the foggiest idea where my future Naval adventures would lead me, but somewhere in the back of my head I knew that I'd probably end up doing my part at the mill in one capacity or another. Imagine my surprise when I returned home to find that everything had changed."

When Phil inhaled to take another breath, Jake took his chance to interrupt.

"The forest had all become diseased and the mill was forced to close. And by the time the woods became safe again, the mill had already reopened in Scoutsville. So instead of working at the mill, I became a forest ranger and worked alongside a handsome youngster named Jacob Spire who I would eventually take at gunpoint, tie to a chair, and torture with pointless, redundant stories. There, we've caught up to the present."

Phil's face remained emotionless, frozen in a stoic, neutral expression. His fingers drummed on the stock of the rifle, the noise resembling melodic rainfall on a shingled roof.

And this is when he blows my brains out.

But instead, Phil ceased his tapping and turned his chin to the left, loudly cracking the stiff bones of his aging neck. A faint smile of relief appeared on Phil's face and Jake knew the time hadn't come just yet. Phil rolled his neck the other direction, resulting in more snaps and pops, and then returned his eyes to his captive.

"Do you know the motto of the United States Navy?"

The question caught Jake completely off guard. "Um," he said, suddenly feeling as if he were on a twisted version of Jeopardy. "I know Semper Fi is the Marines. And then there's 'Be All You Can Be'…but that's the Army, right?"

Mercifully, Phil cut off his nervous rant. "It's 'Non sibi sed patriae.' Do you know what that means?"

Jake just shook his head.

"'Not for self, but country.'"

"Oh...kay."

Phil released a condescending chuckle, an expression usually reserved for those speaking to a child. "They may just be mere words to someone like you," Phil said while raising his chin with pride. "But to those like myself, it's a code one follows throughout their entire life, even after their days of military service have come to an end. Maybe we can't always protect our *entire* nation, but a man can certainly do all he can for his home. And that, sir, is exactly what I did."

When Jake's vision began to become blurry through a film of tears, he realized he hadn't blinked once in the last minute or so. Jake averted his eyes so Phil wouldn't mistake his tears for those of fear. He pretended to be staring out the four-paned window directly behind his captor, though the glass revealed nothing but darkness outside. Not that there would be anything to see in the daylight.

What about Doug?

Doug was probably starting to wonder what was taking Jake so long, and could quite possibly turn around and return at any moment. But while Jake could certainly use the assistance right about now, he hoped Doug would stay wherever he was. Phil would undoubtedly hear the engine of the approaching ATV and spot the vehicle's headlight long before Doug stuck his head through the front door. The younger ranger wouldn't stand a chance.

Phil, who had noticed Jake's diligent vigil he was keeping on the window, turned to see if anything of interest was occurring outside their shelter. With nothing outside but the silhouettes of tree branches against the night sky, he one again regarded Jake with a confident smile on his face.

"Doug won't be coming back," he said, apparently possessing the ability to read Jake's mind. "I'm sure he's far too preoccupied right now. But what was I saying?"

Jake looked the man right in the eyes. "Some shit about Uncle Sam, I think."

"Ah, yes. When I returned home, Embry was not as I left it. The lumber industry was completely extinct. Now, the town's economic survival was entirely in the hands of outsiders. Tourists. Summer vacationers, hikers, and day trippers. But who in their right mind would risk exposing themselves to a fungus that could eat a person's entire body? It seemed Embry was a lost cause, destined to the same fate as so many ghost towns of the Old West. But then I met Seymour Cedar."

For the first time since Phil began his autobiographical rant, Jake's head shot up in interest. "Seymour Cedar? The guy we found axed to death on my first day out?"

"That would be the one." Phil uncrossed his legs and removed the rifle from his lap. With a cracking in his arthritic knees, Phil sat up from his seat and slowly paced to the window. Staring out through the glass, he continued his story.

"I was about your age the day I met him. I'd just gotten a job with the Forest Service, solely because I just didn't know what else to do. Reports of the fungal disease had greatly dwindled, and the chamber of commerce was beginning to discuss how to raise Embry's appeal to become the outdoor vacation destination it'd once been. With the risk of infection so much lower, I figured the best way to help was to get right at the source of the problem: the forest. But the only thing I could think to do was to start exploring the woods and just hope I stumbled upon a solution. Turns out, that's precisely what I did."

Slight prickles of numbness tingled Jake's left buttock, causing him to shift his weight. The ropes allowed just enough movement to relieve the pressure from his tailbone, but the discomfort remained. Annoyed as much as he was confused, Jake breathed deeply through his nose in order to control his frustration.

"How's that?"

Phil rubbed his eyes. "I stepped on a yellow jacket nest. God damn things swarmed me instantly so I took off running.

I had no idea what direction I was heading in, but all I cared about was getting away from those stingers. Hard to say how long I ran but by the time I was sure I'd lost the last wasp, I was staring at a cabin I'd never seen before in my life. There was smoke coming from the chimney so I knew someone was in there. I don't know if was just sheer curiosity or the thought of putting some cold water on my stings, but I didn't think twice about knocking on the door.

"Unfortunately, no one answered so I moseyed around the back and found one of those old fashioned water pumps. My wrist was beginning to swell so I started pumping away and dunked my wrist under. The cold water had just about numbed the sting when I heard, 'Hey! What you doing here?' And there was Seymour, aiming a shotgun right at my chest. I, of course, threw up my hands and said 'Don't shoot! Don't shoot!' And that's when I saw this fuzzy green bracelet wrapped around my wrist."

Jake glanced up from the floor, an astounding expression claiming his eyes and mouth. "You caught it?"

"Yep," Phil said as matter-of-factly as humanly possible. "And though I wouldn't admit this to just anyone, I panicked as if I'd just gotten bit in the face by a rattler. Totally forgot about the double barrels aimed at my midriff. Just standing there, grasping my arm at the elbow and blabbering, 'Oh shit oh shit oh shit!' or some nonsense. Didn't see or even hear Seymour walk up to my side, but somehow he got close enough to grab my wrist and say, 'Look what you've done here. Don't you know that pump pulls water right from Emerald Lake? Well c'mon, ya dumbshit. Let's go.'

"Next thing I know he's leading me inside, sitting me down at his kitchen table, and handing me a tin cup filled with something dark. Looked like black coffee. 'You better drink this,' he said, 'And I'll cook you up some meat. Better make myself some too, just in case.'

"I looked at the cup and saw that it wasn't coffee. When I asked him what it was he grabbed the shotgun again and shouted, 'Drink!' So that's what I did. Though it tasted like old rain water as thick as maple syrup, I downed the whole thing."

"What was it?"

"I'm getting to that," Phil said, putting up a hand. "I didn't know what it was at the time either, but I did know my heart rate was starting to slow, my breath coming a little bit easier now. It'd literally only been about thirty seconds since I finished the mystery drink but I just felt...*better*. It's hard to put into words, but it didn't even occur to me to so much as glance at my infected wrist that had just been burning like it was on fire. Instead I just closed my eyes and enjoyed the high I was getting off Seymour's homemade concoction. Hell, the stuff was better than moonshine. I just savored the air flowing into my lungs. The peaceful sound of the breeze blowing the branches outside. And the smell—the most delicious, most downright heavenly scent I'd ever breathed in, coming from Seymour's stove. I had to know the source of this amazing aroma so I opened my eyes….and saw my wrist. My perfectly healthy, normal-looking wrist."

Phil paused to let this information hit Jake with full force. Jake simply stared back at Phil, waiting for the rest of the sentence. When it didn't come, Jake cleared his throat and said, "Hold on, Phil, back up a second. Either I must not have understood you, or you must not be remembering right, because what you just said is impossible. You're saying you were cured of the fungus?"

Phil winked.

"Jesus, man, are you already getting Alzheimer's? There is no cure for the fungus. We've both read the newspapers. We've both seen the pictures of the loggers with stumps for hands because they had no choice but to amputate. So think harder and try again."

The old man smiled and shook his head like a school teacher facing a student who thinks he knows better. "Yes, Jake, we've both read the articles. And seen the pictures. But you never had the pleasure of eating dinner with Seymour Cedar. And he didn't share with you his discovery, his secret to continued survival in Embry, Vermont. Only he knew of the remedy. And now I did too."

Jake swallowed hard, a bowling ball-sized lump traveling down his throat. "The remedy?"

Phil leaned forward, staring Jake right in the eyes. "Flesh and blood. Human flesh and blood."

There was a beat of silence.

And then Jake erupted in laughter.

"You, sir, are a crazy son of a bitch, you know that?" He let loose a few more hoots. "Soylent Green is people, right? It's people! Fuck me, we're supposed to be friends. The least you could've done is shot me in the head and spared me the longest joke in recorded history."

Phil's face remained stoic.

"I suppose that's how I would've reacted, too, had a glass of blood not instantly cured my life-threatening disease. So I don't take offense to your disbelief."

"Hey, I'm sorry, man. I shouldn't have laughed. And I appreciate the efforts you've gone through to convince me. The tying me up, the gun in my face. It was just because you just wanted me to listen. I get it. But you obviously need some help, Phil. I didn't go to an Ivy League school, but I'm smart enough to realize when a troubled friend is reaching out for help."

The captor cocked his head at the captive. It was impossible to tell what was going through the busted gears of Phil's broken mind, but Jake remained confident that he'd reached him. However, that confidence shattered when Phil finally spoke and said, "You really are a good man, Jake. A good friend, too. That's why I'm telling you this. A lesser man would've already been taken care of by now, but you deserve to know the truth. You deserve a chance."

A sudden thump against the window caused both men to flinch in their chairs. Jake just caught a glimpse of the fluttering wings of a bat before it continued on with its hunt of insects.

ASHER ELLIS

Jake turned his head back from the window. "What do you mean 'a chance?'"

"A chance to join our cause, Jake. I know you care about this town as much as I do. I know you would've done the exact same thing if Seymour had shown you the bodies in his basement. If he'd explained to you how he and his family nabbed a drifter now and then and stored them in their cellar to be consumed later. Wouldn't you have listened if he had proposed that as long as you let them capture a hiker or camper now and then, they'd never let an infected person escape the woods? What loyal Embry native would say no to that? Seymour and his clan were the sole reason the reports of fungal infection had dropped to zero. As long as they were allowed to hunt, tourists would believe the disease had gone completely extinct. So after talking over the best steak I've ever tasted, Seymour and I came to an agreement. He and his family would do their part, and I would do mine."

"Yours?" Jake still didn't believe the old man, but he couldn't help but take the bait.

"As I'm sure you can imagine, I couldn't have every hiker and camper disappearing or it would bring far too much negative attention to our town. And what would that solve? So I started handing out my provisions at the ranger station where every visitor must check in. As you've seen with your own eyes, people will accept anything if it's free. So as long as they took a complimentary stick of jerky or one of our other meat products, I knew they'd be safe for the duration of their visit. And if a vegetarian should come our way, all it took was, 'Oh please, try our jerky substitute.' Turns out soy strips soaked overnight in blood works just as well. But every once in awhile, we get a stubborn son of a bitch, or a poacher or trespasser who doesn't check in, and that's when the Cedars take over. Or I suppose I should say, an unfortunate bear attack."

Phil winked again but Jake ignored it.

"Listen man, I won't pretend to know what's going on

inside your head, but I'm sure you still got enough of your wits left to realize the holes in your story. So let's take a minute and think about it: if human blood or flesh was the only sure way to avoid catching that damn fungus, we would've had to ingest some every work day before heading out into the woods. I mean, come on, we're out there just about every single day. And I don't know about you, but I know my breakfast has been eggs and toast ever since I started working for the forestry department. Not a finger or an eyeball anywhere on my plate. So how do you explain that?"

"Well," Phil said, uncrossing and switching his legs so his left was now under his right, "allow me to answer that question by asking you another: besides a hearty breakfast, what else do you consume to start each day?"

The answer Phil was fishing for was obvious enough. "You're talking about coffee."

Phil nodded. "Exactly. I've been brewing up a fresh pot every morning and offering you a cup since your first day. I doubt you've ever thought twice about that cup I put in your hand, but for as often as we're in the woods, constant inoculations are necessary so the immunity effects don't wear off. Lucky for both of us, I've never seen you turn down my special roast."

Before Jake could offer anything in reply, Phil was unbuttoning the cuffs of both his uniform sleeves and rolling them up past his elbows. Jake was completely unaware that his jaw was hanging open as he stared at Phil's forearms in total disbelief. The aged flesh of his underarms were completely covered in old scars, countless nicks where a straight razor had drawn blood from the tender skin. It was if someone had tried to trace senseless constellations between his freckles and liver spots, leaving his arms looking like a game of tic-tac-toe where both players had been X.

"Holy fuck. Phil…" Jake's statement came out as a whisper.

Phil rolled down his sleeves. "It's not as bad as it looks. It doesn't hurt either, but it does leave me looking like a piece of sharpening leather. But nothing comes without sacrifice. These scars mark my commitment and devotion to my home. I've worn them with pride."

Jake fought back the urge to gag, an unexpected sour taste overtaking his tongue. Phil's self-inflicted mutilation had catapulted this situation into a realm where Jake was an absolute foreigner, utterly unprepared at how to handle the world around him. He was becoming aware that the room was spinning and picking up speed.

I've been drinking his blood. All these years, I've been drinking his blood.

"So now here we are." Phil stood up from his chair, bending his neck to each side with a pair of loud cracks. "And now you know the truth. So what next? That's the question, isn't it?"

He looked down at Jake as if he actually expected an answer.

"Well, Phil, if I didn't know you any better, I'd say you were going to kill me now to keep your secret safe."

The old man smirked, but it was a tired expression, as if pulling his lips up a half an inch left him utterly exhausted. "But you do know me better, Jake. I would never harm you. You're the closest friend I have left in the world."

Despite everything that was happening and everything he'd just learned, Jake found himself touched by the sincerity of his words.

Phil continued. "And that's exactly why I've got you tied up like Houdini. Because I don't want you running off and getting yourself killed. You were dangerously close, too. If I hadn't caught up to you, the Cedars would've punched your ticket for sure. You'll be safe here until morning. Whoever's working the early shift will get here and cut you loose, and then you can call in the cavalry."

Jake blinked once. Twice. Three times. A part of him was still waiting for Phil to burst out laughing and reveal this was all an elaborate prank. But the practical side of Jake's mind, the larger part that dictated the majority of his actions, knew this wasn't going to happen.

"What about you, Phil?"

Phil shrugged. "What can I say, old friend? I'm tired. I'm just so god damned tired. And I guess there comes a time in any man's life when he just has to face the music. I just can't do this anymore. And I've been feeling that way for a long time. I think I was just waiting for the straw to break the camel's back."

He turned before Jake could reply, taking three long strides towards the window.

"I'm leaving the next move up to you," Phil said, facing the glass. "It's about time someone did the right thing, if such a thing even exists."

The unmistakable click of a cocked firearm instantly widened Jake's eyes. From behind Phil's back, he could see the man holding the barrel of the rifle directly under his chin.

"Phil!"

Jake lurched forward, momentarily forgetting his tightly bound state. The chair wobbled, teetering to Jake's right, giving him just enough time to take a single breath before crashing to the floor.

His head connected with solid wood, sending a painful jolt through his skull. Though his vision blurred with dizziness, he could still see Phil slowly turning at the sound of the chair's fall.

He caught Jake's frightened glance, and returned his gaze to the window.

"Remember good ol' Murray Dobson?"

Jake didn't register that what Phil had said was a question until he added, "The man you shot?"

"Of course I do, Phil. He was going to kill you."

Phil's grip on the rifle's stock tightened. "I was going to kill him. He was fighting for his life and would've gotten away if not for you. But you saved me."

"Phil…"

Jake caught Phil's glare in the reflection of the window, his eyes drowning in a sea of sadness and regret.

"Biggest mistake of your life, Jake."

Phil pulled his shoulders up, his stature becoming one of honor and pride. The stance of a soldier. The stance of a patriot.

"Non sibi sed patriae."

Jake's ears rang from the deafening boom of the gun as he watched it all play out in slow motion. The rifle clattered to the floor along with Phil's limp, practically headless body. Once the body and weapon finished their descent, Jake was left alone in utter silence, minus the ringing swan song of his dying ear cells.

No chirping of nocturnal insects.

No thumping of bat wings on windows.

No breeze whistling through the trees.

His world had become one of only sight and no sound. And all he could see was the river of blood flowing from the hole in Phil's head.

The pool that crept steadily towards Jake's face.

CHAPTER
TWENTY-ONE

The world did not return to Leigh in a slow, gentle manner, like waking from an afternoon nap with the warmth of the sun greeting her eyes. Reality did not knock on the door of her consciousness, nor even turn its handle. Instead, it kicked the door open, charging across the threshold of her awareness like Nazi storm troopers raiding a safe house. And it all came from one glass of water, thrown directly in her face. "Gah!" she shrieked, completely oblivious to the nonsensical sound she projected into the room around her. For a moment, all she could process was the ice cold water drenching her skin and stinging the wound on her right temple. But after a few seconds of disorientation, the details of her condition and surroundings began to take form.

She was inside an old fashioned log cabin, dimly lit by hanging lanterns. She couldn't move, thanks to the ropes that bound her to her chair. And an-all-too familiar face smiled down at her, a face that belonged to the body grasping the now empty glass of water.

"Rob?"

On the good days, he'd barely been her friend. Now, standing there with a condescending smile on his face, Leigh didn't know what to call him now. Or even what he'd been all along.

"Sorry about that," he said, retrieving a bandana from his back pocket and using it to dab her damp forehead. "But it's going to be sun-up soon and I couldn't let you sleep all night."

Leigh wrenched her face away from Rob's touch. "What's going on? What the hell are you doing?"

Rob shrugged. "Only what I have to."

Someone weakly moaned right behind Leigh's head. Though the ropes wouldn't let her twist completely around to see her fellow captive waking from his slumber, Leigh could identify the other prisoner from his groan alone. Sam was tied to another chair, his back against hers.

"I'm sorry things turned out for you this way," Rob said, leaning casually against a weathered kitchen table. "I've always liked you, Leigh." He then quietly chortled to himself and shook his head. "You probably never knew that."

Though her awareness was continuing to increase with every passing second, Leigh's confusion had not dwindled at all. In fact, it only grew larger the longer Rob spoke.

"I don't understand."

"Yeah, I know," Rob said. "You never had a clue because I gave you shit every chance I could. But you must believe me, it was all because I didn't want you to go on this trip. I thought if I treated you badly enough, you know, acted like a total asshole, you'd pass and I'd only have to deal with your dumbass friends."

Leigh couldn't tell whether the tears beginning to leak from the corners of her eyes were conjured from fear or anger. Probably both.

"Rob," she said, her voice coming out a mere whisper. "Why are you doing this?"

Rob grabbed the edges of the kitchen table and hoisted himself up. He swayed his dangling feet back and forth like a little kid waiting for a puppet show to start.

"Well, you see, Leigh, this land has a rather colorful history that dates back many years. It all started..." Rob cocked his head to the left, the corner of his mouth following suit. "Wait.

You know what? I think my Aunt Clementine could explain this better than me." He turned to the right. "Bugger?"

Leigh craned her neck to see a strange man in dirty overalls leaning against the wall. The brim of a brown baseball cap concealed his eyes as he looked down at the knife he was using to pick out grime from under his fingernails. Leigh couldn't believe he'd been standing there the entire time.

Rob hopped off the table. "Bugger!"

The man with the knife whipped his head up. "What?" he snapped back through yellow teeth.

"Would you please go get my auntie?"

"Fuck you." The man scowled and returned to the maintenance of his fingernails.

Rob sighed, obviously making a point to release the sound with as much melodrama as possible. He looked at Leigh. "My cousin's a little upset because I had to kill his girlfriend." The word *girlfriend* was accompanied by a quotation gesture.

Leigh flinched as Rob's cousin slammed the knife into the wooden wall of the cabin, the impact causing the glass frame of a hanging black-and-white photograph to fall to the floor and shatter.

"She was supposed to be all mine," he shouted. "All mine!"

Rob rolled his eyes at the other man. "Oh get real, Bugger. Like a woman that fine would ever look twice at a cretin like you. But me, on the other hand…" He turned to Leigh. "Did you know Alex used me to cheat on Marshall? Sure, it was only one time, but she didn't even make me put on a rubber. Shit, I'm surprised I didn't knock that bitch up." Rob shook his head. "That girl had no character. Not like you."

Leigh looked away, her jaw trembling uncontrollably.

Bugger took a step forward. "Stop talking about her!"

"Or what?" Rob looked at his cousin, boredom and disinterest painted across his face.

Bugger snatched the handle of the knife, tearing it from the wooden wall. "Or I'll kill you!"

He didn't wait for Rob to make another snide remark, already charging with the knife raised to his head. With more agility than he'd ever demonstrated before, Rob gracefully leaped over the kitchen table, putting the piece of furniture between himself and his relative. Whichever direction Bugger would dart, Rob would sidestep the other direction.

"Come here, you little fucker!" Bugger screamed in frustration.

Rob laughed like an older brother tormenting his younger sibling. "Gonna have to catch me first. Come on, I thought you were hunter."

Bugger let loose an animalistic howl and shoved the table forward. Its edge jammed into Rob's stomach, pinning him against the wall. With the practiced skill of a veteran circus performer, Bugger flipped his knife into the air, caught the blade between his thumb and forefinger, and reared back to throw it directly at Rob's head.

"Wait!" Rob yelled, but the knife was already on its way. Leigh pinched her eyes shut, knowing that closed eyes would do nothing to shield her from the splash of blood coming her way.

She heard the knife make contact with a heavy *thud*.

But felt nothing. She opened her eyes.

Rob panted like a St. Bernard, his eyes as wide as the full moon. A mere centimeter from his left ear, driven into the wooden wall, the knife protruded, its blade embedded almost all the way to the hilt.

Bugger pointed a dirty fingernail at Rob's face. "I've always been more of trapper than a hunter. Best you not forget that."

The trance of utter fear that froze Rob's features suddenly broke. "You crazy fuck!" The muscles in Rob's biceps flexed as he shoved the table forward, but Bugger easily dodged it with a casual sidestep. "I'm going to beat the shit out of you."

Bugger opened his mouth to retort, but a louder voice boomed over both of them.

"*Robbie!*"

Both Leigh and her two captors whipped their heads in the direction of the voice. In the doorway leading to one of the cabin's bedrooms, the oldest looking woman Leigh had ever seen sat in a wheelchair just as ancient. The giant man in the bear mask stood behind her.

With gray, glossy eyes behind old-fashioned circular spectacles, she stared at Rob. "You watch that mouth of yours when you're in my home. You hear me?"

As if he were a ten-year-old school boy being reprimanded by the headmaster, Rob feebly answered, "Yes ma'am."

The old woman nodded approvingly and turned her attention to Bugger. "And that goes for you, too. Now both of you stop this horseplay."

Bugger raised his hands like a whining child. "But Cousin Robbie killed my girl!"

With a shocking amount of strength, the woman slammed her fist down on the handle of the wheelchair, her huge, arthritic knuckles cracking like firecrackers. "Don't you talk back to me!"

Just like Rob, Bugger also lowered his eyes like a humiliated dog. "Sorry, Ma."

A wave of her hand gestured for the behemoth in the bear mask to push her chair forward into the room. The giant wheeled her past the two squabbling men, right in front of Leigh. They now looked at each other eye-to-eye.

"Now, what do we have here?"

Leigh could only stare into her glaucoma-ridden eyes for so long before having to turn away. Her eyes trailed down to her faded, dusty house dress, a purple garment covered in flowers that actually may have been pretty at one time. Her gaze continued down to her legs, wrapped in stockings with more holes than Swiss cheese, before landing on her heavy, jet black shoes.

Rob hesitantly stepped forward. "Sorry, Aunt Clemmy. These two were a little more trouble than the others."

The old woman gripped the rusty wheels of her chair and pushed herself over to Sam, who was just now coming to. In her peripheral vision, Leigh could see Rob's aunt reach out towards Sam's face. The back of Sam's head hit hers as the woman yanked his chin upward.

"I thought you said you bringing me four. Who's this?"

Sam swallowed hard, awakening to join the nightmarish party.

"What's going on?" he groggily asked no one in particular.

Rob walked over behind his aunt. "He was hitchhiking. I figured you'd guys wouldn't mind one more, with winter coming and all. Maybe you could pickle this one, or make some more jerky."

Sam's hair brushed the back of Leigh's neck as he looked around the room. "Who the fuck are you people?"

A quick shriek shot from Leigh's mouth with the loud slap that cracked behind her ears. It took her a moment to realize the sound had been the woman smacking the side of Sam's head.

"I don't like that language in my home, you understand?"

She didn't wait for Sam to respond.

"But I'll still answer your question, seein' as it's the polite thing to do. We're the Cedar family. My name is Clementine, and these are my children, Bugger and Grizzly. And it seems you've already met my nephew, Robbie."

Although Rob had already referred to Bugger as his cousin and the old witch in the wheelchair as his aunt, Leigh had been too distracted to fully consider the implications of those words. But now hearing him be formally introduced, the ultimate horror of her reality hit her with unmerciful force.

She looked at Rob and could only mutter, "No."

Rob only shrugged in return, the same gesture he might've used if he'd stolen the front seat of a car after someone had already declared shotgun. "I'm afraid it's true, Leigh. This here's my fam. And where I come from, family comes first."

Clementine slowly nodded in agreement. "That's right, Robbie. We've always put our family first, for as long as we've lived in these woods. Even the fuzz of the forest couldn't break what we have. Right after the outbreak, every other single person living in this whole damn forest moved away. But not this family. This family sticks together. This is where we belong."

"But we've seen this fungus," Sam said. "It kills. Quickly. Why the fuck aren't you all dead?"

A second slap met Sam's mouth, but this time Leigh didn't gasp. She was too heavily focused on Rob—the betrayer.

Clementine brought her hand back into her lap and sighed. "You don't listen very good, do ya boy?"

When Sam didn't respond, she continued.

"Now, like I was about to say until you interrupted me with that dirty mouth of yours, like any family, we've got secrets. Not from each other, mind you, but things only this family knows. And one of those things just happens to be the remedy for this Hell-spawned disease."

She then pulled back on her wheels, reversing from the two prisoners. Pulling one wheel so she pivoted to face her family, she asked, "How's it go, boys?"

Bugger cleared his throat. "Rabbit's a good meal…"

"…Squirrel's a good snack," Rob said, taking the second line before handing it back to Bugger.

"But a belly full of man…"

Clementine turned back around to face Leigh, an awful grin splitting her chapped lips. "…And the fuzz don't grow back." Her smiled dropped in the instant after saying the last word. "Well, at least for awhile it don't. You see, unfortunately the remedy ain't permanent. So we try to always stock up the best we can so we can nip it in the bud whenever our skin starts to turn green. That's where my dear nephew comes in."

Rob immediately straightened up, a look of pride washing over his face as he crossed his arms on his chest like a superhero posing for a movie poster. "Happy to do it, Auntie."

Clementine reached a hand out for her nephew which Rob tenderly accepted in his own. She stared at him as she addressed

Leigh. "Isn't he a sweetie? I don't know what we'd do without him. We used to keep a fresh stock in the cellar at all times and that was working well for quite awhile. But then—"

For the first time since entering the room, Leigh saw the strength adorning the woman's features suddenly transform to weakness. Clementine exhaled noisily, doing nothing to hide the obvious sadness pulling like ten pound weights on her eyes.

"Then that bastard Murray Dobson managed to make a run for it. I'll never know how he managed to do it, but he somehow got the jump on my dear, sweet Seymour. With my husband gone, I knew we couldn't risk keeping any live ones here anymore. I mean, what if that were to happen to me? My children would have no one left. And the thought of that is…"

Clementine trailed off, her last sentence lost to a haunting thought she chose to let drift away. Rapidly blinking her eyes, she brought herself back to the present. "But as the saying goes, there's more than one way to skin a cat, and that's when Robbie came in handy. He transfers to a new school every year and brings us a fresh batch of meat."

She playfully slapped Rob's backside. "Just about has it down to a science, don't ya boy?"

Rob practically blushed at this Aunt's compliment. "It's really simple," he said. "All I have to do is make some new friends, drive 'em up to Montreal for spring break, get a flat on the way back, and let Bugger and Grizzly do the rest."

Rob came out from behind Clementine's chair and walked in front of Sam where Leigh couldn't see him. She could still hear his voice, though, as he looked down at Sam and said, "Of course, you made things a little more interesting than usual. But as it turns out, you were nothing but the perfect patsy."

Leigh would've never thought there could be any emotion strong enough to overower the raw fear that claimed her mind and body. But upon hearing Rob's last sentence, all fright and concern lifted like smoke escaping through a chimney. In its place was something far worse.

Guilt.

No, worse.

Shame.

The true enemy had been alongside her the entire time, leading her into this trap. But just as Rob stated, she not only doubted Sam's character, she'd accused him of treachery. She'd questioned his motives, kept a gun trained on his back, and even believed he'd murdered her best friend. But the only crime Sam was guilty of was hitching a ride with the wrong people. In this light, Leigh was as much to blame for Sam's fate as Rob himself.

In the end, she, too, was a villain.

Her voice came out as a whisper. "I'm sorry, Sam."

And Sam—the decent, kind-hearted person he'd been all along—wouldn't let her shoulder the blame. "It's not your fault. How were you supposed to know your friend was related to a family of cannibals?"

Rob returned to his prideful position behind his aunt's wheelchair like a soldier supporting his general. "Ooh," he said, his face grimacing. "You see Auntie doesn't really care for that term."

"Oh, really?" A fiery tenor sparked Sam's voice that seemed to come out of nowhere. Perhaps it was the multiple smacks upside his head that brought back his fighting spirit. "Well, how about this? You're all a bunch of fucking freaks."

Leigh braced herself for the sound of yet another blow that was sure to strike Sam's face, but instead the old woman remained where she was. With the righteousness of a pastor leading a sermon, she simply stated, "We only do what we have to do."

Sam scoffed and Leigh could feel he was shaking his head. While she'd experienced confusion, fear, and overwhelming humiliation, it seemed the only emotion currently affecting Sam was unbridled anger. "You only do you have to do? Sounds like there's more bullshit being served around here than human flesh. C'mon, be honest: you people just do what you like. You only have to take one look at this little prick over here to know he takes far too much pleasure in eating another human being."

Though it took him a second to figure it out, Bugger realized Sam was speaking about him. He jumped off the window sill he'd been sitting on and quickly advanced toward Sam. "You saying there's something wrong with taking pride in your work?"

Sam sneered. "'Work,' he says. Did it ever dawn on you that if you people actually did work, maybe this town would've had a better chance to stay afloat? Or were you too busy killing innocent people for no reason?"

"Sam," Leigh said, stopping him before he could speak another insult. "You need to calm down." Though their chance of survival had been small since the moment she woke up tied to this chair, Sam's outburst was bringing it down to absolute zero.

Clementine removed her chin from its resting place in her hands and spoke up. It was then Leigh realized how oddly quiet the old lady had been during the entirety of Sam's tirade.

"No, it's okay, missy," she said with an eerie somberness to her voice. "Though he could stand to learn some manners, your friend has every right to question our ways. I may be old, but I'm not so far gone that I can't appreciate how difficult this all must be for both of you to take in. And I can't downright say with all honesty that I would believe myself if I were you. After all, talk is cheap. Isn't that what they say?"

She then looked to Bugger and nodded a signal that only the two of them seemed to understand. She turned to the giant known as Grizzly and did the same. The two siblings immediately marched out of the room, Bugger going outside and Grizzly heading down the staircase to the cellar.

Clementine watched as her children exited, and once gone, her gaze returned to her two captives. What she said next were the last two words Leigh ever expected to come from her mouth.

"I'm sorry."

Leigh could only stare at her, speechless, so the woman kept talking.

"I know how strange that might sound, all things considered. But you two should know that all of this—it's nothing personal."

"Nothing personal?" The disbelief in Sam's voice mirrored her own. "You're about to eat us, lady. You can't get much more personal than that."

Clementine sighed and folded her hands in her lap. "I think you'd find me a whole different person if my children weren't always around. The truth is I've never wanted to do any of this. And when my Seymour was still alive, I never had to. He took care of everything. Always told me this was not 'women's work.' So all I had to do was the cooking. And by time the meat made it to my kitchen, it was just that. Meat. Could've come from anywhere. That made things so much easier."

Leigh searched Clementine's wrinkled face for deceit. This had to be a trick, just another mind game for her own amusement. But Leigh could not find any evidence of trickery in the old woman's eyes.

"Seymour explained to me time and time again that what we were doing was absolutely necessary, but I never could shake that guilty monkey from my back. It had just about consumed me when Seymour left us to fend for ourselves. And that's when I made my decision."

Leigh swallowed, her dry mouth making the action far more difficult than usual. "What decision?"

Clementine leaned forward, staring her right in the eyes. "I decided that my children were never going to know the guilt I carried with me every day. There were going to have to continue my husband's work, there was no way around that. In my old age, I lacked the strength and speed that a hunter needs. So it was up to them. But I was damned if I was going to raise those two believing there was anything wrong with what we do. No, my children were going to be happy."

From behind her, Leigh could feel Sam shrug. "Ignorance is bliss, right?"

"As God as my witness," Clementine replied, straightening herself in her chair.

The back of Sam's head rubbed back and forth against Leigh's skull, his soft hair brushing across her neck.

He was shaking his head.

"M'am, may I be the first to congratulate you on a mission accomplished. A little murder seems to make that sicko son of yours happier than a pig in shit."

Clementine frowned, but when she spoke, her voice did not rise in anger.

"I'll admit," she said, "Bugger can get a little out of control. And the fact that he can take things a little too far is entirely my fault. But it's far better than what he could've become. It's better than living with the guilt."

A soft thumping noise emanated from underneath their feet and began to grow louder. Grizzly was beginning his ascent up the cellar stairs. Upon hearing the noise, Clementine sprang forward in her chair, a sudden urgency coming with her words.

"I just wanted to clear that up before my babies got back. So don't waste your breath telling me 'this is wrong,' or, 'you can't do this.' I know the price of what we do. I've known it most of my life. But I *can* do this. And once my children return, I will."

She turned toward the opening cellar door.

"For their sake."

With Clementine's final word, Grizzly emerged at the cellar door's threshold. Leigh inhaled a sharp breath when he she saw what the lumbering giant carried in his arms.

A man dressed in a forest ranger uniform.

Clementine returned her gaze towards Leigh and Sam. That callous, soulless look had returned to her eyes as if her confession had come from an entirely different woman. In the presence of her children, Clementine embodied method acting at its finest.

"It'd do no good for you two to hear me jaw on anymore about our remedy, would it? Because seein' is believin', right? No, what you two need is a demonstration."

The ranger was young, perhaps no older than Leigh herself.

His ankles had been tied together, as well as his wrists behind him. A slab of duct tape covered his mouth. But while all these details were unsettling, the worst belonged to his wide eyes, bulging with fear. This man was alive, awake, and totally aware of everything happening to him.

And about to happen to him.

Grizzly slammed the man down on the table in front of Leigh, the one which Rob and Bugger had fought so viciously over. The man released a loud "umph!" from his nostrils as his head harshly connected with the solid wood. From this close, Leigh could read the man's name tag.

Douglas Graham.

"What are you doing?" Leigh screamed, turning toward Clementine. "Answer me, you bitch!" Leigh knew the crass insult would greatly offend the old woman and that was exactly what she wanted. Pulling Clementine's attention away from the young ranger was all she could think to do to help the man.

But Clementine just smiled as if she hadn't even heard the foul language. "Patience child," she said. "You'll see."

Rob sauntered over to the table. "So…" He leaned closer to the man to read his name tag. "Douglas. It appears you found the note I left for you at the outpost."

"*You* left?" Sam spoke from behind Leigh, his words much calmer than before. "But I wrote the note. It said to come to the hunting camp."

In three long paces, Rob walked over to Sam, digging for something in his pants pocket. He retrieved a wrinkled scrap of paper with scribbled handwriting, pinched between two fingers.

"You mean this note?" Rob brushed the paper against Sam's cheek. "If you recall, I was the last one out of the station. But before I left I switched the note, which led Ranger Rick over there right to us. It's too bad you guys were still asleep when he showed up. Grizzly clubbed him right off his four-wheeler."

"But he works for the forest service," Sam said. "Authorities will know if anything happens to him."

The lantern light reflected off Clementine's glasses, hiding her eyes behind a flickering glare. "I wouldn't worry about that," she said without a trace of anxiety. "Robbie isn't the only one on the outside with our interests in mind. We've got someone who'll be able to sort this out."

The cabin's front door suddenly swung open. Sweat pouring from his brow and breaths coming in heavy gasps, Bugger grunted as he plodded into the room, a long, bulky burlap sack resting on his shoulder.

"Grizzly!" His voice shook with exhaustion. "Get me a chair."

The larger sibling immediately retrieved a nearby seat and placed it front of the kitchen table. With heavy steps that shook the entire floor, Bugger trudged over to the chair and threw the sack off his shoulder. Now that it sat upright at the table, Leigh noticed how much the bag's shaped resembled that of a human body.

"Damn," Bugger said as he gasped to catch his breath. "Why'd I have to be the one to go all the way to shed? Just about busted my back."

His mother simply raised a hand. "Oh, hush. You'll live." She then motioned to Grizzly to approach the sack. "Now then, it's time to greet our newest guest."

"Actually," Rob added, "I believe they've already met."

Grizzly untied the knots clinching the top of the bag and pulled it down. When the bag reached the man's waist, Grizzly stepped away so Leigh could see who it was.

She could not find the breath to scream.

Somewhere underneath inches of thick, damp fungus sat Dale Preston, the tree man of Embry, VT, looking worse than ever. Buried beneath so much invasive fungal growth, any doctor would've assumed that Dale Preston had long expired. But then again, they would've had to notice the slight, rhythmic movement of Dale's chest. And they wouldn't have missed the way the grassy hairs around Dale's nostrils shivered every few seconds.

Though now more plant than human, Dale was still alive.

Bugger arched over so he could look at Dale at eye-level.

Or rather, where his eyes would've been.

"Now what did I tell you, buddy?" As Bugger spoke, he made sure to keep his distance from the contagious hunter. "Didn't I tell you not to take a dip in the lake? And just look at you now." He reached over to a rusty cleaver, its blade buried in a cutting board. With a vigorous tug, it came free. Bugger lifted it front of Dale's face, as if Dale could see anything.

"I bet you're just begging for this, aren't you? Just one quick chop to your neck and all the pain goes away."

Leigh couldn't believe her ears when a hissing noise came from Dale's mossy lips like air escaping a flat tire. Dale was actually trying to speak.

"Oh, save your breath, fungus face." Bugger flipped the cleaver into the air, the blade doing a full rotation before the handle landed back in his hand. "This isn't for you. No, you have something far better in store. Something that'll make you feel all better."

Bugger turned to his mother. "Now, ma?"

Clementine returned a slow nod. "Go right ahead, son. It's about time these two see the truth with their own eyes." She tapped Grizzly's arm. "Turn them so they can both see."

Leigh felt her feet leave the ground as Grizzly effortlessly lifted the two chairs and spun them counter-clockwise. She now had to crane her neck to the right to see Douglas Graham pinned down by Grizzly's massive arms. Sam, now twisting his neck to the left, was seeing the third prisoner for the first time.

"Leigh," he whispered, "close your eyes."

Mother Cedar slammed the armrest of her wheelchair. "You do and I'll cut them right outta your skull."

Knowing Clementine would keep that promise, Leigh dared not even blink.

They started with his ear. The cleaver's blade must have been dull because it look three big whacks to sever the cartilage. Douglas screamed through the duct tape sealing his mouth shut and trembled as if he were lying on a wire frame bed connected to a car battery. But even with the slick blood rushing over Grizzly's hands, the giant held him in place as Bugger pinched his ear lobe and tore away the remaining strands of tissue.

Leigh kept telling herself it was just a movie. She was just watching that Quentin Tarantino flick that Marshall made her and Alex watch last semester. But in the film, the camera panned away when the psycho cut off the cop's ear. Leigh had imagined what the amputation must have looked like, just like Tarantino intended.

She pictured something gruesome, bloody and nasty—but nothing like the look of absolute pain on the victim's face as the tissue fibers snapped like rubber bands.

Bugger, who'd been straddling Douglas as he performed his ghastly operation, swung his legs over his patient's body and hopped off the table. He approached Dale, holding out the ear like a biscuit for an obedient dog.

"For Christ's sake," Clementine suddenly hollered. "Wear a glove, you fool."

Sheepishly, Bugger marched over to a dust covered cabinet and retrieved a pair of worn-out leather work gloves. Returning to Dale, he slowly moved the ear toward his fuzz-covered lips.

"Open wide," Bugger said as if addressing a child. "Here comes the airplane!"

Dale's mouth hesitantly parted and accepted the ear on his dark green, swollen tongue. The fungus covered lips closed and the mound of mushrooms on his chin began to bob up and down as he chewed.

Leigh gagged once. Twice. And then threw up a rancid, white, semisolid fluid, the only thing left in her stomach. Sam remained frozen.

"Good Lord, girl," Clementine said as she shook her head. "Pull yourself together." She then looked over at Dale and saw that he was still chewing. "Bugger, damnit! That piece is too tough. Give him something he can swallow."

"Sorry, ma." Bugger paced back over to Douglas and

pulled up the ranger uniform tucked into his pants. Douglas's stomach and obliques were well-toned. But Bugger was still able to pinch a chunk of fat from the man's stomach, which he immediately began to slice off.

Again, Douglas screamed, slamming the back of his head so hard against the table that Leigh was surprised he didn't knock himself out. Which was probably what he was trying to do.

The sliver of flesh, like the ear, didn't come off with a quick incision. The muscles in Bugger's forearms and biceps tensed as he sawed away the skin with the edge of the cleaver. This time, when the hunk of meat was removed, it didn't come with the same dry, snapping noise as before. It was wet, like slicing off a bite-sized piece of extra rare steak.

The flesh finally came free in Bugger's hand, resting in his palm like a peach-colored slug. Douglas's screams, while at first loud and furious, turned to weak whimpers as he started to cry.

Leigh began to weep as well.

"Stop," she said between sobs. "For God's sake, please stop."

But Bugger ignored her pleading, too busy removing what was left of Douglas's ear from Dale's mouth and replacing it with the slippery morsel from his torso.

"There ya go," he said to Dale. "That should slide right down."

And indeed it did, with a sickening gulp. Leigh retched again, but this time expelled nothing. Douglas, now weak from his struggles, looked to her with beseeching eyes. Through all his pain and suffering, the man didn't seem to notice that Leigh was as helpless as he. There was nothing she could do for him except pray that these sickos were finished.

Unfortunately, that was not the case.

"Hmm," Clementine said, studying Dale. "I think we need to speed this up." She looked to Bugger. "Drench him down. Use a foot."

Before Leigh could even begin to figure out what that could mean, Bugger was back at Douglas's side, the cleaver coming down with mighty force. It connected just above the left ankle. Though it appeared Douglas had no fight left in him, the man thrashed against the painful blow, actually prying an arm free from Grizzly's powerful hold. The giant regained the limb instantly, but the flail somehow managed to loosen the tape covering Douglas's mouth. Now with the tape dangling from the corner of his lower lip, Douglas was able to release a tremendous scream.

"*NOOO!*" He wailed as the cleaver slammed into his ankle yet again. "Stop! Please, *stop*! Don't!" But his screams did nothing to stop the blade from coming down with one final hack that severed his foot clean off. Bugger caught it just before it hit the floor. Grizzly clamped a colossal hand over Douglas's mouth to cease his shouts.

Rob leaned down to his aunt's ear.

"Uh, Aunt Clemmy?" he asked timidly. "Does he have to be alive for all of this?"

Clementine turned a pair of understanding eyes up toward her nephew. "Oh, I'm sorry, Robbie. I forgot you're not as used to this sort of thing as we are. But I'm afraid it's all completely necessary. You see, with a case as bad as this one here, the meat and blood have to be as fresh as possible."

As Clementine explained her mad reasoning to her nephew, Bugger tilted the amputated foot over Dale's head so that the blood within rained down over him. It was like watching a twisted Gatorade commercial, but the winning coach was being soaked with something far more gruesome than lemon-lime sports drink. With the last drop of blood emptied from the extremity, Bugger tossed it into the corner of the cabin like a discarded beer bottle.

"Wow, mama," Bugger said, stepping back to admire his work. "You were right. That worked fast!"

Leigh managed to lift her head, which felt like it weighed one hundred pounds, and glanced over at the Tree Man still sitting in his chair.

Though splotches of fungus still spotted his face and

body in a green patchwork of fuzz, the Tree Man had almost completely vanished. Dale Preston had reclaimed his body, his distinct features more easy to see than ever before. And not only was the fungus retreating from its all out attack, Leigh could see the sanity and comprehension returning to Dale's mind. His expression was one of a man who'd just stepped out from a hot, relaxing Jacuzzi.

The expression didn't last long as Bugger slammed the back of his head with the handle of the cleaver, knocking him unconscious. Then Bugger pointed at the mutilated Douglas, whose muffled screams still continued under Grizzly palm.

"Might as well take care of that one too, Grizz. He's served his purpose. Right Ma?"

The moment his mother returned an agreeing nod, Grizzly raised a brick-sized fist high above his head. A second later, it came crashing down on Douglas's skull with a thunderous *crack!* Douglas's body twitched three times before lying still.

Wheeling her chair over so that her face was only inches from Sam's, she asked him, "Now do you believe me?" A cocky grin spread across her face as she used her head to gesture over to the unconscious Dale.

Sam merely shrugged. "It truly is remarkable. But you're still all a bunch of sick, murdering, redneck fucks."

Before Clementine could offer any retort, either with her voice or the back of her hand, Bugger sprinted past her and snatched Sam's face with his blood-slicked hand. His fingers dug into Sam's cheeks, pushing hips lips apart like those of a fish.

"Oh, come on now!" Bugger said, furiously shaking Sam's face. "Have you ever even *tried* man flesh before? You just don't know what you're missing. It's real tasty. Especially the way Ma makes it."

Clementine patted her son on the back. "Why thank you, sonny boy."

"Hell," Bugger continued, "and not only that, but it's real good for you. Makes you big and strong!" He pulled Sam's face towards Grizzly. "Just take a look at my sister."

Through his fish-shaped lips, Sam slurred the word Leigh was already repeating in her own mind.

"Sister?"

As carefully as one would handle a beautiful, delicate vase, Grizzly grabbed the bottom of the bear mask and pulled it upward. Locks of red, greasy hair tumbled out, falling onto Grizzly's shoulders like dying serpents. The mask rose up over Grizzly's head until Leigh and Sam could fully see its face.

Her face.

Leigh had never been so cruel to make fun of another's appearance or call attention to someone else's unfortunate physical flaws. But as she stared at the female juggernaut before her, Leigh couldn't help herself from thinking:

That's the ugliest woman I've ever seen in my life.

One narrow eye was lower than the other, her protruding brow towering over both of them like a newspaper stand awning. Her nose was pulled up and pushed in as if it had been hit square on with the business end of a sledgehammer. A severe harelip severed her upper lip, revealing a single, jagged tooth underneath. A strand of drool hung from the corner of her mouth, dangling saliva that she didn't seem to notice.

"Oh my God."

Clementine wheeled over next to her daughter who knelt beside her. As the mother spoke, she ran a hand though the clumpy strings of Grizzly's hair.

"Oh, God had nothing to do with her size. You see, when my daughter was only an infant, she came down with a real bad case of the fuzz. Covered most of her body, in fact. So for a whole year she ate nothing but human flesh until I was sure the illness was gone. But wouldn't you know it? It's been years since she was cured but she still won't eat anything else." Clementine wiped away the clinging drool with the hem of her dress. "I guess she's still scared of catching it again."

Bugger released his grip on Sam's face and pointed a teasing finger at his sister. "You big baby!"

"Now don't get started," Clementine yelled at her son. "We still got to deal with these two."

The words bubbled like battery acid on Leigh's brain. After seeing one man's harvested flesh fed to another man like dinner party hors d'oeuvres, who knew how these people would *deal* with them.

"What are you going to do?" she asked.

As if the whole weight of the world had fallen upon her shoulders all at once, Clementine leaned back in her wheelchair like she was about to take an afternoon nap. A look of maudlin sadness came over her.

"Well, the truth is, honey, I'm getting' old. And soon not even our remedy is gonna be able to do any good." The words came from the mother's mouth with as much gentleness as a grandmother receiving a visit from her grandkids.

But the illusion did not last any longer than it took the woman to speak her next sentence.

"So I figure if I'm ever gonna see any grandchildren, now's the time. And that's where you come in."

An icy hand squeezed Leigh's heart, prickling her skin and tightening her buttocks. She darted her eyes to Bugger, who had molested her in the cellar just hours ago. She still could still feel his rough, filthy hands on her skin. His horrid, rancid mouth on her nipples. The idea of going through that again—and worse—

She couldn't do it.

"No," she whispered. She had never said anything that ever sounded so pathetic. But Sam's voice was a different matter all together.

He wrenched in his chair, trying desperately to loosen the knots that held him tight. Frothy saliva spat from his mouth like that of a rabid dog. "I swear to God, if anyone lays a hand on her, I'll fucking kill all of you." He pulled his body forward as hard as it could go, but the ropes did not budge an inch.

"I'm gonna fucking kill you!"

Clementine furrowed her brow in complete awe. "Heaven's child!" she said with an amused smirk on her face. "What makes you think it's *her* I need?"

Sam's frantic struggles stopped as suddenly as they had begun. The words froze him like liquid nitrogen. It took him about five seconds to figure out the meaning behind the old lady's question, but when he did, he could look nowhere else but at the Grizzly's revolting visage.

"Oh, hell no."

It was quite a sight to see someone as intimidating as Grizzly run over to the cabin wall and bury her face in her arms while great big sobs racked her entire body. Her moans scraped at Leigh's eardrums like a dull fork scratching an aged blackboard. If not for the green flannel shirt and dark wool pants, Grizzly might've resembled a high school senior stood up by her prom date.

Clementine called over to her daughter, "Oh don't you mind him, girl. You're beautiful. He just hasn't gotten to know you yet, that's all." She then looked back to Sam and grinned. "But he will."

Grizzly's sobs quieted, but she remained facing the wall in shame. Satisfied that she'd at least calmed down, Clementine turned her attention towards Leigh. "As for you…"

Bugger was practically jumping in place. "Can I do it now, Ma?"

"Do what?" Rob took three long paces so that he stood between Bugger and his mother.

Clementine removed her glasses and gingerly rubbed her brow. "Yes, I suppose it's time. But do it in the barn. We've already got a big enough mess in here." She tried to wheel around Rob but he extended a foot to stop her left wheel.

"Do what in the barn?"

His aunt looked down at his sneakered foot blocking her way and then back up to his eyes. "Fair's fair," she sighed. "You went off and killed Bugger's woman, so he's gonna get his turn now."

Clementine turned her chair to navigate around Rob's
foot but her nephew leaped in front of her and grabbed the
armrests. "Hold on a minute."

The fire behind the old woman's eyes became hotter with
every passing second.

"I thought Leigh was gonna be kept alive to keep the family
going."

Leigh expected the woman to cry out with an order to
respect her authority, but Clementine warmly smiled. "Now
why would I want to go through all the trouble of keeping an
outsider in my home for a whole nine months while we wait
for a baby to pop out of her when my Grizzly girl could have
the chance to experience motherhood? No, the boy will do his
job, and this one here goes."

"That's right!" Bugger's joy had reverted his behavior to
that of a seven-year-old. "Ma said it was okay!"

Before Rob could mutter another word of protest, Bugger
was pushing past him, a jackknife in his hand.

Leigh squirmed at the sight of the blade.

"No!"

But after squeezing her eyes shut and bracing for the cold
bite of the knife, all she felt was the sudden relief of the ropes
around her wrists breaking apart. Just as she realized Bugger
was cutting her free from her chair, he hoisted her over his
shoulder and started carrying her away.

Away from Sam.

"Sam!" she bellowed, catching the frightened glance of her
friend still securely bonded to his seat.

Again, he tried to break free but he knew just as well as her
that it would do no good. "Leigh!" he screamed. "Leave her alone!"

As Bugger fumbled for the knob on the front door, Leigh
pounded as hard as she could on his backbone with her fists.

"That tickles," Bugger said between chuckles. "You want
me to tickle you?" The point of the jackknife blade just barely
touched the exposed skin of Leigh's her lower back. She

immediately stopped her attack upon feeling the sharp metal, going limp with defeat.

Before the front door swung open, Leigh watched as Clementine pointed a bony finger at Sam and said to Grizzly, "Go get your man." As easily as Bugger lifted her, Grizzly hoisted Sam over her own shoulder and carried him into the back bedroom. Clementine followed closely behind, wheeling herself into the room.

Rob tried to follow. "Aunt Clemmy…wait!"

But when Clementine reached the door, she quickly pivoted around and replied, "Now Robbie. You stay out of here. This is not for your eyes."

Leigh and Sam exchanged one final glimpse before Clementine slammed the bedroom door shut, leaving Rob shaking the securely locked knob and screaming, "Aunt Clemmy? Aunt Clemmy!"

Rob's voice faded as Bugger carried Leigh outside, down the porch steps, and towards a large barn about a hundred feet from the cabin. When she saw the brilliant red light silhouetting the trees to the east, she immediately thought the forest had caught on fire. But then she realized the light wasn't dancing like flames, but was merely the warm, welcoming colors of daybreak. It was just the sunrise of another beautiful September day in Vermont.

CHAPTER
TWENTY-TWO

Air noisily rushed in and out of Jake's nostrils like a bicycle pump in full use. With a slowly advancing river of blood creeping up on him from behind, Jake had managed to scoot himself halfway across the dusty floor of the ranger outpost. Jake had struggled greatly, having only the use of his knees to pull not only his own body weight, but that of the chair still attached to him like a leech. But although his aching muscles begged for reprieve and his exhausted lungs threatened to call it quits at any moment, Jake kept an unwavering focus on the prize ahead: an opened, cardboard box with the word *supplies* written in black Sharpie across its side.

Loosening the ropes with squirming or wriggling wasn't going to free him anytime soon. Phil had made sure of that before blowing his brains out in a Jackson Pollack splatter across the outpost's window pane. Jake knew his only chance of salvation lay waiting inside that box, be it in the form of a knife or anything plastic he could break into a jagged edge. Of course, it may just contain cans of food and bottled water, in which case he wouldn't be going anywhere until another ranger came passing through.

But he had to try. He had to get free as soon as possible and report everything he had learned this night. He had to tell the rest of the department. The town of Embry. The world.

But where to begin?

Jake released an unexpected chuckle, an obvious sign of stress relentlessly chipping away at his composure. The laughter was an unnecessary exertion of energy that halted his progress towards the box as he stopped to rest and get the goddamned giggles out of his system.

Christ, what a night.

A pleasant warmth spread across his face like a fleece blanket fresh from the clothes dryer. For a moment, Jake forgot all about the endless tasks that lay ahead and the flow of blood pursuing from behind. A reddish-orange beam of light penetrating the window and crossing directly in his path pushed all of it from his troubled mind, replaced with the revitalized optimism that comes with a new day. The darkness of night trounced by the glory of morning.

The quick rest hadn't done much for Jake's body, but his mind felt like it had just come off God's assembly line. The morning light had burned away the doubts and hysteria, allowing Jake to reclaim his plan of attack. If he ever wanted to put the Humpty Dumpty of his world back together again, first thing was first: free himself and get back on his feet.

Which means you got to reach that fucking box. So let's do it.

Jake groaned and threw his weight forward, crawling another six inches towards the cardboard container. Then another six inches. Then another foot. And just when his lower back seized in cramps, pain like a cobra's fangs sinking into the tissue on both sides of his spine…

…his forehead connected with a heavenly smooth surface. The box.

But Jake's physical tribulations weren't over yet. Craning his head upward to the point where the tendons in his neck felt as they though they would snap, Jake lashed out with his jaw at the opened flap above his head. Like a disobedient dog snatching at a treat, Jake clamped his teeth into the pliable, cardboard flap, its rough edge digging into his lower lip. Not wasting any time for fear his muscles would utterly fail him, Jake pulled downward with all the strength left in his body. His applied force, with the natural assistance of gravity, delivered the results he'd outright prayed for: the box flipped over, spilling its contents onto the floor.

Jake's eyes darted from object to object, determined to find anything that could help him. But "supplies" can mean a lot of things, and the case of this upturned box, it meant matches, glow sticks, bottled water, and dynamite. Sticks upon sticks of dynamite.

"Shit."

Jake let his head come to rest on the hardwood floor. He'd intended to shout the word in an act of furious frustration, but the overwhelming weight of defeat had allowed for hardly a whisper. After all the effort it took to cross what felt like a mile-long room, Jake's only reward had been a way to blow himself up.

Looks like I should make myself comfortable.

A radio sat up on a table to his left, but it only served as a way to further tease and remind him with the impossibility of his escape. On the table high above him, the radio might as well have been balancing on the top of the Empire State Building. And even if he'd managed to stand his chair back up on its four legs and reach the desk, he had no way of pressing the buttons and switches necessary to make a call.

No, Jake knew he wasn't going anywhere. All he could do now was lie on his side and stare at the plethora of useless items before him, the worst being the red sticks of explosives. They carried as much value as a pair of snowshoes on a desert island. But even modern snowshoes had sharp, metal spikes on the bottom that could be used to crack open coconuts or crab shells. All the dynamite offered was nitroglycerin cocooned in sawdust and a long fuse.

Then again, maybe blowing myself up isn't such a bad—

A single stick poking out from underneath a box of matches caught his eye. Though the same color, shape, and size as the rest of the identical dynamite splayed across the floor, this stick had one very drastic difference that Jake cursed himself for not noticing sooner.

There was no fuse protruding from its top. Instead, a white, plastic cap adorned its head like a soldier's helmet. Though Jake couldn't read from this distance what was printed on the stick's side, he didn't need to identify a label to know what he was looking at:

That's a goddamned flare!

Whether the flare had been misidentified or purposely thrown in the box by a lazy ranger who didn't care to thoroughly organize the outpost's equipment, it didn't matter in the slightest. All that mattered was that Jake now had a means of escape.

Of course, it was far from an ideal method. Jake's surge of excitement diminished to a meager sizzle when he thought about what using the flare would entail. He was confident he'd be able to use his hands to remove the cap and strike the flare on the cap's coarse striking surface, but in order to burn the rope on his wrists he'd have to torch far more than that. He would literally have to put his hands to the torch's red hot flame. He could only hope that the ropes would sever instantly. The pain would probably only allow for a second or two of burning at most. But it was either that or remain lying on the floor with his new roommate. And he didn't think Phil would be much for conversation.

Taking a deep breath before commencing his procedure, Jake threw all the weight he could to his left, attempting to flip himself over. When he only lifted an inch before returning to the exact same position, Jake knew he'd have to use his toes to scoot himself around one-hundred and eighty degrees.

The task was difficult and time-consuming, but luck on was on his side, allowing Jake to get just enough leverage with his feet to complete the entire rotation. With his back now to pile of box contents strewn across the ground, Jake reached out with his hands and felt for the stick with the plastic cap. It took several tries.

But Jake found it.

Holding the stick with his dominant right hand, he pulled off the plastic cap, being careful not to drop it. His fingers allowed him to rotate the cap so that he could feel the roughness of the igniting surface underneath. He lined up the flare to the flint. Everything was ready.

Jake shut his eyes, attempting to control the nervous breath that rushed in and out of his lungs. He tried to assure himself that it would all be over in the blink of an eye, that it wouldn't even be as bad as getting a shot of Novocain before a cavity removal. But when impenetrable doubt followed each reaffirming thought, Jake smiled and opened his eyes. There were just no two ways about it.

This was going to suck.

"Fuck me."

Without giving himself the chance to second guess his actions, Jake struck the flare against the coarse surface as hard as he could.

And touched the sun.

Jake lunged forward and screamed the moment the hiss and color of the flare filled the room. His wrists and bottoms of his palms felt as if he'd dunked them in a vat of molten lava. It was pure heat. The most intense pain Jake had ever felt in his life. It seared more than just the skin that touched the heat. The fire seemed to engulf his entire body, igniting his nerves everywhere with the sting of a thousand hornets. The prick of a thousand needles.

But though the pain seemed to last an eternity, the strength of the ropes did not. The rope had been dry and old. The combination of the flare's fire with all of Jake's body weight lunging forward was far more than the binding could bear. The ropes gave and Jake flew forward, almost bashing his chin on his knees.

The flare automatically dropped from his grip the moment the rope released his wrists. Jake brought them to his chest, desperately trying to shake away the lingering singe of pain that remained. The skin on his palms had turned a deep red, and bubbles of fresh blisters ran along his wrists. But considering the direct exposure to the flame his hands had just endured, his injuries were much less severe than he'd expected. The process must have been far quicker than his pain had suggested, leaving him a small, second-degree burn at the most.

Ignoring his flesh that begged for cooling, Jake went straight for the ropes binding his feet to the legs of the chair. Fortunately, the flare had hardly touched his fingers which made untying Phil's expert knots all the more easier. But with the amount of adrenaline still pumping through his system, Jake was sure he could've have easily ripped the ropes apart like the Incredible Hulk.

Standing upright and feeling the floor underneath his shoes had never felt so good, but Jake didn't spare any time savoring the sensation. He was too busy digging up a bottle of water from the mess of the cardboard box, ripping off the cap, and drenching his tender skin. The water was the nectar of heaven, instantly cooling the burn. Jake repeated the process with two more bottles before drinking a third in four large gulps. The last bottle in the box he used to douse the flare, applying what was left to his burns and his still-parched mouth.

Though he wanted nothing more than to call it quits and get some much-needed rest, Jake didn't let his mind consider the idea for more than a second. Instead, he focused on the first aid box near the outpost's front door. Inside he found gauze pads, some medical tape, and a bottle of antiseptic. Pouring the disinfectant on his wounds would certainly reignite his pain, but Jake applied it generously, telling himself over and over that the sizzle was a good thing. And after the close encounter with the flare, the cleansing liquid felt like a mild sunburn in comparison.

With his injuries cleaned and wrapped securely, Jake marched over to Phil's splayed corpse. Touching or even getting anywhere near his ex-coworker's body was the last thing he wanted to do, but Jake knew he had no choice when he eyed the radio attached to Phil's belt. It was clear that avoiding the blood completely just wasn't going to happen, but the first aid kit had not been without a pair of latex gloves. Jake assumed the person responsible for stocking the kit had never intended the gloves to be used for corpse handling, but they did not job nevertheless. With his hands fully protected, Jake removed the radio from its blood-soaked holster and switched it on.

He tuned it to Doug's frequency. "Doug, come back."

Only static answered.

"Doug, it's Jake. Answer if you can hear me."

Again, nothing.

"Shit," Jake said, tearing the radio from his ear in frustration. The questions that Doug's failed response brought were practically endless. Why wasn't he answering? Had he found the tourists who'd left the note? Were they okay? Why hadn't he returned or sent another ranger to Maple Ridge when Jake hadn't met him there?

Only one thing was for certain: Jake wasn't going to find any answers here. His best course of action was to jump on his ATV and continue where he'd left off before Phil showed up to crash the party. Though heading directly back to the station and calling in back up was tempting, he first had to make sure Doug and the stranded group of hikers were okay. After hearing Phil's appalling tale, he knew a fungal disease was the least of their concerns.

Phil's rifle lay in a pool of blood a few inches from his ruined skull. With the gloves still on his hands, Jake retrieved the weapon and doused it with the disinfectant. He then wiped it clean and checked its cartridge for ammo. It was loaded.

Minus one bullet.

Jake slowly turned to face the dead body of his fellow ranger.

Many might have considered it a foolish thing to do considering the destroyed state of Phil's cranium, but Jake still knelt over Phil's face and pulled the lids down over his open eyes.

"Rest in peace, old friend."

When the familiar warm wetness of tears beginning to collect in the corner of his eyes, Jake quickly removed his hand from Phil's cool face and stood back up. Shifting the rifle to rest on his shoulder, Jake brought his straight fingers to his brow, offering the old navy man one final salute.

Rifle slung across his back, Jake grabbed the note still lying on the radio's table and made for the outpost's front door. He read the note as he walked, wanting to know his exact destination the moment his ass hit the seat of his ATV. He'd just passed through the door's threshold into the welcoming light of morning when he stopped dead in his tracks.

HELP!!!

We are a small group of day hikers in need of medical treatment. One of us has become very sick. The Cedar family has been kind enough to let us stay at their home while we await assistance. They are located on the far west side of Emerald Lake. You will see their chimney smoke from the shore. Please hurry!!!

Jake didn't bother to read the last two words. He was already gone.

CHAPTER
TWENTY-THREE

Once inside, Leigh discovered that the "barn" was more of a makeshift garage than anything else. Instead of the walls being lined with stables or farming equipment, antique lumberjack machines inhabited most of the space. A diesel powered log-splitter sat abandoned in a far corner, a thick layer of dust and grime concealing years of accumulated rust. A long, two-person cross-cut saw stretched along the building's left wall like the remaining smile of the vanishing Cheshire Cat.

We're all mad here.

Piles of axes, hatchets, and bark removers sat scattered all across the floor like a colony of ant mounds. Even an old, long out-of-service pick-up truck slept tucked away between two stacks of crates, its hood propped open, revealing an empty cavity where an engine should have been. In fact, the only material suited for a farmland barn was the old, moldy haystack that lay near the barn's entrance.

Bugger threw open the barn's door and hurled Leigh to the dirty ground. All she could focus on was her captor as he loomed over her, a demon grin spreading across his face as he reached for yet another knife strapped to his person.

And this one was big.

"No…"

Bugger nodded, the ecstatic anticipation never leaving his eyes, his eyes never leaving Leigh, who slowly crawled backwards away from him.

"Oh, yes," he whispered.

The blade of the knife reflected the beams of morning sun that snuck in through the cracks of the barn walls. Leigh kept crawling as Bugger took slow, deliberate steps towards her. She was a mouse caught in a cat's game—a swift and painless death nowhere in her immediate future. Bugger had all the time in the world. And he intended to use it.

Leigh's hand landed in puddle of tepid water but she didn't notice. Nothing could tear her attention away from the combination of intense lust behind Bugger's eyes, a combination of two kinds: flesh and blood

She shrieked uncontrollably when he darted forward.

He retreated a step and laughed. "What'd you say? I didn't catch that."

Though Bugger's advance came in short, drawn-out steps, the wall behind Leigh was fast approaching. She knew when her back hit that wall it would be the end of the line. Literally. She would have no where to go and no way to defend herself against Bugger and what looked like a prop stolen from *Friday the 13th* in his tight grip.

"Please." Her voice came out as if she were lying on a quarter-operated, vibrating motel bed. "Don't do this."

Bugger's eyes closed in absolute elation. He inhaled a deep breath through his nostrils as he savored Leigh's helplessness and fear. "That's right," he groaned in pleasure. "Keep talking."

With her assailant's eyes closed, Leigh seized the opportunity to whip her head back and steal a glance at the environment to her rear. The wall was now a mere ten feet away. Once she reached it, she would be pinned between a wobbly worktable and a large pickle barrel. But it was the table that caught her eye—or rather, what lay resting along its corner closest to her: a wooden mallet.

A weapon.

Still, Leigh would have to somehow take her attacker's attention away from the blunt object, reach it with her hand, and deliver a blow powerful enough to buy her the time needed to get away. All before that oversized blade cut into her heart like a butcher's knife through a stick of butter.

Mission impossible.

Or is it?

From the menacing expression imprinted into Bugger's facial features, Leigh could tell he wanted two things from her. Her only chance at survival was to divert his focus to the thing that wasn't her blood.

"Come on, Bugger, you don't want to do this. Not yet."

Bugger practically giggled. "What, you don't think this is fun?"

"Sh-sure it is." Leigh closed her eyes and swallowed hard.

It's years from now. You're in court, trying to win over a jury. And how do you do that?

Make them see only what you want them to see.

"But I know of a better way we can have fun."

She stared at his crotch, bringing as much hunger to her eyes as she could possibly conjure.

Bugger stopped in his tracks.

And then burst into laughter.

"How stupid do you think I am?" He followed his question with a few more hoots and hollers. "I may not go to fancy schools like my faggot cousin, but I got enough brains in my head to know when a bitch is trying to trick me."

He took two more steps forward. Leigh matched them by backing up.

Just a few more feet…

"It's not a trick!" The sincerity in Leigh's voice surprised even her. "Haven't you ever heard of passengers jumping each other when their plane is about to crash? People want to fuck before they die."

She lowered her chin so that she stared up at Bugger from beneath her brow.

"And I want to fuck you."

Again, Bugger stopped. But this time he didn't laugh or even crack a smile. He simply stared at his prey, attempting to detect deception in her words.

When he took a challenging step forward, Leigh brought her finger to her mouth. Though she couldn't even stand a tongue depressor during a doctor's visit, sheer desperation allowed her gag reflex to allow her finger to travel all the way down her throat to the last knuckle. Her eyes never left his.

Removing the finger from her mouth, she felt her back lightly graze a hard surface behind her. She'd reached the wall.

Leigh stared up at her captor, imagining Alex's trademark pout and trying to mimic the expression as best she could. "Are you such a monster that you wouldn't give me one last lay before I go?"

Leigh had no idea who was speaking anymore, but it definitely wasn't her. She wasn't this good an actress. Hell, she wasn't this good a liar. And she wouldn't have in a million years thought to add, "Oh, who the fuck am I kidding? I just wanted to do it once before I died."

Bugger almost dropped the knife in his hand but recovered before it could fall from his fingers. Clearing his throat like a nervous schoolboy, he asked, "You mean…you never?"

"And it looks like I never will."

It last only a moment, but Leigh couldn't miss the change in Bugger's expression that confirmed that her act of seduction had worked. But the hidden side of her that had emerged to take over her actions wouldn't let him see her satisfaction, instead keeping the look of lust pasted on her face. She'd keep up this charade until he was on upon her. And then, with his face buried in her chest, she'd reach for the mallet and come down on his skull like a judge's gavel delivering a sentence of eternal darkness.

Leigh still believed she couldn't bear his touch again, but she didn't have to. This new woman could. *She* could do anything in order to survive. Leigh just had to go along for the ride. It was *She* who was in control.

But then Bugger didn't put his knife away. And he didn't go to lower his pants.

He just smiled and said, "Nope. I guess not. But don't worry. I'll be just as happy to fill every hole after I slit your throat. Maybe even that one too."

She was gone. In fact, *She* had never even existed in the first place. There was no new woman being born within Leigh's consciousness. No femme fatale or black widow finally getting a chance to come out and play. Leigh was just and only herself, the same person who she'd always been and who she would die as: alone with an evil she'd utterly underestimated. Bugger was more than a redneck or a sadist or a rapist.

He was the destroyer.

Even the prospect of raping a virgin seemed tame in his eyes compared to the chance to deny his victim her dying wish. Blood and flesh—these were byproducts. Party favors. How foolish she'd been to think she could convince him to give her anything, even a final mercy fuck. In Bugger's world, giving did not exist. There was only loss—his insatiable craving.

So it turned out that Sam was right. To Bugger, cannibalism was more than a remedy to a horrible disease. It was the act of taking that drove him. The ultimate symbol of consumption.

And now he was about to consume Leigh.

She closed her eyes, expecting her loving parents to be the last thing she pictured. Or maybe her brother who'd sacrificed so much for her in the past. Or maybe that field behind her grandmother's house where she used to lie as a child, watching fireflies dance above her head.

But when she closed her eyes, all she saw was the army jacket of a past war, a baseball cap of an extinct team, and the kindest smile to ever warm her heart.

Sam.

"Hey!"

The sudden shout jolted Leigh's open just in time for her to see a fist connect with Bugger's jaw. Something in the cannibal's face cracked as he staggered backward, tripping on his own two feet. Right before a pair of black-panted legs blocked her view, Leigh spotted Bugger falling to the dirt floor, confusion twisting his features as it did hers. For a split second, Leigh believed her vision of Sam to have materialized, her wish to have come true. Her knight in shining armor had arrived to save her.

But above the legs, Leigh discovered a torso adorned in a denim vest with a *Dead Kennedys* logo sewn to its back, and she realized a much darker knight had arrived on a red-eyed steed.

Rob.

Staring through the space between her unlikely savior's legs, Leigh watched Bugger stumble to his feet, shaking the dizziness from his head. Unfortunately, his bearings were not the only thing he regained as he stared in disbelief at the barn's latest guest. He also reclaimed his impressive knife, which had somehow remained at his side after the punch sent him tumbling.

"Robbie?" he said, rubbing the left side of his jaw. "What the fuck are you doing?"

Rob frowned, his hands going to his pockets. "I can't let you do it, cuz."

"You son of a bitch." A wad of saliva shot from Bugger's mouth tainted pink with blood. "Ma said I could."

Rob shrugged his shoulders, the gesture reeking of that immature cockiness that had infuriated Leigh so many times before. "She ain't *my* ma."

It was almost painful to watch Bugger's uneducated mind try to grasp the logic behind Rob's statement. The busted, ancient machines scattered in the barn had a better chance of running than the gears within the woodsman's mind. Angered by his own puzzlement, the muscles bordering Bugger's mouth twitched as if to push the perplexity to the side.

"Okay then," he said, that grin full of yellowing teeth and bloody gums once again returning to his face. He tossed the knife into the air, the blade flipping three times before the handle returned to his grasp. "If that's how you want to play, let's play."

The image of Rob and Bugger circling could have been plucked from so many movies Leigh had seen in her short lifetime. No matter what the film's content, it was always the same scene: the leaders of two opposing sides somehow find each other in a vast, chaotic battlefield. Although the battle rages around them, men killing each other every other second, the two sworn enemies somehow find the space to pace around each other before one of them decides to strike first.

That was what occurred next—Bugger bearing his teeth like a feral animal, Rob returning an unimpressed smirk. Despite the hate apparent in both men's eyes, there was something holding them back, delaying the violence that so wanted to present itself. There was no doubt to what that reason was; Leigh had met her just moments ago.

Old Clementine Cedar wouldn't be too happy about her son and nephew killing each other. And the victor would have to deal with the matriarch's repercussions.

As if on cue with Leigh's thought, Rob said, "We don't have to do this, Bugger. But if anyone's going to touch Leigh, it'll be me."

Frothy foam sprayed from Bugger's mouth.

My God. Is he really rabid?

"No!" Bugger screamed. "You took mine so I get this one."

Rob held his hands out to his sides like a police negotiator. "'Fraid it doesn't work that way."

"Yes it *does*! Ma said so!"

The regression that Leigh had previously observed in the cabin had returned, transforming Bugger into a bratty six-year-old who wasn't getting his way. Rob now played the part of the tolerant adult, patiently explaining to his toddler the golden rule of parenting: *Because I said so.*

"Oh boy," Rob said, an exaggerated amount of exasperation delivered with the phrase. "Is she going to be furious when I tell her about this."

"But she said…"

Leigh couldn't believe what she was hearing. Though she would've sworn it impossible, it seemed she was actually witnessing Rob outsmart someone.

Well, he outsmarted you, didn't he?

The criticism was like a slap to the face. She'd been so mesmerized by the sudden turn of the events that she'd completely ignored the opportunity his presence was creating.

A distraction.

However, it did not take a lengthy examination to realize the building only had one entrance—and it was directly on the other side of the face-off. As involved with one another as they were, Leigh seriously doubted they wouldn't notice if she made a run for the door. The escape attempt of their common prey would be more than enough to make them forget, at least momentarily, about their differences.

No, if she were to make a break for it, the two men would first have to be engaged in physical combat. Bickering back and forth just wasn't going to cut it. But it continued.

"You're going to be in so much trouble," Rob said.

"What?" Bugger slammed his palms against his brow repeatedly. "No, wait! Mama said—"

"But I won't tell her if you put down the knife."

For a moment, it looked as if Bugger was seriously considering Rob's proposition. He glanced down at the blade in his grip as if it had betrayed him, having transformed from a loyal friend to a treacherous enemy that had landed him in a horrible dilemma. But the illusion did not last long as the glint of its metal reflected across his eyes, burning the thought of deception right from his brain.

"No!" He screamed. "You're full of shit."

Hands slapping down on his thighs to show he'd given up, Rob simply replied, "Suit yourself. I'm going to go get her right now."

And then, despite the insanity of the maneuver, Rob turned his back on his psychopathic, knife-wielding cousin, and casually sauntered for the barn's sliding door.

Leigh had as much time to question if Rob had lost his mind as it took to inhale a single breath. The moment it had left her lungs, Bugger was screaming a voice-cracking war cry and sprinting toward Rob's back, his knife ready to do its bloody business.

What a fitting end for a backstabber: a stab in the back.

But just as the tip of the blade was about to puncture the back of his neck, Rob spun, grabbing Bugger's wrist and bringing the furious attack to a screeching halt. Rob used Bugger's own momentum to throw his cousin over his shoulder, hurling him to the dirt.

A cloud of dust accompanied a painful *"oof!"* as Bugger's body impacted the earth at Rob's feet. Despite the sand particles floating in the air, Leigh could see the knife fall from Bugger's grasp when his abrupt landing jarred it free. Rob, too, spotted the loose weapon and immediately sent it flying away with a field goal kick.

Foot still suspended in the air, Rob couldn't defend himself against the tackle that brought him painfully to his knees. Bugger was upon him again, unfazed by his previous tumble.

The two men rolled across the barn floor, tangled like two mutts in an illegal dog fight. This was the moment Leigh been waiting for, the chance to sprint to the door and flee into the forest before either captor knew she was gone.

She scrambled to her feet. Placed one foot in front of another, putting weight on her back toes like a sprinter waiting for the gunshot. Took a deep breath...

And Bugger hurled his opponent away from himself, sending Rob soaring to a patch of ground directly in Leigh's path. Before Leigh could even consider attempting to jump over Rob's body like a track hurdle, Rob was springing to his feet.

A large knife he'd landed next to now in his hand.

It didn't even register at first that Rob was speaking to her when he shouted, "Don't move, Leigh. It's okay now. Everything's under control."

Keeping the blade pointed at his enemy, Rob glanced at Leigh and flashed a reassuring smile. When their eyes met, Leigh was overwhelmed by the pure madness that stoked his stare like burning coals.

He really thinks he's the hero.

What happened next was nothing short of magic. Of the blackest kind.

A circular saw blade appeared in the back of Rob's hand.

There was no way to tell in what order everything took place. It all happened so quickly. Rob screaming out in pain, blood spraying across his lips and cheeks, a jagged disc buried in the flesh of his right hand, the knife dropping to the ground. The only event that Leigh could place in correct sequence was what happened first: Bugger throwing the saw blade with freakish pinpoint accuracy. Who knew where he had been hiding the blade—it certainly hadn't been visible anywhere on his person. It was as he'd pulled it from his sleeve like a master magician. Maybe he had. Thanks to Leigh, his lovely assistant who provided the necessary distraction, no one would ever know.

But now the magic show was over. Whimpering like a fox caught in a trap, Rob gingerly pinched the edge of the saw blade and tried to extricate it from his hand. He didn't even notice Bugger charging at him.

The punch caught him right under his jaw, a perfect, knock-out uppercut. Leigh winced as she heard the sickening crack of Rob's teeth gnashing together, no doubt breaking and slicing the inside of his lip. Bugger connected with such tremendous force that Rob took flight, his airborne route leading him right to a pile of moldy hay. He landed almost silently, the wet straw cushioning his fall like a pillow.

With his enemy dazed, Bugger took his time reclaiming his

knife and walked over to the haystack as if taking a leisurely stroll. Only when Bugger was merely feet away did Rob become aware of his approach, his groans ending and his eyes popping open with fright. He tried to scurry backwards through the damp hay, but the hard wooden wall behind him would allow no further retreat.

Bugger had him trapped.

"Bye-bye, Robbie!"

Perhaps it was the stress—the severe shock of the incessant traumatic events taking toll on her exhausted mind—but her brain just couldn't process information at normal capacity and longer. That had to be reason the scene before Leigh's eyes played out with the speed of a slow motion replay.

Bugger charged, bringing the knife down with all the fury of Hell. Due to the frame-by-frame playback of Leigh's sprained consciousness, she saw with clarity the wooden handle just barely sticking out from the depths of the moist straw. She saw Rob slowly reach for the handle, the fingers of his uninjured left hand gripping it tight. With Bugger no less than two steps away, the muscles in Rob's left bicep hardened as he brought something with considerable weight from underneath the hay, sending strands of straw shooting into the air like confetti. But even with the flying silage impeding Leigh's vision, she immediately discovered what was at the end of that handle.

And so did Bugger when he ran at full speed into the four sharp tines of a farmer's pitchfork.

Leigh flinched at the sight of a quartet of bloody holes appearing in a perfect row across Bugger's back. The holes widened as Rob drove his arm forward, further piercing the fork through his cousin's body. Leigh heard something like a nail being driven through a tin can full of jello as the rusty metal punctured flesh and scraped bone. Over the nauseating sound, Bugger released a short "*Ulck!*" noise from his mouth before staring down at his midsection in complete disbelief. Rob had jabbed him like the last remaining bite of a steakhouse dinner.

As abruptly as it had slowed down, the world regained its speed.
"GRAASHHH!"

The word Bugger screamed through a throat full of liquid
had no meaning short of total rage. Despite being completely
impaled the fork, blood pumping out from the perforations
in his back, Bugger began slashing out with the knife that had
somehow remained in his grip. The blade came so close to Rob's
face that the hair on the side of his head actually danced with
the breeze created by Bugger's swipes. Still, despite the dying
determination to cut his cousin's throat, the long handle of the
pitchfork kept Rob a safe distance from the knife, the swing of
the blade just short of his flesh.

Bugger managed to slice the air six times before his arm
slowed, his eyes rolled back, and the knife finally dropped from
his hand. It disappeared into the straw, a very large needle in
the haystack.

With a heavy grunt, Rob tossed Bugger's dead body to
the side as if he too were made of hay. Springing to his feet
with more energy than Leigh would've thought possible at this
point, Rob delivered one final kick to the corpse's gut.

"Should've thrown the knife at me," he said, gasping for
breath. "Dumbass."

The question hit Leigh the moment Rob looked over at
her, blood oozing from the corner of his maniacal smile.

Why didn't I run?

The answer came effortlessly, its proof still obvious in the
two feet she stood on, still immovably fixed to the floor:

She was literally frozen with fear.

Rob, his bottom lip split open from Bugger's powerful
uppercut, spat thick, red saliva onto the ground and wiped
away the red trail running down his chin. With one, quick tug
and a sharp, excruciating yelp, he yanked out the saw blade still
embedded in his flesh, leaving behind a dark, bleeding gash. As
he painfully walked toward Leigh, Rob brought the hand down
to his waist, wrapping the ragged cut with the bottom of his

t-shirt. Leigh watched the material become dark as the wetness immediately seeped through.

"Are you okay, Leigh?"

Leigh was aware she was backing up, yet again, away from the exit. At least this time she was on her feet, but that fact would become pointless the moment her back reached the wall.

"Get away from me, Rob. Just stay away."

The expression on Rob's face might've been comical in another scenario not nearly as grim. He actually looked hurt by Leigh's words, as if he had done nothing to deserve such a response.

"No, no, it's okay." His hand extended out in reassurance. "It's okay."

"Fuck you!"

Leigh's words came without thought, the tanks of logic within her mind running on empty. She was now solely fueled by emotions, her actions dictated by the factions of fear and anger battling inside her. And it seemed anger had gained the upper hand.

"Fuck you," she repeated. "You've lost your fucking mind. Don't you dare come near me."

Again, Rob seemed perplexed by Leigh's outburst. Had a bystander been witnessing the scene, they would've surely labeled Leigh as crazy and Rob as the stable one trying to reason with her.

"Leigh." Somehow the sereneness in his voice was far more threatening than if he'd were screaming. "You've got it all wrong. My cousin was the crazy one."

He stopped creeping forward.

"I love you, Leigh."

Leigh stopped walking backward.

"What?"

The runaway, crazy train that Leigh had boarded the moment she entered the twisted world of the Cedar family was somehow still picking up speed. Even with everything she'd endured up until this point, Rob had surprised her yet again. His eyes were simultaneously rock solid and chaotically unstable, like a cement foundation built on a fault line. It made it impossible to determine if was speaking with total sincerity or just trying to bait her into another trap.

He must have easily seen the mystification that covered her face like a veil. "It's true. I love you. I always have. And I never wanted to hurt you."

When a hot, wet streak ran down her left cheek, Leigh knew she had begun to cry. The action was strictly unintentional, and though she was experiencing more fear than she'd ever felt in her life, the tears hadn't announced their arrival in the slightest. So now it was official: her authority over any function of her body had been rendered to absolute zero.

"Rob," she whispered. Laryngitis had suddenly claimed her vocal chords. "Just stay back." She wiped away the tears fogging her vision, the looming figure before her warping like an abstract painting.

"I saved you." He took another step towards her. "Bugger was going to hurt you and I stopped him. Now we can be together."

Even more shocking than her own tears were the ones slowly falling down Rob's face, rolling down the sides of his nose and mixing with the blood leaking off his lips. "I don't want to do this anymore." Rob's shoulders jerked as his sobbing intensified, racking his entire body.

A strange sensation tickled the depths of Leigh's gut. It was only a suggestion of an emotion—an incomplete transmission sent from her brain with the weakest signal. But the feeling struck her with just enough force to introduce itself as the most unwelcome guest of all:

Pity.

"I love my family, I really do." Rob's eyes had become nearly as red as the bottom of his stained t-shirt. "But I just can't help them anymore. They'll just have to find another way to get their food, because I'm done with this."

The rubber heel of Leigh's sneaker collided with a barrier behind her.

The wall. She'd run out of room to retreat and now could only stand and face her weeping pursuer, a man who looked like he could just as easily fall to his own knees as strangle every breath of air from her body. However, his last words could not have come at a more opportune time. Maybe Leigh wouldn't need to escape him if she could further encourage his change of heart. All she had to was feed the fire.

"That's…that's good. You don't need to do anything you do want to." As Leigh spoke, she fought the urge to tear her eyes from Rob's glare of madness. She wanted desperately to scan the area for any sort of opening for a getaway, but she knew she couldn't forfeit this chance to earn Rob's trust. And it seemed to be working.

But there was a problem: Rob was still advancing.

He wiped his eyes, a newfound energy springing them open as round as the morning sun still rising in the sky. "Yes!" he practically shrieked, his voice cracking as if he had just reached puberty. "We can be together. We'll leave right now. Just you and me."

Rob's face was inches away from the tip of Leigh's nose. She could smell an odor wafting off of him, a sickening combination of blood and sweat.

The scent of madness.

Leigh's breath came hard, then not at all. It held tight in her lungs, too terrified to share itself with such a deranged man. Leigh was out of room, out of time. Nowhere to go, trapped between a psycho and a hard place. The two halves of her mind had declared an all-out war, logical reasoning versus physical action, in a battle to determine what she did next.

Lash out.
Say something.
Distract him.
Run.

But Leigh could do nothing but stand frozen in place, remaining breathless as Rob reached out for her. Just above a whisper he said, "Take my hand."

Somewhere outside in the forest, the unmistakable throaty squawk of a crow filled the quiet air between the trees. Its cries continued as it flew overhead, calling out for another bird of the blackest feather, a companion to share its darkness.

CHAPTER
TWENTY-FOUR

Samuel Tucker got a bum deal.

That was what it would read on his headstone.

Hands tied to each bedpost with lengths of thickly wound rope, Sam lay face up, stark naked on the queen-sized bed centered in the cabin's bedroom. Unlike the rest of the house, this room was kept surprisingly tidy, the entire space void of clutter or filth. The bed was neatly made, bordered by nightstands supporting unlit kerosene lamps and facing a charming antique bureau. A rocking chair sat in the room's rear left corner, accompanied by an old fashioned record player resting on a roll top desk. The record player looked to be such an early example of the technology that it could easily be an authentic Edison phonograph. Judging by this room alone, as misleading as it may be, one might have referred to this cabin as nothing short of cozy.

Of course, this illusion was broken the moment Sam turned his head to the wall to his right to see the grimacing old woman waiting in her rusted wheelchair. In any other scenario, there would be nothing menacing about the sight at all. But, oh, how much darkness the truth did bring. It transformed the woman from a handicapped senior citizen to the Anti-Christ—though maybe that title was best reserved for the disfigured she-hulk returning to the room with thunderous footsteps. Sam didn't know. It didn't matter. He was going to die very soon. That much he was certain.

The door slowly opened with a prolonged creak. Sam craned his neck upward to see Grizzly, now adorned in a periwinkle nightgown, standing in the threshold. She shyly stared downward at her feet.

"Oh my goodness," her mother said, clasping her hands together. "You look lovely, dear. Doesn't she look lovely?"

Sam didn't have to look at the old woman to know she was speaking to him. "Oh, just beautiful." The words came dry, emotionless.

Clementine groaned, restraint apparent behind her voice in an effort not to upset her daughter. "You don't know how lucky you are." She spun her chair towards Grizzly. "You put the ranger and the hunter back in the cellar?"

Grizzly nodded, her eyes still trained on the floor.

"Good." The wheels of Clementine's chair squeaked as she moved closer to the bed. "Now then, no need to be nervous, darling. Mama will tell you what to do."

The muscles in Sam's buttocks clenched. This was actually going to happen.

He was going to be raped.

But although the physical implications were nothing short of nightmarish, waves of nausea striking him with just the thought of it, worse still were the reasons behind the violation. This demented family wanted his seed. And the moment they had it, it would make Sam a contributor to this fucked up gene pool. This he could not take.

How the hell did I end up here?

A voice within him chuckled at the question. In the strangest, most screwed up way possible, he knew his fate made sense. It was undeserved, unjust, and completely unprecedented, but in the life of Samuel Tucker, that was all just business as usual.

Another day, another shit sandwich.

Had it ended when a foundry accident took his father's life, Sam would've never suspected he'd been dealt such a lousy hand. Sure, he would've loved to have a father past the age of seven, but a single parent home was no reason to turn his life into a sob story. He still had his mother, and that made him far more fortunate than a lot of children in the world. So no games of catch in the backyard, but life went on.

Until his mother's death when he was fifteen. He'd never liked the guy she'd been seeing at the time. Sam never spotted any bruises on her mother's arms or had to overhear horrendous shouting matches, but the man simply reeked of deceit. He borrowed money never to be returned, stayed out late without explanation, and every time Sam caught his eye, he was always greeted with the same perpetual smile that the dirtbag wore like a Halloween mask. So really, it came as no surprise when he killed himself and Sam's mother in a drunk driving accident. A soul crushing tragedy that poisoned Sam with hate and anger for the next three years—yes, but was it surprising? As much as it pained him to say it, Sam could admit that his mother had been playing with fire. Only he had gotten burned as well.

But even still, Sam didn't find it possible to feel too sorry for himself. Thanks to a mother who'd raised him right and a father who'd left him enough to pay expenses, Sam was able to further his education after high school. And even at the young age of twenty-two, Sam knew such an advantage made him fortunate, despite everything else.

But you can't escape a bad sign you're born under, can you?

Because in a roundabout, indirect fashion, choosing to enroll in those college courses was what had landed him here: helplessly buck naked and surrounded by lunatics who planned to murder him and eat his corpse. To think that if he had kept falling further into the rebellious troublemaking of his early teen years, the worst place he could have ended up would've been prison. At this point, the idea of a jail cell was looking like a four star hotel.

If I hadn't decided to go to school.
If I hadn't needed a ride back to campus.
If I hadn't gotten in that GOD DAMN VAN.
No.

He would never regret climbing aboard that vehicle full of drug-smuggling college kids for one simple reason:

It had brought him to Leigh.

Leigh...

There was no way of knowing for certain, but the odds were she was already dead. Since he could do nothing to help her, he prayed the sicko who dragged her outside had made it quick—nothing like what he was about to endure. Though she had once thought of him as a traitor, as a fucking *bad guy* for crying out loud, Sam could take solace in knowing that she had realized the truth before she was forever taken from him. As suspicious as some of his acquired survival skills might've seemed in the wrong light, they had only been derivatives of a self-reliant lifestyle. Before the end, Leigh had come to see that Sam wasn't a criminal or an evil-doer or a mistreated monster waiting to get revenge on a cold, cruel world.

Let the record show Samuel Tucker was a good guy.

Though the journey into his thoughts had proven a temporary escape, reality returned in its full ugliness as Sam realized both Grizzly and Mother Clementine were looming over him. They were staring at his crotch.

Grizzly grunted, the sound laced with inquisition. Her mother leaned forward, straightening her round spectacles to get a better look. In the microsecond it took for Sam to blink his eyes, Clementine's expression had turned from one of puzzlement to pure rage.

"Oh, for God's sake," she said. "Get it up, damnit!"

Sam slowly looked to the area of his body that currently held the attention of everyone else in the room. His eyes were greeted with the sight of his penis lying across the flesh under his belly button, as limp as a drowned earthworm. At first he didn't get it, his mind too exhausted to immediately understand. But after darting his eyes back and forth between the menacing women and his wilted organ, he finally comprehended the situation.

These crazy bitches needed him to get an erection.

Fear seized his insides, squeezing some part of him deep inside his gut and bringing sharp cramps to his abdominals. What they were asking was impossible.

"I can't." Sam's voice came out as a pitifully weak whimper.

Just as he was beginning to consider the consequences of not following through with the old woman's order, a ground-shaking thump rattled the floor, the vibrations running up the bed frame and into Sam's bones.

Grizzly was stomping the floor.

"God damn you!" Clementine shouted over the thumping of her daughter. "Make it work! Now!"

The fear wrapped around Sam's heart like a boa constrictor suddenly loosened, replaced by the contempt of an emasculated man.

"Listen!" The volume of Sam's shout surprised even himself. "I can't do it with you standing there watching me."

The boney, vein-covered arms of the maniacal matriarch folded across her chest.

"Well, I ain't leavin' you alone with my daughter. I know your type. You like to play rough, don't you?"

What the fuck is she talking about?

"So start doing your job or I'll cut it off!"

Sam had known it was just a matter of time until that exact threat reared its ugly head. Castration would, of course, prevent any chance of him performing his half of the dirty deed, but Sam had no doubts that Clementine wouldn't think twice about reaching for a knife.

Sam craned his head away from the chair-bound witch and the ugly-as-sin daughter. He'd never been less aroused in all his life, and if he were to have any chance to excite himself, he could not spare even half a glance at his hideous captors.

In order to pull this off, he'd have to become nothing less than a Zen master—separate his mind from his body. Drift off to somewhere far, far away where a banquet of beautiful, voluptuous naked women waited to please him.

Just use something as a focal point. Don't look away from it and concentrate on the dirtiest thing you can imagine.

Sam's eyes landed on the pile of his own clothes lying on the floor at the base of the bed. By keeping his field of vision limited to the mound of laundry, Sam used the image to imagine they were discarded in his own bedroom. A young Jenna Jameson had just ripped them off his body before binding his wrists to the bedposts. She was teasing him now, gently licking the flesh of his inner thighs, just barely brushing her tongue against his balls. He so desperately wanted her to take him in her mouth, to swallow the entire length of his shaft that had become as long and thick as that red stick that stuck out from the pocket of his discarded jeans.

What the fuck?

Sam had just begun to feel his loins awakening when the sight of an out-of-place object shattered his fantasy to pieces. Sam lifted his head from the pillow, straining to get a better look at the item on the floor directly underneath his left shoulder. The tip of a faded red rod poked out from under his crumpled jacket.

A stick of dynamite.

The scene flashed before his mind's eye. Leigh was just about to light the dynamite's fuse, but Sam snatched it from her grasp just in time.

And then slid it into his pocket.

"Boy, you got until the count of three to get ready for action!"

Sam whipped his back to face the snarling old lady.

"Wait! I can do it. I just need my right hand, okay?"

Clementine stared at him suspiciously.

"It has nothing to do with your daughter. Your daughter's gorgeous. I just always need to use my hand, no matter who

I'm with. I'm serious."

She continued to stare, unblinking, her expression impossible to read.

"Just untie my hand, all right?" Sam glanced over to Grizzly and winked. "I'll make this happen."

After the longest five seconds of Sam's life, Clementine turned to Grizzly and nodded. The brute shuffled over to Sam's side, an old fashioned barber's razor in her hand. A moment later, Sam's right wrist was free.

"Thank you," Sam said, rotating his wrist to get the feeling back in his hand. "Now just give me half a second and we'll be in business."

He rolled over onto his side away from them, bringing his free hand to his groin.

And began pumping.

Even with the furious jerking, Sam's penis remained lifeless in his grip. But this was of no concern as he stared at the dynamite stick, trying to gauge its distance. He was almost certain he could reach it now with his loose hand. However, he knew Clementine and Grizzly were both staring at his back and would notice if he stopped his charade and reached for the stick.

He would need a distraction.

"How's it goin', boy?"

"Getting there," Sam answered, peering back over his shoulder. "But, um…"

Here goes nothing.

"Would you mind putting on some music?"

As expected, Sam was answered with a moment of stunned silence followed by Clementine muttering, "Come again?"

Sam cleared his throat. "Well, I was just thinking, it's your daughter's first time, right? I just thought some music might make things a little bit more romantic. I find it always helps me." He nodded his chin towards the ancient record player.

"Oh, hush! She don't need music and neither do you. Now come on!"

His shoulders fell slack with Clementine's response, pushed down by the weight of failure. It had been worth a try, but it had also been his only idea. Even if he had the mental strength left to think of another ruse, he doubted he had the time.

Sam stopped touching himself. What was the point? It wasn't going to work. All he could do was close his eyes and wait. So he did.

From the darkness of his closed lids he heard a sound, something that was part moan, part snarl. It had come from Grizzly's mouth, no doubt a protest to Sam's lack of participation. Another threat from her mother would come at any moment now. Or maybe not. Maybe she'd just go straight to the cutting.

It was only when the mother did speak that Sam realized Grizzly hadn't been snarling at him.

"Now honey, I didn't mean you don't deserve romance, I just—"

Grizzly once again slammed the ground with her foot, the bed frame dancing across the wooden floorboards.

"Okay, okay!" Clementine released the brake of her wheelchair. "If it'll help make this special for you, I'll put a record on."

More squeaking from the chair's rusty wheels. The old woman was moving away towards the phonograph.

Grizzly, however, hadn't budged and couldn't seem to take her eyes off her gentleman caller.

Please, God...

"Well, come pick one out if you want it so badly."

With the obedience of a well-behaved child, Grizzly lumbered over to her mother's side. Both of them hunched over a wooden crate of vinyl records. They did not see Sam whip his hand down to the floor and snatch up the dynamite—his speed matched that of a crocodile snagging a baby antelope who wandered too close to a murky river's edge. There had been just enough time to stuff the stick under the bed's top sheet before the crackle of needle on vinyl filled the room.

"Ah, Billie Holiday," Clementine said with a sigh. "Excellent choice."

Over pops and snaps of the vinyl's cracks and dust, the soul singer crooned, "*Crazy he calls me...*"

"Isn't that lovely?" The old woman began to wheel herself back over to the side of the bed.

Sam shrugged. "It's no 'Sexual Healing,' but it'll do."

The bed shook as Clementine's chair collided with its sideboard. Sam could see her shadow towering over his body and onto the floor before him. Though he knew she was sitting on the other side of the mattress, Sam could swear he could feel her sour breath blowing down the backside of his neck.

"Roll over and face me, boy. It's show time."

Sam tensed, the entire room becoming silent except for Billie Holiday's tearful lyrics.

"*The impossible will take a little while...*"

He couldn't roll over to face them. Not yet. There was still one more thing that needed to be done first, one more miracle that needed to be answered.

After a long, deep breath to steady his nerves, Sam closed his eyes and said, "Uh yeah, I'm just about ready to go. But I think we're missing some candlelight."

"No!" Clementine's response came so quickly it practically cut off Sam's last word. "There'll be no more stalling."

"I just thought your daughter would like some—"

"I said that's enough!"

This time Sam didn't even get the chance to be disappointed by the old woman's denial of his request. Grizzly was already stomping her feet and letting out a string of frenzied moans. Her whining came high-pitched and liquidly, the combined vocalization of a sparrow/sow hybrid.

Before her mother could offer a placating explanation or a scolding demand to stop her hysterics, Grizzly was pacing over to the bureau near the door and grabbing something that rattled in her hand. Sam peered over his shoulder to spot a box of matches in her grip, which she slammed into the chest of her elderly mother.

Clementine looked down at the box of matches and back up to her daughter. "Now don't listen to him. He's only trying to…"

This time it was Clementine's turn to be interrupted. The sound piercing from Grizzly's lips could only be compared to that of a boiling tea kettle. She banged her fists against her misshaped forehead, yanking at the dirty clumps of her sparsely haired scalp.

"Okay, fine!" Clementine dropped the matchbox into her lap and reached for her wheels. "Quit your wailing and I'll light the lamp by the bed. Lord have mercy."

"Yeah, that'll be great!" Sam pretended to be as enthusiastic as possible as he gave Grizzly a flirtatious wink. She flashed a smile missing its two front teeth, and clapped her hands like a little girl delighted at a puppet show.

Grizzly moved aside to let her mother pass as she wheeled around to the other side of the bed, rolling right over the heap of Sam's clothes. With her chair mere inches away, Sam made sure to keep a hand over his crotch to hide his still nonexistent erection.

Clementine's bony, arthritic hands drew a match and struck the box's flint with a surprising amount of strength. She removed the lamp's glass chimney and brought the flame to its thick, cotton wick. It ignited instantly, filling the room with a soft, flickering glow. It reflected off the lenses of the woman's glasses, making her look even more like a visiting tourist from Hell.

"I can't believe I'm going through all this trouble," she said, extinguishing the match with a shake of her wrist. "Guess it just shows you how much I love my daughter."

A thin, grey tendril of smoke snaked its way from the match's burnt head into Sam's nose. There was something oddly pleasant about its scent. It simply might've been its innate state of being in this world spun completely out-of-control—its existence the natural reaction to an action before it. This was the smell of order. Of logical progression. Fire gives you smoke, every single time. If only the rest of world worked in such an objective formula. A good man gets a good life.

But there is no force more subjective than nature. Sam was living proof of that.

"Well, you're a wonderful mother," he said, brandishing his most obsequious smile.

The woman scoffed, a scowl accompanying the sound. "Now don't you think flattery's going to get you anywhere. As soon your job's done here, I'm gonna turn your meat into jerky." She leaned forward, her vinegary breath overpowering any lingering trace of the sulfuric smoke. She bore her teeth in a grin of total malevolence, so close Sam could see the wiry white hairs that bordered her upper lip.

"You'll be your child's first meal away from the tit."

Sam tilted his body as forward as the binding ropes would allow. All pretense drained from his smile, replaced by a sincere frankness.

"The things we do for our children."

Through the reflective lenses of her glasses, Sam could see Clementine's ashy, clouded eyes actually widen with surprise.

No. pretense

With *revelation.*

The speed of a camera's shutter wouldn't have even been able to capture the moment. But Sam saw it. The twitch of her eyebrow, the quiver of her bottom lip. All reactions to the only thought that could falter a dominator's poise.

Something isn't right.

Now!

His hand flew from his crotch with the speed of a striking cobra. Sam didn't feel the weight of the chair nor the woman sitting in it when he pushed out as hard as he could. The nerves of his fingers didn't have time to register the cool touch of the chair's metal frame, nor the flaky rust that rubbed his skin. Before those sensory signals could even reach his brain, Clementine was already rolling backward, propelled by Sam's mighty shove. She slammed into the wall behind her, the kinetic force repelling back into her body and sending her forward onto the floor.

As much pleasure as the sight would've brought, Sam couldn't spare any time to see her withered frame plummet to the ground, falling into a heap not unlike his own clothes. He was already reaching into the sheets for the dynamite, his fingers gripping the prize like the sword in the stone. Nor did he hear the end of her descent, her body landing on the floor with the loud snap of a breaking bone. His conscious thoughts had come together into a single, unbreakable notion. Nothing else existing but the one goal he focused on with fanatical commitment.

Reach the flame.

He stretched out his arm towards the uncovered, burning wick of the lantern.

And then Grizzly was upon him.

The only thing stopping her from crushing his skull into a pulpy mound of blood and brains was the foot he'd thrown up between their colliding bodies. She was impossibly heavy, as if her blinding rage actually contributed to her physical weight. Her uncountable pounds pushed down on Sam's bent leg, driving his bony kneecap into his chin. A distant part of his mind was aware his hamstring was literally snapping under the pressure. But pain did not deliver the message.

He could feel nothing of the injury that would've crippled an Olympian athlete. Nor could he could feel the putrid air of Grizzly's breath that blew from her screaming mouth like a jet engine, nor the hot, viscous drool that landed on his forehead and ran over the bridge of his nose.

Reach the flame.

"Get'em, Grizzly! Kill the bastard!"

In spite of her numb, useless legs and the fractures of several brittle bones, Clementine Cedar found the strength to crawl across the floor towards the bed. Using only her spindly, skeleton arms, she dragged herself closer and closer.

Reach the flame.

His arm trembled. The fuse of the dynamite danced over the tip of the lantern's wick, teasing to ignite but not sparking to life. Perspiration dripped into Sam's eyes, his glowing target blurring through the lens of sweat. His shoulders cramped, the strength of a bear trap's jaws biting into his muscles.

He wouldn't be able to hold his position much longer. In the fight between the demands of the body and the orders of the mind, the body always won sooner or later.

A sudden powerful force rocked his vision. Grizzly was lashing out with her Sasquatch-sized fists. And although Sam's legs kept her from delivering full force, her blows still dizzied his focus. But the punch brought more than a warm, torrent of blood from his nose.

It brought clarity. Sam knew what he had to do.

He relaxed his legs. All of Grizzly's crushing weight landed on his chest, pushing every breath of air from his lungs. Her thick, calloused hands immediately found his throat.

But he didn't need oxygen to finish his task. To cease the spasms causing his hand to quaver above the lantern, he needed to relieve the physical stress on his legs. Now, even with the coming darkness of asphyxiation, his hand was as steady as a surgeon's.

"Crazy he calls me..."

The fuse ignited.

Sam spun, catching a glimpse of Clementine directly below him as she crawled over the pile of his clothes. With Grizzly's bulbous nose touching his, he brought the dynamite forward, its fuse raining light like a fourth of July sparkler. Head ready to explode from blood pressure, vision blackening with every passing second, Sam gritted his smiling teeth—

And slammed the stick of dynamite so far into the Grizzly's open mouth that he felt its end jab into the back of her throat.

She looked down at the sparking fuse protruding from her cracked lips, disbelief raising the hairless brows above her black eyes. Her stare darted back up to Sam.

Who blew her a kiss.

"Suck it, bitch."

Samuel Tucker never got the chance to flip-off the foundry owner whose failure to comply with safety standards robbed him of a father. Nor he did he ever get the chance to slug the face of the deadbeat who'd taken his mother on a one-way ride. But on that morning, in the bedroom of a cabin in the woods, Samuel Tucker finally got even with the world.

The explosion destroyed the entire room and everything in it, the justice denied him in life finally arriving with his death.

Paid in full.

CHAPTER
TWENTY-FIVE

"What the hell?"

Rob turned toward the sound of the explosion that shook the ground. He'd been seconds away from grasping Leigh's hand when the blast occurred. From the corner of her eye, Leigh could see the mallet to her left during Rob's entire advance, but his unwavering stare had not allowed her any chance to reach for the weapon.

Then the entire world outside the barn was apparently blown to smithereens. The detonation claimed Rob's attention, the distraction lasting only a moment.

But it was long enough.

With the blast still echoing against the trees trunks, Leigh darted her hand to her left, not daring enough to take her eyes from Rob's preoccupied face. As Rob's brow furrowed with concern, Leigh's fingers searched the surface of the worktable.

Come on. Come on. Find it.

Something smooth and cylindrical found its way under the crook of her knuckles. When Leigh wrapped her hands around the wooden shaft, she could feel a significant weight pulling down on one end and knew she'd located her prize.

It was not a moment too soon.

His gaze trailing behind, Rob slowly turned back to her. "Come on, Leigh, let's go see what—"

Leigh swung the hammer with all her strength, making direct contact with the Rob's right cheek bone. Harsh vibrations stung her palm as it connected with the hard patch of skull under Rob's eye, sending tremors all the way up her arm. But Leigh barely felt it, her attention focused entirely on the sight of Rob slouching to the left and falling to the ground.

If she had drawn blood, she didn't see it. In fact, she had no idea at all how badly she'd injured him. Leigh was already sprinting towards the barn's door, not taking a second glance at her slumping enemy.

At first, her legs seemed to rebel against her, refusing to operate as quickly as her mind demanded. Fear and stress had taken their toll, seizing her muscles with incapacitating cramps.

But the instinct to survive would not be denied. It overpowered any resisting forces within Leigh's body, ordering her protesting nerves to shut their screaming mouths. Only one thought repeated itself over and over in her mind.

Please let him be unconscious.

It would be another prayer unanswered.

Over the pounding of her feet on the ground and the heart in her chest, Leigh could just barely make out Rob's voice behind her. At first, his voice came out weak, almost groggy, as if he had just awoken from an afternoon nap.

"*Leigh…*"

The next sound she heard as she reached the barn's heavy door was as different as night is to day. Again, it was Rob's voice, but now he didn't sound hindered at all.

He was pissed.

"LEEEIGGHHH!!!"

Had she had the courage to glance over her shoulder, Leigh wouldn't have been surprised to find Rob transformed into a snarling werewolf. His voice sounded guttural, feral, the sound of pure rage. Whatever haze he'd suffered from Leigh's blow to the head had completely vanished, replaced with the utter urge to kill.

"Get back here!"

Leigh could practically hear his vocal chords ripping to shreds. "You BITCH!"

If the door had been closed an inch more, Leigh wouldn't have been able to deftly slip through the slim crack without pausing to push it open. As it were, she was able to turn her body sideways and force herself through the opening, her shoulders scraping the splintered wood.

The slam behind her suggested Rob's body was too large to do the same.

Leigh found herself blinded by the sun the moment she stepped outside. She put her hand up to shield her eyes and that was when she saw it: half of the cabin blown away, jet-black smoke billowing from the flaming crater.

Sam...

A thunderous slam of wood hitting wood cracked behind her. She looked back to see Rob ripping the entrance of the barn open, the sliding door almost flying off its hinges.

Leigh didn't know what scared her more—the bloodthirsty smile on Rob's face or the black iron blade of the massive ax in his hands.

For the second time in just as many minutes, the destroyed cabin bought Leigh precious time. Rob couldn't help but look over at the explosion's aftermath when the corner of his eye caught the flicker of the flame.

"Jesus Christ," he muttered to no one in particular, his eyes seemingly hypnotized by the burning timber.

Leigh's legs acted entirely on their own, anticipating the request that was just about to arrive.

Run.

The cool morning air chilled the perspiration glazing her skin as she took off into the woods. Branches whipped across the tender skin of her cheeks and chin, leaving red scratches.

Leigh did not need to look back or even hear his footsteps to know Rob was right behind her. While the curtains of leaves and tangled arms of the tree branches impeded her progress with every blinding flash of green and brown, Rob knew how to dodge the obstacles the forest put before him. He'd been in these woods many times. Maybe even played this same game of cat-and-mouse with a past victim. This idea became more and more probable as he closed the gap.

"I gave you a chance," he said, his voice even closer than Leigh had assumed. "I could've made you happy."

Leigh darted ninety degrees to her right, zigzagging between the thick underbrush. She'd once seen a nature documentary about how some prey escape predators by quickly changing direction and catching their pursuer off guard. She didn't know she was able to recall such information at time like this, but she didn't question it.

Leigh looked back, trying to catch a glimpse of Rob's location, but there was no sign of him. She could still hear him though, his panting breath and the snapping twigs under his shoes seemingly coming from every direction.

And then he was upon her.

Strong fingers caught her ankle, buckling her knees and sending her to the forest floor below. Leigh clenched her eyes shut in painful anticipation—not of the abrupt landing, but the fall of the rusty ax that would immediately follow.

"Watch your step, Leigh!"

Her eyes sprang open. Rob's voice was still a few feet away.

Leigh looked down at her feet to see a tree root wrapped around her ankle in a lover's embrace. A short distance beyond her tangled foot, a drape of branches and brush parted to reveal a heavily sweating, ax-bearing maniac.

Rob stopped in his tracks upon spotting her. Through the growing edema that swelled from his right cheek bone, Leigh could still see the whites of his insanely wide eyes. Dark streaks smeared the handle of the axe, blood from his hand wound running against the grain of the wood. The dirt, grime, and dried blood that darkened his face made the teeth of his mad grin appear even brighter.

Rob took a step forward. There was probably no point to keep running. Rob was far too close now to ever escape him. Any attempt to get away would be a waste of time. It made more sense to just get it over with and not drag out her tormented end any longer.

But she ran.

Leigh ripped her foot from the tangled root and made for the evergreen stand ahead. Even if his axe would be on her any second now, it would be better not to see it coming.

A long bough of a pine tree stretched out exactly in her eye line. Raising her hand, Leigh pushed the branch aside, the flexible soft wood bending but not breaking with her push.

Behind her, Rob hoisted the ax over his head.

Leigh took one last leaping step.

And the pine branch shot back like a whip, slicing Rob directly across the eyes.

"Fuck!" Rob screamed, the pain bringing his hand to his brow and halting his pursuit. The whipping branch had momentarily blinded him just before he was about to end the chase. Now he could only rub his eyes and wait for his vision to return.

Leigh continued to bound over fallen logs and moss-covered stones. The thrashing tree limb had been nothing short of a gift from God. Or maybe just a little help from Mother Nature. Whoever had aided her escape wasn't important. All that mattered was that Leigh had another chance to survive this nightmare, and the feeling that fate was on her side rejuvenated her exhausted lungs and legs with the fuel of hope.

A moment later when God reached down and plucked her into the sky, she realized just how wrong she'd been. God had chosen a side.

And it wasn't hers.

Leigh bobbed in the air four times before she understood what had happened. The clutches that squeezed her left ankle and dangled her six feet above the ground hadn't been sent from the heavens. It was merely the business end of a snare trap, a rope that stretched from a tree branch high above.

And Leigh wasn't going anywhere.

Whimpering as she struggled to reach the loop around her ankle, Leigh choked on her own breath when she saw the upside-down image of Rob leisurely strolling up to her side.

"Well, hello there," he said, the ax casually resting on his shoulder. "It appears I caught something. But what strange species is this?"

Long, hot streams of tears ran over Leigh's eyebrows and into her hair. She could feel the blood rushing to her head, dizzying her vision.

"Wait! Rob! Don't!" Her hands shot forward as if they could do anything to stop his attack.

Rob chuckled as he brought the axe off his shoulders and into his hands. "Look at this. It talks!"

"You don't want to do this, Rob."

"Of course I do." Rob squeezed the axe's handle, twisting the wood in his sweaty palms. "I mean, what else am I going to have for dinner?"

Leigh's mouth ran on autopilot, frantically blabbering in a last desperate effort to save her own life. "I'm sorry, Rob. I was wrong to attack you. We should be together, I see that now."

Rob inhaled as if to speak another sarcastic remark, but instead froze with Leigh's last comment. She saw the hesitation in his eyes and it brought forth more words.

"It's true. Please forgive me, I was scared before. But now it's all so clear. You and I are the same. We should be together."

He smiled at the sound of that, the aggression just barely leaving his eyes as he stared downward to the ground, his mind seemingly lost in space.

"I'm sorry, Rob. I'm so sorry. I made a mistake, but it'll

never happen again."

Looking up from under his eyebrows, Rob bared his most ghoulish grin yet. Satan himself would've envied the evil behind the smile.

"No," he said, lifting the axe into the air. "It won't happen again."

Leigh wanted to shut her eyes, but fear propped them open like a door jamb. She could do nothing but watch as Rob brought the axe behind him, winding himself up to deliver a decapitating swing.

Here it comes.

The axe had completed half of its journey towards her head when Leigh suddenly plummeted to the ground, her descent accompanying the explosive crack of a gunshot.

Rob passed over her crumpled body, the momentum of his swing twisting his body in a complete three-hundred-and-sixty degree rotation. He'd called his shot, swung for the fences, and connected with nothing but air. He'd hadn't even brushed the frayed end of the severed rope that hung above his head.

Leigh looked up from the heap she lay in at Rob's feet. The same confusion that claimed her expression doubled itself on Rob's face. She knew he must be thinking the same thing: Had he missed and sliced the rope? No, it was impossible. Even if he'd swung a little high, the axe would've buried itself into Leigh's chest or stomach. Something else had broken the rope.

The gunshot.

A twig snapped behind her. Rob looked up from Leigh, surprise widening his eyes. With a strange, out-of-place airiness he might've used if a salesman had knocked on his front door, Rob asked, "What do *you* want?"

A second later, he got his answer.

Leigh shrieked as blood shot out the back of Rob's head, the explosion of a second gunshot echoing through the morning air. The final, puzzled look on Rob's face remained frozen in his features—the wideness of his remaining eyeball, the half-open position of his mouth. The ax fell from his limp grip, landing inches away from Leigh's hip. Wobbling in the air as if denying his own demise, Rob followed, collapsing to the ground.

He landed facing Leigh, the blank stare of his only eye looking directly into both of hers. She found she couldn't breathe as she stared into the black, quarter sized hole that oozed the last of its blood. Part of her expected an evil spirit to crawl from the small void and make its escape, or maybe a slug-like parasite that had controlled Rob's actions all along.

But no such thing occurred. The man lying next to her was only a fresh corpse, a lifeless body that could never harm anyone ever again. Still, she found she couldn't take her eyes away from his, even when the stranger slowly approached on foot.

Above her, she heard a man's voice say, "Miss? Are you okay? Can you hear me?"

The sunlight backlighting the figure above her turned his form into a dark silhouette. Though she could not see his face, when he knelt down to examine her, a nametag on his right breast pocket became easily legible.

Jacob Spire.

It would be the last thing Leigh would see for awhile. She closed her eyes, her consciousness slipping away. Warm, gentle fingers lightly touched her neck, looking for a pulse. Feeling a human touch that didn't want to harm her was the final comforting nudge that led Leigh to pass out.

So when the man said, "We're going to get you out of here. Everything's going to be fine," she thought she was already dreaming.

CHAPTER
TWENTY-SIX

Leigh could've sworn the minute hand was actually ticking backwards as she stared at the clock resting on the wall above the blackboard. She'd long stopped listening to Professor Henderson drone on about the case of Williams vs. the State of Maine, her mind far too preoccupied to focus on any lecture. There were only three minutes left until the class concluded, but they'd somehow extended themselves to fit what felt like half an hour. Normally, Leigh wouldn't have nearly as anxious to leave the classroom, as she usually took her time colleting her things and looking over her last assignment.

But today was different.

Today was their one-year anniversary. And she knew Sam would already be waiting for her when she returned to her room.

Just as she was considering grabbing her bag and marching out behind Henderson's turned back, the professor spun from the chalkboard, clapped his hands, and proclaimed the discussion to be finished.

"Class dismissed. Enjoy your weekend."

Leigh couldn't remember grabbing her bag, rushing through the classroom door, or even leaving the building. In fact, her entire trip across the UVM campus to the door of

Hamilton dormitory was all a blur.

Skipping a leisurely ride up the elevator, the three flights of stairs proved no challenge today. Even with a bag full of textbooks weighing her down, Leigh felt as light as air itself being blown up the stairwell.

And then she was at her door.

Leigh brushed back her air, removed her glasses, took a deep breath, and entered her room.

As usual, she was greeted by the poster of Johnny Depp that hung above her bed. But today she was not interested in the movie star, as attractive as he might be dressed as a swashbuckling pirate. Today, nothing could distract her from the man hiding beneath her sheets and comforter.

"I see you under there," she said, taking the strap of her book bag off her shoulder. She threw the bag haphazardly onto the desk that sat on the opposite wall, kicked off her shoes, and prepared to pounce on her blanket covered lover.

"Make room!" she said, taking a step forward.

It was the only step she would take.

Something was wrong.

No—everything was wrong.

Her desk didn't sit against the wall across from her bed. It had always been at the foot of her bed, bordered by her cabinet refrigerator. Something else was supposed to occupy the space where her desk rested now, something that changed the entire layout of the room.

A second bed.

Alex's bed.

But Alex is dead…

Though the light bulb above her cast the room with its sixty-watt luminescence, the room now seemed much darker. It was as if the light were being filtered through a black curtain, darkness trickling through the air like underwater blood from a shark bite.

Leigh slowly turned back to the hidden mass underneath the bed covers. She didn't know what was going on, but she

THE REMEDY

knew Sam would make everything all right. He always did.

She pulled back the blanket. The sheets followed.

Leigh could feel herself screaming—the air rushing from her lungs, the tendons in her neck tightening, threatening to snap. But she could hear nothing, as if her life had instantly transformed into a silent movie. The only sense still functioning was her sight, and she wished it too had been taken from her.

The fungus-engulfed head and shoulders of Eliza rested on her pillow like a bloody patch of mushrooms, a severed stump of flesh leaking red and green fluids that ran together into a sickly shade of brown.

Something behind her cracked with volatile ferocity as the noise of the world came crashing back into her ears. Leigh spun towards the sound just in time to see the wood of her door splinter into a ragged gash. The wound was immediately followed by another as something hard and sharp continued to crash against the door.

Leigh looked down to her shoes when she realized she couldn't move them an inch. Despite her desire to flee, her traitorous feet refused to budge. She was frozen. Stuck.

Trapped.

A final scrap of sliced wood flew from the door to complete a gaping hole. A familiar face grinned at Leigh through the jagged portal.

Rob.

"Don't worry about her," he said, using the blade of his massive ax to point at what was left of Eliza. He stared at Leigh with his only eye, the other empty socket glowing with a blinding, crimson light. "She's out of the picture."

Leigh looked away, hoping she could find anything she could use to defend herself. But nothing was within her reach, her room now impossibly empty. The only thing that still remained was her dorm room's single window. But instead of her third floor view of Hamilton's parking lot, all she could see through the glass was trees.

261

Dark, endless trees.

She was back in the forest.

Leigh released an almost inaudible whimper as her lungs locked with fright. She'd turned from the window to find Rob's face an inch from her nose. This close up, she could see right into the wound of his eye. Green tendrils of mold crawled out from the hole, as if they were living snakes reaching for Leigh's tender flesh.

"They're all dead," she moaned.

"Yes," Rob whispered, bringing the axe above his head. "Now we can be together."

Again, Leigh tried to cry out. And although she could hear the sound that escaped her mouth this time, it wasn't a scream.

It was rhythmic, gentle, machine-like.

And it followed her into the next world.

Beep. Beep. Beep.

Upon waking, Leigh didn't have the slightest clue as to where she was. But wherever she had been taken, she could tell the moment her eyes fluttered open that it was warm, comfortable.

Safe.

Taupe-colored walls bordered her on all sides. A television high on the wall across her from her showed a daytime talk show, its volume muted. The window to her left let in soft rays of light that ran across her face and reflected off a panel of machines to her right. One of these machines included a narrow, green screen where a line would jump every second or so.

Beep. Beep. Beep.

A heart monitor. Leigh was in a hospital.

As if she needed further proof, a tube sticking out from a bandage on her wrist ran upward to a bag of clear liquid suspended above her head. It was when Leigh traced the I.V.

trail with her eyes that she noticed the man standing at the door, peeking out into the hallway through the partially open crack. The white doctor's coat adorned his upper torso.

"Hello?" Leigh couldn't believe the weakness of her own voice, or how much strength it took to mutter a single word.

The doctor turned from the door and shut it, a smile instantly forming on his face when he discovered his patient awake.

"Ms. Swanson," he said with a tranquil tone. "I'm so pleased to have you back with us."

The doctor walked over to the side of her bed, his shoes sounding an impressive *clomp* with every step. Though her vision still blurred with drowsiness, Leigh could make out his dark hair and slight five o'clock shadow. He was much younger than she expected.

"Where am I?" she said, attempting to straighten herself against the wall behind her. But when every muscle in her back throbbed with an ache that reverberated down her legs, it cancelled any plans of sitting up.

"Please relax, Ms. Swanson." The doctor placed a gentle hand on her shoulder. "You're in Saint Andrews hospital on the outskirts of Embry, Vermont. You were transported to this facility immediately after you were found."

"Found?"

The doctor looked up to examine the bag of intravenous fluids, but something about his uncomfortable stature suggested he was trying to avoid eye contact. "Yes, miss. I'm sorry to say you were an unfortunate victim of physical assault." He tapped the bag and watched the liquid drip down. "Things might seem a little hazy at the moment but your memory will start to clear up as you get your bearings."

Leigh clenched the sheets in her fists turning her knuckles a bloodless white. Like the ax-wielding Rob of her nightmare, memories began to tear down the door of her consciousness.

The chase through the woods.

The snare trap.

The man with the rifle.

"I…" she began to say, having to stop to swallow through her dry throat. "I remember. Someone saved me."

The doctor nodded. "That would be Mr. Jacob Spire, a ranger of the Forest Service. Apparently, his department found a note requesting immediate assistance in the area you were found."

The note. The one Rob wrote to lure poor Douglas Graham to the chopping block. He'd replaced the one Sam had written.

"Sam…" Leigh whispered.

The doctor adjusted the collars of his coat. "Excuse me?"

"Where's Sam? Is he okay?"

Staring down at her, eyebrows bent with confusion, the doctor opened his mouth to answer but then hesitated, as if searching for the right words. Finally, he said, "I'm afraid I'm not sure who exactly you're talking about. With the exception of your assailant, whom Mr. Spire was forced to take down, you were found alone.

He turned a shoulder, making his way to the foot of her bed where her chart sat in a plastic sleeve. As he walked away, Leigh heard him mutter, "Although the police did discover the…remains…of bodies found in a nearby cabin home. I gather there was a quite an explosion."

Tears wanted to leak from her eyes. She could feel their pleas to be released. But a combination of fatigue and an overwhelming sense of numbness prevented her from crying a single drop. It may have been the painkillers pumping through her circulatory system, but Leigh found all she could do in response to Sam's demise was mumble, "No. No. No."

Whether he didn't hear her or was just pretending not to, the doctor plucked her chart from its sleeve and said, "That's all I know. But there are police officers in the lobby who'll be able to tell you more. In fact, they're very eager to speak with you. But I made it clear to them that I wouldn't have anyone bothering you until you felt you were completely up to it. So feel free take your time. They can wait."

Leigh could hardly hear what he was saying. At best she caught every other word. Images of her horrible nightmare were returning to distract her. The trees surrounding her room, their branches scraping the window.

I'm still in the woods.

"They're all dead."

The doctor cleared his throat, shifting his weight from one foot to the other. "Well, the good news," he said, "is that, in spite of everything you've been through, you miraculously suffered very little physical damage. With the exception of a few bumps on the head and a variety of light scratches…"

He pointed to a bandage on Leigh's arm that she'd yet to notice. The gauze wrapped around her bicep like the cloth of a mummy, though she could feel no wound beneath it.

"You should be feeling better in no time at all. All you need is a little rest. But in the meantime—"

He strolled to a small table near the window that Leigh had failed to notice before. Upon it sat a covered tray which the doctor retrieved and brought to her side. He placed it on her lap, using latches along the bed to lock it in place.

Lifting the tray's lid, he revealed a plate of pot roast. Carrots, celery, green beans, and grilled onions came together with the gravy and bits of steak to form an appetizing, steaming medley. The dish was accompanied by a side of homestyle mashed potatoes.

"I know you probably don't feel like eating," the doctor said, placing the lid to the side. "But your strength would return much faster if you were to eat at least a little something. After all, you're in good enough condition that an I.V. isn't necessary anymore."

Leigh looked down at the plate of hot food. The steam from the meat and vegetables wafted into her nostrils. Though the doctor was correct in assuming she wasn't in the dining mood, the needs of her body spoke louder than the troubled state of her mind. She hadn't eaten anything in more than twenty-four hours, and the intravenous fluids dripping into her bloodstream weren't stifling her appetite in the slightest.

Still, there was no possible way she could look at the meat without seeing Dale Preston being fed the freshly harvested flesh of Douglas Graham. Leigh knew right then and there that she'd be a vegetarian for life.

"I suppose I could try to keep down a few bites of the potatoes," she said, reaching for the fork.

The doctor folded his arms across his chest. "Like I said, even a little will help. You can save the rest for when you're feeling more to up it. But how about something to drink? I bet you're thirsty."

The thought of liquid pouring down her parched throat brought a smile to Leigh's face. "Yes," she said, blowing on the mound of potatoes on her fork to cool them off. "That would be nice."

A pitcher and a plastic cup stood next to each other on the table where the tray had been retrieved. The doctor promptly returned to the table to pour Leigh a glass of dark, purple liquid.

"It appears we have grape juice," he said, topping off the glass. "I can get you something else if you'd like."

Leigh shook her head. "No, grape juice is fine. Thank you very much, Doctor…?" It occurred to her that she didn't know her physician's name.

The man smiled, handing her the glass of juice. "Benson," he said. "Doctor Benson."

She accepted the cup and brought it to her lips. Though the juice was far from ice cold, it still relieved her dry mouth and throat. She hardly tasted the fluid as she gulped down almost the entire glass, concentrating solely on the feeling of replenishment.

Dr. Benson extended his hand to retrieve the empty cup. "That good, huh? Here, let me get you a refill, and then I need to check on another patient."

A moment later, Leigh had another full glass.

"If there's anything else you need," Benson said, making for the door, "please don't hesitate to page for a nurse."

Through a mouthful of potatoes, Leigh said, "Thank you, Dr. Benson. I appreciate that you're trying to make me feel better."

Before he disappeared out the door, Dr. Benson looked back one last time. "Don't worry, Ms. Swanson. You'll be all right."

And then he was gone, the door slowly closing shut behind him.

Now alone, Leigh placed her fork down on her plate. The food had momentarily distracted her from everything else, demonstrating yet again how a good meal could sometimes be just what the doctor ordered. But now that she was by herself in the uncomfortably sterile hospital room, the flood gates of her memories couldn't be closed any longer.

Her grief bounced from one subject to another. Alex's carefree character. Marshall's laidback attitude. Eliza's strong spirit.

Sam's warm embrace.

They were all gone.

And, somehow, she alone had survived. It didn't seem right. Not in the sense that she deserved to live anymore than her friends—their demise was unjust without question. No, it was something else. Just the fact she was lying in this bed after everything that had happened seemed as dreamlike to her as the nightmare with Rob in her dorm room. On another day, in other circumstances, this eerie, surreal sensation would've unnerved her to no end.

But today Leigh welcomed it. The numbing feeling of distance from reality was the only thing preventing a total breakdown, a force-field to repel a barrage of pain and remorse.

She reached for her fork and found her fingers couldn't grasp it. Her whole body trembled, her hands shaking like a seizure victim. Quick, short breaths were the only amounts of air she could suck through her lips. She'd hyperventilated before so she knew it was happening now.

Perhaps that force-field wasn't as strong as she'd thought.

Leigh would've surely screamed if the room's door hadn't reopened just then. A heavyset woman with red, curly hair entered wearing nurse's scrubs and a cheery grin.

"Good morning, sunshine," she said, walking the quick pace of someone over-caffeinated. "I'm Nurse Vicky. How are you feeling?"

Leigh took her first deep breath in several seconds. "Not bad," she answered. "All things considered."

Nurse Vicky paced over to remove the I.V. and halted as she eyed the tray on Leigh's lap. "Where'd you find that?" she asked with a puzzled smile.

Leigh looked down to the food. "Dr. Benson gave it to me. He just left a couple minutes ago."

Instead of the nurse's expression changing to one of understanding, her brow furrowed even more. "Doctor who?"

Leigh hesitated before answering. Did she get the doctor's name wrong? No, she didn't think so. "Benson," she said, speaking the name as clearly as she could.

The nurse tilted her eyes towards the ceiling, as if her memory was hiding somewhere up there. After a moment of rolling her eyes back and forth in concentration, she finally jolted with a twitch of comprehension. "Oh, Benton! You must mean Dr. Benton. I'm sorry, I'm working my way through the second half of a double. Your doctor is Willard Benton, I remember now."

Leigh searched her mind again. It was plausible that in her groggy state she'd misheard the doctor state his name, but now she realized she must be more out of it than she'd initially assumed.

She pointed to the plate of food. "Am I not supposed to have this?"

The nurse shrugged. "I would've thought it was too early to offer you solid foods, but if Dr. Benton gave it to you, then it must be fine."

Vicky snagged a pair of latex gloves from a box resting on top of the heart monitor. "Now, if you'll just stay still for just a second," she said, snapping the latex around her wrists, "I want to take a quick peek at this."

With professional tenderness, she gently lifted the bandage covering Leigh's bicep. Leigh noted how quickly the nurse could slow her mile-a-minute speed to a deliberate, careful pace when examining a patient. She watched, quite impressed, as the nurse cautiously loosened the wrapping and leaned in closer for a better look.

Vicky's comforting smile fell so quickly, Leigh didn't even see it drop.

It simply vanished.

"That's..." The nurse struggled to find the right words to finish her sentence. "Odd."

It wasn't exactly concern washing over the nurse's face. It was more like wonderment. Perplexity. Still, when the subject is one's own body, no one likes to see uncertainty in the eyes of a medical expert.

"What is it?" Leigh asked. "Is something wrong?"

"No." The nurse spoke more to herself than to Leigh. "Nothing's wrong. But that's what's so strange."

"What do you mean?" Leigh didn't even realize she was yelling. She ripped her arm from the nurse's grasp and peered down. Minus a couple of freckles, her skin was completely flawless.

"Now calm down, sweetheart," Vicky said, placating her patient with a pat on the head. "This is a good thing. I just need to have the doctor take a look at this."

Leigh looked away from her perfectly healthy arm to the nurse who jogged over to an intercom next to the room's door. "Paging Dr. Benton," Vicky said while pressing a round, blue button. "Dr. Benton, would you please report to room 202?"

Dr. Benton must not have gotten far after leaving Leigh's room just moments ago as the door opened less than a minute later.

Except a middle-aged man with a graying beard and salt-and-pepper hair walked briskly to Nurse Vicky's side.

"Dr. Benton, come take a look at this."

The nurse led the stranger to Leigh's side, who looked up at him with wide, frightened eyes.

"Who are you?" Leigh asked, her voice shaking.

The bearded man half-smiled and spoke in a purely professional manner. "I'm Dr. Benton. It's nice to meet you."

"But you're not—"

The doctor firmly gripped her arm. "Excuse me just a moment, miss, I need to look at this." He pulled up the bandage with far less care than his nurse, but the same baffled expression washed over his face as well.

His word of choice was "remarkable."

Leigh knew the tears were going to arrive any second, as the symptoms of hyperventilation had already arrived. "Please," she said, looking back and forth between doctor and nurse, "someone tell me what's going on."

The doctor pulled the bandage back down and stood up at her side. "Everything is fine," he said, calmly, rocking back on his heels.

"Then why do you both look so surprised? And where's my other doctor?"

Dr. Benton threw a puzzled glance at his nurse. "What is she talking about?"

Nurse Vicky shrugged. "I'm not sure. She said a Dr. Benson paid her visit before I got here and gave her that food. I just figured she meant you."

Dr. Benton looked back down to Leigh. "There is no Dr. Benson practicing at Saint Andrews. My name is Benton, and I am your assigned physician."

Leigh stared up at him, speechless. She wanted to ask another question, but her thoughts had piled on so heavily it was as if a traffic jam had developed in her brain.

The doctor overlooked her silence and kept talking. "I suppose, considering this fortunate turn of events, I can now be completely honest with you. I'm always happy to share good news with my patients. It's the best part of the job."

Dr. Benton paused his speech to chuckle, and his bemused expression suggested he expected Leigh to share the laugh.

When Leigh only stared at him in total bewilderment, he cleared his throat and continued.

"When you were admitted to this hospital, your examination showed you had no suffered no serious injuries: no broken bones, no internal bleeding. Nothing. Your physical state was surprisingly normal—minus one abnormality, located on your right bicep."

He pointed to the bandage.

Leigh inhaled a sharp breath that she could barely release. "What?"

The doctor sighed. "You had contracted a fungal disease. One that we here hadn't seen in a very long time. At first I couldn't believe my eyes. Or rather, I didn't want to believe them. You see, that particular fungus was so intrusive and so destructive that it once practically shut down this entire town. Not only is it lethal…" He shook his head as if he didn't believe his own words. "But until today we thought it to be incurable. But here you are. As healthy as a horse."

The doctor offered one last smile before motioning for the nurse to join him at the far side of the room. With their backs to Leigh, the two looked over her chart, discussing low voices so Leigh couldn't eavesdrop.

Not that she would've heard a word they were saying even if they were shouting. Leigh was too busy trying to process the onslaught of information she'd just been assaulted with in a matter of minutes.

I caught the disease.

I'm better now.

But there's only one remedy.

She looked down at the tray of food in her lap, the aroma of the gravy-soaked meat still wafting into her nostrils.

There is no Dr. Benson.

Leigh stared at the "pot roast," her lower lip trembling, her right eyelid twitching. Bile began to work its way up her esophagus and would've surely burst through her mouth had it not been for a sobering thought at the very last moment.

I didn't eat the meat. I only ate the potatoes.

Though it didn't answer how she'd cured herself of the lethal, man-eating fungus, it did eliminate the possibility that she had consumed human flesh. No matter the origin of the mystery meat steaming in front of her, Leigh had only partaken in the mashed potatoes and a glass of...

Leigh slowly reached for the cup resting above the corner of the plate. She picked it up and swirled the liquid around the glass. When nothing looked out of the ordinary, she glanced at the doctor and nurse to make sure they were still engaged in conversation, and extended her arm out past the edge of the bed. Turning her hand completely over, the juice in the glass poured out in violet cascade, splattering on the tiled floor.

Nurse Vicky turned in reaction to the noise, racing over when she saw the purple mess. "Oh honey, you spilled your juice. Don't worry I can get you some more."

But Leigh didn't hear a word she said, nor see a glimpse of the nurse retrieving a roll of paper towels.

All she could focus on was the rim of the inverted glass.

Thick, dark liquid dripped much slower than the juice before it. She followed its descent to the floor to find it leaving deep red splotches on the linoleum.

Dr. Benton reached for door's handle. "Nurse, once you've finished cleaning that up, please report to my office." Out of the corner of her eye, Leigh could see him staring at her as he said, "You get some rest. There are policemen who still want to talk to you but they can wait as long as I say. The important thing is that you're going to be okay."

He left without another word.

I'm going to be okay.

Nurse Vicky gently pried the glass from Leigh's fingers. "You want some more, dear?"

With wide, unblinking eyes, Leigh slowly turned her head to meet the nurse's gaze. "Why not?" she said, a grin slowly forming on her face. "You know what they say, don't you?"

Nurse Vicky shrugged. "What's that?"

Leigh's lips parted into an even bigger smile. She let a deep breath fill her lungs and recited,

"Rabbit's a good meal,

"Squirrel's a good snack,

"But a belly full of man..."

She leaned forward, her eyes narrowing.

"...And the fuzz don't grow back."

When Nurse Vicky told her after an awkward silence that she'd never heard that one before, Leigh erupted into a fit of uproarious, gut-busting laughter.

She was still laughing when the policemen arrived at her door.

CHAPTER
TWENTY-SEVEN

You couldn't have asked for a better day.

After the gray, rainy, gloominess of yesterday, today's clear skies and bright sunshine seemed like the forecast of another planet. But that was Vermont for you. A Twenty-four-degree change in twenty-four hours was business as usual.

But though the sun shined as brightly as a midsummer's day, Jake Spire felt no warmth whatsoever as he sulked through the automatic double-doors of Saint Andrews Hospital and into the parking lot outside.

The sun was too bright. It hurt his eyes.

The birds were too loud. They hurt his ears.

He could hardly breathe out there. Walking across the parking lot, the heavy soles of his hiking boots noisily clomping against the pavement, Jake kept his eyes trained to his feet. Though the temperature rested at a perfectly comfortable seventy-two degrees, Jake's forehead ran slick with sweat. The collar of his ranger uniform squeezed unbearably tight against his throat.

Relief came only when Jake was back in the cab of his truck, sitting on the vinyl seat behind the wheel. With the truck's doors securely closed, the claustrophobic sensation overtaking his body seemed to lift slightly, his breath coming more easily and deeper.

Today, the outdoors was not synonymous with freedom. The sky threatened to fall on his head, the earth promised to swallow him whole. Perhaps in time this feeling would pass. But maybe not. After everything that had conspired in the last day, the idea of spending the rest of his life safely tucked behind a desk was more than appealing. Evil could follow you indoors, sure, but combating the greed of corporate America would be a walk in the park compared to what Jake had just been through. When it came to pure destructive force, nature could bring mankind to its knees any day of the week.

Jake reached for the key in the ignition, planning on turning the engine over and pulling out of his parking space. But when his hand found the warm metal of the vehicle's key, he hesitated, staring at his hand.

A bandage concealed an inch-long cut on the back of his thumb. *You had to do it. You saved her life.*

Jake had been repeating this mantra in his mind ever since the ambulance came to rush the girl for immediate care at Saint Andrews. Even as the ambulance doors closed, a policeman tapping its side to tell the driver he was good to go, Jake knew would he was going to do. He'd known the moment he saw the patch of fungus on her arm almost immediately after she'd lost consciousness.

It had been far easier than he'd initially predicted, though finding the doctor's coat slung over an office chair had made quite a difference. He'd known gaining access to Leigh Swanson's room would've been extremely difficult, perhaps impossible, as Jake Spire, forest ranger. Even the policemen he'd passed in the waiting room weren't allowed to bother the girl with questions. Why should he be allowed to her bedside?

Spotting the coat through an open office door had been plain, dumb luck. He'd snatched up the coat without even bothering to check if the coast was clear. Even then he was sure the disguise wouldn't make a difference—the first nurse he encountered would surely ask why he was masquerading as a medical professional. But that old saying had turned out to be one-hundred percent true: the clothes make the man.

The coat had even been one size too big for him—another small miracle. Running almost to the back of Jake's hands, the long sleeves amply concealed the gauze wrapped around both of his wrists. The sting of the burns from the night before still lingered underneath, the bandages making it appear as though he'd slashed his wrists in a failed suicide attempt. But throwing the physician coat over his shoulders, the suspicious injury instantly vanished from sight.

From there it had been all too easy. The girl was still sleeping when he'd entered with the food and juice, having already visited a restroom stall to slice the flesh under the knuckle of his thumb and bleed into the pitcher. For a brief moment, he'd considered using actual flesh to cure the girl's ailment. But the thought passed with the question of where to acquire such a thing, since the only source to come to mind, the Cedar cabin, was in no shape to explore.

But there was another way, a method he'd learned from a dear old friend. So for one last time, Jake had continued Phil's secret work.

Phil.

It was not this name that brought the tears. When thinking of his deceased coworker, his sadness became filtered with a strange sense of pride. What Phil had done was wrong; any form of justice, be it a man's or God's, would have all ruled the same. But in the end, Phil had taken responsibility for his actions, seen the error of his ways. His death had been at his own hands. His own choice. It wasn't much to hold onto—a scrap of plywood in a stormy ocean—but it was something.

What brought the mournful sobs and his face to his hands was a different name, one that belonged to someone much younger. Someone innocent.

Doug.

Jake had driven his ATV as fast as the narrow path to the Cedar's house would allow. But Phil had delayed his journey for far too long. By the time Jake had reached the cabin, it was too late.

It was just too late. Doug was dead. Everyone was dead.

Except the girl. And if Jake had shown up a single second later, she would've been one more casualty to add to the body count.

But you didn't. You saved that girl's life. You took the shot.
Again.

Jake took a deep breath through his nose, realizing it was a mistake too late. All he could smell was a sickly sweet aroma: the varnish of a rifle's stock.

He practically had to kick his door off its hinges in order to stick his head out of the truck in time. A burning, sour combination of orange juice and half a bear claw travelled up his throat, moving from his stomach to the pavement near his shoes. Once the gags and dry heaves passed, he swung his legs back inside and reached out to shut the door. A young E.M.T. jogged by. He had most likely witnessed the entire incident, but didn't seem fazed in the slightest. They were in the parking lot of a hospital, after all.

Jake's hands shook uncontrollably. When he tried squeezing the wheel to steady them, the tremors moved up his arms into his shoulders, racking his entire body. He hoped the glare of the afternoon sun shining off his windows hid him from the occasional person that strolled by his truck. He didn't want anyone to see him.

His red, bloodshot eyes looked back from the rearview mirror. Jake punched it, its swiveling base turning a full ninety degrees towards the passenger seat.

He didn't want *anyone* to see him.

Jake didn't bother checking the clock when he finally started his engine, so it was impossible to say how long he sat there shaking and sobbing. But when he turned on his right turn signal to leave the property of Saint Andrews Hospital, the tear reservoirs of his eyes had completely run dry. Phil's suicide, Doug's murder, the girl's ruined life—none of it succeeded to summon the strength needed to cry any longer.

Jake simply drove in silence.

He had to get out of this town. With the bullet fired from his rifle, he'd killed more than the college-age psychopath about to put an axe through an innocent girl's head. He'd killed a cannibalistic legacy, a macabre conspiracy that had gone on for far too long. But with these deaths also came the demise of an entire community.

Without the Cedars to take out the trash, the fungus would return. The delayed doom of the town would finally arrive, driving away all tourism, commerce, and, ultimately, its citizens. If the girl recovering in room 202 of Saint Andrews Hospital wanted to reveal the disease's only remedy, so be it. But Jake was done.

A freshly painted sign sped by on the right side of the road. *Now leaving the town of Embry. Come back soon!*

Jake shook his head as he reached for the power button of the truck's radio. "I don't think so."

He wasn't really in the mood for music, especially the Creedence album in his CD player that he'd heard a million times before. But he didn't silence the song, singing along to the lyrics in hopes they might down out the cries of regret that echoed throughout his haunted head.

EPILOGUE

The Buck n' Doe wasn't the cheapest place to drink in Embry, nor did it offer the liveliest crowds. If one was looking for dollar drafts or a place to pick up women, Macky's or the Freemont Club were always better choices. But what the Buck did offer that you couldn't find at any of those other watering holes was a circular fireplace right in the middle of the room. From the months of April to August, the pit fire novelty became obsolete, lowering the pub's occupancy to a handful of loyal old drunks and barflies. But come the first evening chill, which usually arrived mid-September, the stoked fire created the best drinking atmosphere in the county. And of course, Dale Preston always occupied the closest seat.

Dale sipped at his "Autumn Stout," a microbrew he could only find at this tavern. Ever since the rescue workers had dug him up from the collapsed basement of the Cedar cabin, Dale had vowed to never at any moment waste his second chance at life. And that meant no more spending his hard-earned dollars on cheap swill that tasted more like pond water than real beer. If he was to drink, and he didn't plan on stopping anytime soon, he'd do it right from now on. Even if it cost a little extra, he was going to taste the hops he was paying for.

The crowd tonight was light, but that was to be expected on a Wednesday night. And Dale wasn't going to complain.

After the ambush of policemen and reporters he'd endured over the last few days, he greeted some peaceful solitude with open arms. He'd hardly had a chance to process what had happened in that cabin in the woods, a large part of his mind still insisting it'd all been a dream.

No. A *nightmare*.

He couldn't remember much, but he knew he should be thankful for that fact.

And he was.

His memory was like an old, damaged VHS tape—white lines of static obscured what images still remained. He remembered diving into Emerald Lake to escape the men who killed Red. He had a vague recollection of getting lost in the forest trying to find help, stumbling upon two strangers whose faces he couldn't picture.

And then, as if the tape had just snapped in half, there was a gaping stretch of blackness. A total blank.

Dale didn't need the expert opinion of a doctor to know this was due to shock. He'd seen guys lose control of their chainsaws, take a chunk out of their hide, and pass out from pain and panic. When they came to, they could hardly remember the details of the accident, as if it had happened while they were asleep. The human brain just had a way of knowing when to spare you memories you didn't want.

The last thing Dale *did* remember was waking up in the dank cellar of that dreadful house. Whatever had blown apart the roof above had probably pulled him from his slumber as well, though he couldn't be sure. All he knew was that when his bearings returned, thin beams of light punctured the darkness that had engulfed him. The explosion left him trapped in rubble, far too heavy to move an inch in his weakened state.

Had it not been for the jars of pickled meat he'd found with his fingers, Dale would've surely expired before the rescue crew unearthed him from his tomb.

He took another drink of his savory beer and licked his lips.

The taste of the meat was still on his tongue. Though his damaged memory brought little clarity to many of the past events, the flavor of the preserved meat lingered with vivid intensity.

He'd known just after taking his first bite that he'd tasted this before, and that the déjà vu wasn't just the fabrication of his imagination—the same way one can instinctually tell the difference between any old memory and a dream. There was all the reason in the world to suspect his broken mind was simply making it up, but something about the memory felt right.

It was more than just the meat's taste—it was how it made him feel immediately after swallowing it. It was an unprecedented revitalization, as if pure, unfiltered strength was being injected into his very soul. Had the rescue workers not arrived when they did, Dale didn't doubt for a second that, given time, he would've been able to lift the heavy rubble himself.

And there was more.

Despite the solid black of the darkness impeding his sight, Dale knew the hellish fungus didn't cover a single inch of his body anymore. And though the stunned doctors and medical technicians couldn't believe Dale's healthy condition, he knew it was all due to this mystery meat that had been within an arm's reach.

But the foundations of denial, no matter how solid and strong, crumble over time. Even if it follows you all the way to your death bed, the truth always comes forth before your last dying breath.

Why call it "mystery meat?" You're only fooling yourself.

He'd known what it was. And though accepting that fact hadn't been easy, it didn't compare to another truth he had no choice but to confront.

He liked it. Even when he had figured out what he was consuming, he'd savored the pleasure that came with every bite.

But still, that was nothing. After all, he was going to die. He needed to eat *something*. So of course he stuffed his face with a smile. Throw a drowning man a floating carcass and he'll smile too.

No, those pills were easy to swallow, given all things considered.

The horse pill, the big one he'd been struggling to digest for days now, was still trying to make its way down his throat, threatening to close off his airways if he didn't accept it soon.

He was still—

"Dale?"

At first he didn't recognize her. But that was to be expected. It had been twelve years.

"Cindy?" He said her name with complete reserve, knowing just how embarrassed he'd instantly become if he mistook her identity. "Cindy Burnett?"

The woman enthusiastically nodded her head, a lipstick-bordered smile revealing bleached white teeth. "Go Wildcats!" She raised a fist into the air.

The woman had aged well, her face only slightly rounder than the teenage image still branded into Dale's mind. She'd done admirably well at keeping in shape, her stomach still toned flat, if not just an inch wider. And her breasts—they'd succeeded with flying colors to match the high expectations of Dale's wet dreams.

"What are you doing in Embry?" Dale asked, still in disbelief that his high school crush was standing before him.

Her smile lowered but didn't drop completely. "Unfortunately, I'm in town because my grandfather passed away."

"I'm sorry to hear that."

Cindy shrugged, raising her hands, palms up. "What can you do? I'll miss him terribly, but I know he lived a long, fulfilling life. Anyway, at least I ran into you. This is wild! It's so good to see you!"

Dale raised his glass. "I'll drink to that. But I'm still surprised you came to the Buck. You're an old local, you should've known how dead it would be."

"Yeah, same old scene." She placed her purse on a nearby table and took the chair right next to Dale's. "But I haven't eaten all day, and the Freemont stopped serving dinner. So here I am."

Dale raised his eyebrows over his beer in response.

"Have you eaten yet?" She playfully flicked his shoulder.

He wanted to verbally reply but he had yet to swallow the beer in his mouth, so he nodded his head "yes."

The pouty lips that overtook Cindy's face reflected the mirror image of the girl Dale had lusted over in high school. "Shoot. I was hoping you'd want to join me."

Dale swallowed so hard it actually hurt the back of his tongue. Before he squeezed his eyes shut to bear the painful gulp of the frothy liquid, he caught an eyeful of Cindy's smooth, milky legs.

"Now hold on," he said, feeling the fluid splash in his stomach.

And something else with it too.

That pill. The big one.

It had finally made its way down.

"I had a little something earlier, but I could eat again."

Cindy's eyes narrowed. "Are you sure?"

"Oh, absolutely," he said, taking one final glance at the delicious skin of her meaty thighs.

"I'm still hungry."

ABOUT THE AUTHOR

Asher Ellis is a screenwriter, educator, and author of the novels PET, Curse of the Pigman, and Cracker Jack. He has written multiple award-winning short films, including Exit 7A, which was featured in the feature-length horror anthologies, The Portal and Conjure X. His penned short film, My Name Is Art, was featured in Amazon's first annual "All Voices Film Festival," celebrating underrepresented communities. When not writing, Asher enjoys hiking through the woods of his home state of Vermont (which he insists are not full of cryptids and cannibals).

www.ingramcontent.com/pod-product-compliance
Lightning Source LLC
Chambersburg PA
CBHW060526260626
47161CB00003B/772